A
Hustler's
QUEEN
RELOADED

Also by Saundra

Her Sweetest Revenge

Her Sweetest Revenge 2

Her Sweetest Revenge 3

If It Ain't About the Money

Hustle Hard

A Hustler's Queen

Anthologies
Schemes and *Dirty Tricks* (with Kiki Swinson)

Published by Kensington Publishing Corp.

A Hustler's QUEEN RELOADED

SAUNDRA

www.kensingtonbooks.com

DAFINA BOOKS are published by

Kensington Publishing Corp.
119 West 40th Street
New York, NY 10018

All Kensington titles, imprints, and distributed lines are available at special quantity discounts for bulk purchases for sales promotion, premiums, fund-raising, and educational or institutional use.

Special book excerpts or customized printings can also be created to fit specific needs. For details, write or phone the office of the Kensington Sales Manager: Kensington Publishing Corp., 119 West 40th Street, New York, NY 10018. Attn. Sales Department. Phone: 1-800-221-2647.

The Dafina logo is a trademark of Kensington Publishing Corp.

ISBN-13: 978-1-4967-3409-9
ISBN-10: 1-4967-3409-2
First Trade Paperback Printing: September 2021

ISBN-13: 978-1-4967-3410-5 (e-book)
ISBN-10: 1-4967-3410-6 (e-book)
First Electronic Edition: September 2021

10 9 8 7 6 5 4 3 2 1

Printed in the United States of America

A Hustler's QUEEN RELOADED

Chapter 1

The sun bouncing off DaVon's pretty white teeth was everything to me. The rounding of his lips as they lifted his cheeks into that handsome warm smile sent tingly, bubbly chills up my spine. Both his strong hands, one on either side of my waist, eased around me. Suddenly my feet were off the ground and the wind beneath them. The fresh air, the smell of the daisies, was overwhelming. "I love you," I whispered to him, looking down into his big, deep brown eyes.

"I love you too, Precious." He smiled at me again. Unable to resist any longer, I lowered my face to meet his soft lips. Just as our lips touched, he swung me around. Our laughter filled the air as the wind soothed me, but the turns became faster and faster. Too fast. "Wait . . . DaVon . . . Baby, where are you?" I screamed his name but was only met with an echo. No longer outside in the sun, I was surrounded by devastating darkness.

"Where am I?" I screamed again. Cold and scared, I folded my arms tightly around myself as my eyes tried unsuccessfully to adjust to the darkness. I heard a drip, then another immediately followed.

"*Precious.*" I heard my name in the distance. It was DaVon's voice. My eyes caught the beam of a far-off bright light. "*Precious.*" His voice again. My eyes again searched for him.

"Yes, baby. I'm here. I'm right here." Finally, I could see a light in the distance. I realized I was inside an old warehouse or some kind of demolished building. "DaVon, DaVon." I screamed his name over and over and started to run in the direction where I heard my name being called. "Tell me where you are. Please, baby, call my name again. Please, please!" I pleaded with him. "DaVon," I shouted again. Then I saw the light. It was bright. Too bright.

Opening my eyes, I lay still as I made out the familiar sound of my ringing cell phone. And just like that I was waking up in my bed from yet another dream. Another delayed nightmare. I was alone. And DaVon was still gone away from me, forever. Sniffing back hurt, lost hope, and fear, I realized once again I had been crying in my dream, and the evidence was my face soaked with tears.

Pushing my Calvin Klein sheets off, I sat up in bed and reached for my cell phone, which refused to stop ringing. I noticed the number was one of Mob's burner cell phone numbers. Since Clip had been murdered, Rob and Mob were the only members of the crew who were allowed access to me.

"Yeah." I answered the phone, my tone a bit groggy. If I didn't know business was at hand, I would not have answered. I was not in a talking mood.

As always, my tone spoke volumes. Mob got straight to the point. "Aye, shutdown was one hundred. Shit getting back to normal." For that I breathed a soft sigh of relief. Police had been patrolling one of my block areas pretty tough. A few murders had taken place recently in the area, and election time was around the corner, so the district attorney wanted to send a message to make sure their presence was felt. Because of all the mayhem, I had no choice but to tighten ship, and Mob made sure to keep the peons in line. "And confirmation on the setup today?" That was code for meeting.

"Yep. We good." I confirmed our meeting with the crew for later that day. With that I ended the call. I was still shaken from my dream and wished nothing more than to be able to lie in bed all day. But it was another day, and that meant business had to be handled. I hung one leg followed by the other over the side of my bed and stood. That was when my day started.

Turning on the shower, I stepped inside and allowed the warm water to run down my face. With my eyes shut tight, my thoughts slipped back to my dream. I could feel the sun on me, I could feel the wind as DaVon turned me. Then the damp, cold room reared its ugly head. Opening my eyes, I shuddered at the thought. Turning my back to the warm water in the shower, I allowed it to run down the crease of my back. I cleared my thoughts. I had to have my head on right when I exited my front door.

Downstairs I headed straight for the kitchen, "Good morning, Anna." I greeted Anna as soon as I entered the kitchen. Anna was Maria's sister who had moved up to LA from Arizona to help Susanna after Maria had died. Neither Maria's nor Rebecca's bodies had ever been found. And to spare Susanna the pain, I decided not to tell her about Quincy and Keisha's bragging confession of their murders. When Anna had arrived in LA, she volunteered to take Maria's old job, to which I had willingly agreed. And I was glad I did. I liked her right away, and she reminded me of Maria in so many ways.

"Good morning. I was wondering if you were sleeping in today. I whipped you up some breakfast steak tacos."

"Mmm. And it smells delicious." Anna was not hired to do any cooking but occasionally when she felt the urge or if I asked her to, she would cook. And she was good at it, just like Maria.

"I think I need to cook for you a bit more often. You turning into skin and bones." Anna fussed at me. She was convinced I was losing weight, but I ate constantly and didn't see any change in my weight.

"I'm fine. If I eat any more, I will be a cow." I joked. I didn't have a knack for eating healthy. I ate what I liked, which was mostly Mexican or stir fry, which I devoured like it was going out of style. And I didn't take it easy on anything fried, or bread. I loved it all. That was one of the reasons why no matter how busy I got, I made the gym a priority.

"You eat the tacos and I'll be convinced."

"I promise I will. But in the meantime, I have to get going." Grabbing a taco, I rushed out the front door with Anna yelling for me to take more with me.

A half hour later, I pulled into the parking lot of one of our spots that I used for meetings. I made it a habit never to use the same spot too often, and I was the only one who knew the actual meeting place. I never gave that information out until I was in traffic driving to the spot on the morning or day of the meeting, which meant they only had about half an hour to get there. And I only gave that info out to my right hand, who then distributed it to the crew members who were allowed to attend. That was one of the things I picked up from DaVon: Never get too comfortable using the same locations for anything. Comfort could never be afforded. Alertness, suspicion, and plain never trusting could be the saving grace to any hustler in the street.

Bringing my all-black Mercedes SUV to a halt, I checked the scene. There were a few whips outside that I noticed. Plies's silver Beamer was on point, so I was sure he was already inside. Reaching across the seat, I retrieved my white Chanel crossbody purse and climbed out into the ninety-degree LA heat.

Inside I was greeted by Plies and Mob. "Hey, Precious, good to see you." Plies stood to greet me.

"What's good, Precious," Mob chimed in right behind him.

"I'm good. This LA heat ain't, though."

"It never is." Plies grinned and stood back on his legs. His iced-out diamond-studded chain almost blinded me as it moved with him. The thing was easily one hundred thousand and a bill. With no doubt Plies was a good-looking guy. Six feet tall, nice medium build, with chestnut skin. Word on the street was that the ladies were fighting over him. I could see why.

"Look, I'ma check on the supply while you two chop it up." Mob had been holding me down until I figured out my new right-hand situation. He was in the building only as a precaution.

This meeting was the preamble to the meeting that was taking place later in the day with the crew. Today would be the day I would announce to everyone that Plies was my right hand. Plies was known in LA for doing a lot of business and putting in his share of work, not to mention being loyal. He had been Clip's guy in the streets, and before Clip was killed and was planning to take over, he had made it clear that Plies was going to be his partner in crime. It only made sense for me to bring him in to hold me down. Mob had held me down no doubt. But even he could agree it took more to being a right hand than met the eye. But make no mistake: Mob was a major part of the crew and operation. And I didn't take it lightly.

"I'm glad you could make it today. It's time to get to work." I got straight to the point. Time was of the essence.

"And I'm ready. I'm ready to get supply tripled on the

blocks. Crew even tighter. And help you continue to build in the city."

"That's what I need to hear. I'm glad to bring you in. Clip had nothing but good things to say about you, and a lot of that is confirmed through the streets. So I know you gone be able to handle everything I'm about to throw your way."

"Just run it down. I'm all ears."

"We expanded a while back before Clip . . . expired . . ." I paused for a brief moment. I still struggled with saying he was killed or was dead. Just didn't seem right. But at that moment I wanted to smack myself. *Expired* sounded like a horrible way to describe his state. I needed a drink. "We expanded," I started over. "But more opportunity has presented itself and we just acquired three new territories. I have been filling those blocks with workers and distributing. The first two rounds of product have moved through fairly quickly, and we are on the reup."

"Okay, that's what's up. If two rounds went through quickly, we should be able to triple in another week."

"Exactly. So we on the move with no minute to waste. Later today at the meeting I'm making your position clear. It's time to work."

"So which nigga's throat I'm gone have to cut first?"

I smiled at his inquiry. "Let's hope none." My crew was solid, and I never really had any problems out of them. But I too had wondered if new authority would be an issue. Reclaiming my serious tone again, I made my position clear. "Just rest assured we ain't letting nothing or no one stand in our way. Bullshit is not on the table. Now Mob, who you are very familiar with, is going to be your right hand."

"Yeah, me and Mob are acquainted through Clip. We good."

I knew this as well. I was truly glad to bring Plies on and I had hopes that everything would be cool. Clip had never steered me wrong in the past. Clip was like DaVon's baby brother, but in the game the word *trust* was nonexistent. Sadly, it was the ways of the street that made it so. But in some ways I had to say DaVon trusted Clip, so I held him in high regard. But Plies had to know this crew was not just about blocks, money, and power. It was about my love for DaVon, and that was something different.

"Listen, I understand the street lusts for money, respect, and power. If that is your motivation, this situation ain't for you. Because I will only say this once. This business is special to me. The consequence for putting it in jeopardy is personal to me. . . . that means expiration." There was no other way for me to put it. I would put a bullet in him myself, and that was a promise.

"I can respect that." The look in his eyes seemed sincere. With that, I made my exit.

Chapter 2

The short meeting I had with Plies was enough to get my taste buds going. That one taco I had managed to guzzle down for breakfast had long worn off. Thankfully, I had prior plans to meet with Promise at one of our favorite Mexican restaurants. Casa Sanchez was located on Centinela, and they had some of the best Mexican food on the south side. I could remember my dad bringing me as a kid. As soon as I turned on Centinela the cuisine's scents seemed to be floating down the block. The juices in my mouth instantly started to flow.

Inside, Promise was nowhere in sight, so I had the hostess seat me. The sooner I was sitting, the sooner I could at least order me a cocktail. No sooner had I ordered my drink than Promise approached the table.

"Tell me my eyes are playing tricks on me. There is no way you beat me here," she teased me. I was normally running late and could never get her to understand it was for good reason. I always had something going on at all hours of the day. My time was never idle.

"Stranger things have happened. Besides, I'm starving and I need a drink. In fact, I just ordered a cocktail. And being the great sister that I am, I went ahead and put in an order for your cocktail as well," I playfully bragged.

"Well, I thank you for that. I have been craving a drink since I woke up this morning." Promise sat down, took off her Gucci sunglasses, and set them on the table. "I swear, it is so hot out there."

"Say no more. I think I felt a sweat bead on me already this morning," I added. The waitress approached the table with our drinks.

"Do you need a minute to look over the menu?" the young girl asked. She was wearing a huge grin on her face. She kept looking from Promise to me. I was sure our twin status amused her.

"No, I think we are ready." I spoke up. I didn't want to waste another minute getting our order in. I was hungry. We ordered some our favorites: chicken fajitas, salsa with queso dip. We loved to mix it together. The taste was indescribable.

"So can you tell me why you had me waiting?"

"You better stop it. Now you see what you put me through. How many tables and booths have I had to hold down?" She smiled mischievously at me.

"Oh, excuses." I played at being mad. "This is how people act when they become a celebrity."

"See, whatever, you got jokes." Promise beamed. "Anywho, I'm glad you could make it today. I missed you something awful while I was away. Matter of fact, give me a hug." Promise stood up and I followed. We embraced. I loved my sister so much, and I thanked God every day that she put in the effort and found me. For that I would always be grateful to her. The one thing I knew for sure: My sister loved me and I loved her. Nothing and no one could change that or come between us.

The waitress approached, pausing at the sight of us. "Never mind us." I laughed. The waitress set our food down in front of us and asked if we were good before walking away. We dug in without hesitation.

"So how was the trip?" I asked while pulling the foil off my steaming hot corn tortillas. Promise had just made it back from Atlanta, where she had gone to check on some new hair products she was thinking about bringing into the salon.

"It went good. Actually, even better than I originally thought. The products were great, like I hoped for. Oh, and the wholesale and distribution price that we will get them at was even better. I already put in my first order, and they should arrive in a few weeks. I'm really excited. I can't wait to use some of the new products on my clients."

"I'm glad to hear that part went well. Buying product, and good quality product, can be difficult at times. And especially getting it at a good price." I could remember Dad sometimes struggling to get some of the cleaning products he needed for the machines. For the most part, he had good trustworthy vendors. But there had been times that he claimed the products were watered down and overpriced. "So how was the city? I know you ain't spending all your time doing business. Come on, spill the tea."

"Girl, you know your sister, right? Atlanta is everything you hear about it, a straight party town. But, Precious, when I say they country . . . they are country. I had to ask a few people to repeat themselves. If I had not known better, I would have thought I was in a foreign country." Promise laughed.

"For real." I giggled. "Promise, you are crazy. But I have heard them talk before on TV. Plus, I had this girl in my class in high school who was from the South. She had that country accent."

"Yeah, it was cute, though. Other than that, I had a blast. Oh, and they have that real soul food. I think I had the best fried catfish I ever tasted down there. We gone have to fly out there together sometimes just to party and eat. The town is lit. No exaggeration."

"Aye, I'm with that. I can deal with the country as long as there ain't no bugs. That is where I draw the line. The first time something bites me or flies up in my face or hair, I'm on the next flight out." We both started laughing. "Wait, did you hit Magic City? I hear that's the biggest party out there. Major tourist attraction."

"Nope. And really, I wanted to, just didn't have the time. I'm telling you there is just so much to do down there. You could never get bored. When we fly out there, though, that's gone be at the top of our list. Magic City."

"Bet. I can't wait." I sipped my margarita in anticipation of hitting up Atlanta.

"So, what did you do while I was away? Besides work," Promise asked before biting into her fajita.

"Well, I won't shock your world and confirm that was all I did. But really, besides that I spent a lot of time racking my brain trying to figure out this new business venture. And I can tell you nothing pops out at me. I don't have a clue what it will be." I placed both of my elbows on the table and rested my chin in the palm of my right hand, frustrated once again about what to do. I had to come up with something. I took in a deep breath and let it out. I couldn't believe it was that complicated. "All I know is I need it to be legit. I must have something legit besides the dry cleaners so I can put this business degree that I invested my time and energy into to good use." I took another much-needed sip of my margarita. With each taste it proved to get better. Either that or my ambition had jilted me in my time of need.

"Why don't you open up a restaurant and sell fajitas, as much as we eat this shit." We both laughed at her silliness. "I mean, we addicted to it. Why wouldn't another fool be?"

"You silly as always. Actually, it's not a bad idea,

though, if you really think about it. I'm sure I'll be the first one up in there every day eating up all the food. With me gobbling it all up, I'm just not sure how we would profit." We both continued to giggle. "But nah, I'm cool on that. I have to think of something, though. And I would rather it be sooner than later."

Promise gazed at me with concern. "Look, don't stress about it, you will think of something . . . but until then, you can keep pouring your good ideas into the salon. Because business is great, and I have you to thank for a lot of it."

"No doubt, I always want you to win. Tell you what, how about we celebrate the salon's continued success with one more margarita before we get out of here?"

"You ain't said nothing but a word." Promise signaled the waitress just as she was about to pass our table.

I really wasn't up for a meeting with the crew after lunch with Promise. My stomach was tight, and I was way too full. A quick nap would do me good. But those margaritas had mellowed me out and would do the trick to get me through. When you ran an empire and a business, there was not much time to sleep. The reality was people depended on me to eat, and I would make sure they did. No matter what.

Chapter 3

Mob standing outside waiting on me was the first thing I noticed as I pulled into the spot. I wasted no time putting the truck in Park and hopping out. Getting this done in a timely matter was a must. "Guess you ready to get down to business." I addressed Mob, who was clearly anxious to get the meeting started. Mob was never one to stand around idle; he thrived on staying busy. I liked that about him. One of the things I did not like and would not tolerate was a lazy crew member or slacker. And I made sure it was no secret.

"No doubt, everyone already inside. Heads up, though, my man Plies's presence got everybody's attention. Ain't nobody asked, but I know they thinkin' somethin' up." Mob twisted his lips up in a sarcastic motion. For a second I wondered if he was nervous. But I knew better. Men— they all played tough but were softer than females, on the real. I would have laughed but I never showed emotion during business. I wondered if anybody would be stupid enough to put their foot in their mouth about my decision. For their own sake I hoped not. It would not be a good idea.

"Well, listen, my day has been long already. I want this meeting to be short and to the point. Anything other than that is an issue." He had been around me long enough, so he knew my language. I didn't have to say much to make my point.

He nodded in agreement. "Nothin' but a word."

Mob opened the door for me, and I strolled inside without a care in the world. The building was quiet. Approaching the room where the meeting was being held, I looked over at Mob. Standing outside the door in complete silence was the tone. Normally, you could hear the guys inside carrying on conversations, but there was nothing. Mob reached out and pulled the door open to the room where all the guys were seated. I stepped inside and all eyes were glued to me. That part didn't surprise me. They always gave me their undivided attention. Sometimes I still wondered if it bothered them that a woman was in charge of them. If it did, I would never know, because none of them had the balls to say so. But the silence made the room feel stuffy and tight. I looked around, slowly taking in faces, and everybody was seated according to plan. Mob always followed my orders and to the absolute T. I pulled my chair out, still examining the setup. Plies was seated to the right of me because he was now my right-hand man. To the right of him was Mob, because he was Plies's right hand. On the left across from Plies sat Case and Rob. Both were block runners on the team. Everyone else at the table was replaceable but nonetheless ambitious.

"Thank you all for your presence today. Business is prospering, as I'm sure you all are already aware. But it can always be better. As I always say, 'never get comfortable.' If we stay hungry, we stay at the top. With that being said, the new territories opening up was a good addition. They are already bringing in revenue, and we are staying tight on manpower and supplies. However, I am shutting down two of the old territories, effective immediately. As you know, the murders in that area have had the block hot. No heat has come to us, and the money is still rolling in, but I decided it's time to move out. The three new territories will triple in revenue in no time, so we are good." I locked eyes around the room for facial responses and body movement. Nothing. It was time to open the floor. I always wanted to hear concerns or whatever. "The floor is open."

Case wasted no time jumping in. "Aye, some new nigga who think he a rival go by the name Lil Phat, that lil nigga been slipping in our territory selling product. Few customers claim he ripped them off, and a few claim to be sick, claim they ended up in the ER off what they copped from him. He in our territory, so it got them questioning if he works for us and if it's our stuff they copped."

I looked around the room for some sort of confirmation. Not that I thought he was lying, but I always asked. "Any truth to this? Or is it just rumors?" Customers thinking our product was or could be tainted was bad for business on every level.

"I had been hearing the same shit as Case. So, I ran up on him in the club few nights back, dude was showcasing to some bomb-ass wannabes lookin' for a come-up. I hemmed him up, he was shooting his mouth off. Never really would admit to shit, though. Say niggas in the street jealous of him and trying to bring him down. Ain't none of us personally ever seen his ass on our block. I still warned him to fall back, but that nigga already done violated. His move slick." Mob shook his head with contempt.

This was something I would not tolerate. "Lil Phat, or whoever this character is. If you know him, when you see him, remember this from me. He dead on sight. Because when he jeopardized the brand by making anyone question if it could have been our product that made them sick, he sabotaged us. He fucked with this brand, so he bites the bullet." I was done with that part of the conversation. Every head around the table nodded in agreement. And comments like "no doubt" and "that nigga done" floated around from every lip at the table.

"Now, I want all of you to welcome to our crew, Plies. He my new right-hand man, and he here for your support and stability. I'm sure most of y'all, if not all of you, are familiar with him from the streets. He got yo' back. Plies, you got the floor."

"Ai'ght." Plies took the lead. His voice was full of confidence, and his eye contact with the crew was legit. He didn't display cocky or fuck boy. Either would probably be a deal breaker for me. "Like Precious said, I got yo' back. I'm ready to work. Let's continue to run LA. I hear nothing but good things already about the crew, so let's keep that reputation. I been in these streets a long time. I'm ready to share all that knowledge to strengthen our core. And I ain't never above learning." His delivery was intentional and well said. I was satisfied.

With that I ended the meeting. There was no more to be said. Before departing, all the guys shook hands with Plies. This type of gesture from the crew showed their support in his new role and that there would be no hard feelings. I appreciated that. I would have hated to have to clip somebody from the crew because of spite or jealousy. I didn't tolerate that kind of behavior either. The delivery of his speech was great, and time would tell if everything was all good. And I would be watching him with my eyes wide open but not stressing. Having him along would ease some of my load, but all decisions were mine. So I could never be too far away, because if he made one wrong decision, things would have to be corrected. And fast.

Chapter 4

The sun beaming through the windshield of my car was really giving me energy, and I needed it so much to push back the cloud that was trying to put a damper on my day. I had woken up missing my dad. It felt like his spirit was all over me, and there was nothing I could do to shake it. I could hear his voice, that big baritone voice he had, in my head just as clear, him calling my name to come and do this or that. Me giving him my undivided attention as he carefully explained things to me. Our bond that we shared as father and daughter. But also, our friendship. I just missed him so much. I still struggled with the fact that he'd lied to me about my mom and my sister, but on days like today, none of that mattered. I just wished I could call him up and talk to him or ride over to his house for a visit. On days like this I would go to his house where I could feel close to him. So as soon as I climbed out of bed and got myself together, I made his house my destination.

I pulled into the driveway, turned the radio down, and sat in the quiet before getting out. I made the drive to check on the house at least four times a month. I had a company that I used to keep up the lawn and outside work. I really was proud with the work they did. The landscaping was almost perfect. And Anna came by once a week to dust and do the housekeeping. I knew the house was never dirty, but it comforted me knowing his house was being cared for regularly. I even tried to spend at least one night a month. Most of the time Promise would stay with me. We would watch movies, have way too much food, popcorn, and drinks, and we both would share stories about our childhood. She would share about mom and I would share about dad, which sometimes made us laugh or sometimes caused us to cry.

I checked the mailbox first. I still had the utility bills sent to the house, and of course people still sent junk mail and shopping ads, all of which ended up in the trash without me even looking at them. I wanted to do everything I could to keep the house alive. Once inside I headed straight for the kitchen to pour myself a drink. I usually kept a fresh bottle of wine in the refrigerator. Anna stopped by the market once a week for fresh wine and cheese, in anticipation of my visits to the house. I really appreciated that. The gushing sound of the wine filling my glass soothed my thoughts. Once it was filled to my liking, I put the top back on the bottle, retrieved my glass from the counter, and set out for the living room. Walking down the hallway I had a sudden feeling like I might get to see Dad walking beside me. But I knew that feeling to only be the aching in my heart for the missing of him. The wine would calm that pain, at least for the time being.

Kicking off my shoes, I reached out and grabbed the remote off the end table, then plopped down on the sofa with my left leg curled under me. With my eyes shut for a brief moment, I breathed a sigh of relief. I had made it to my destination, it was peaceful and quiet, and hopefully I could get down to business and think. With my dad so heavy on my heart I knew it would not be easy but definitely worth a try. I took a huge gulp of wine and slowly swallowed. As the wine traced its way down my throat, I racked my brain for business ventures. By the third swallow I had almost frowned at the realization that nothing was coming to mind. But before I could form the slanted lines with the corners of my lips, a smile intersected as I remembered the look on Promise's face when she introduced her idea of me opening a restaurant. I knew it could work, but feeding people came with too much red tape. And that was one trap I was not ready to navigate.

But a hair supply store could be profitable, and to be honest there were not enough of them in Los Angeles. At least that was my opinion, which I was certain many would disagree with. I mean, there was a fair share around, but in a city like Los Angeles where appearance was number one? And I knew hair was big business firsthand, especially good quality hair. As much as I despised Keisha, I had to be honest, her decision to open a hair supply store had been phenomenal. Her profits had been huge, her clientele loyal, and she had been in the process of opening another store when things went left. Had she still been around I could easily predict she would probably be on her second store. And now that she was no longer open in that area, I was sure there was a need. On the other hand, a designer heel and purse boutique could be profitable as well. Hmm. That was really something for me to think about. Suddenly my frustration was different. Now ideas were jumping out and red-flagging me from all directions. Looking at the wineglass that I had been drinking from, I realized there was only one sip left. Finishing off that last taste, I stood and strolled to the kitchen for another round. Maybe the last round would help me reach a conclusion to my business venture decision. Or maybe I would finish off the bottle and add more frustration to the one I was trying to drink a conclusion to. I was anxious to find out.

Anna was coming down the hallway with her things in hand, preparing to leave when I entered the front door. She smiled at the sight of me. She said I always looked so serious, so I always gave her that extra smile in return. "Señorita," she greeted me as she sometimes did. "I thought I was going to miss you. It's getting late."

"Yeah, I been a busy woman today. How was your day?" I asked, stopping a short distance in front of her.

"Good so far. I keep so busy with more things to do." She waved off her tasks with an *it's nothing* hand gesture. "Oh, and don't forget I'm not coming in for the rest of the week. I'm going to Texas to visit with my family." The smile that covered her face confirmed her excitement.

My mouth dropped open in surprise at the mention of that. She had informed me over a month ago, but time had flown by and I had forgotten all about it. "Aww, that is this week. I forgot all about it. I'm going to miss you, but please enjoy. Do you need anything? You got enough money?"

"Yes, I am fine. I been saving for this trip for over six months. I wanted to be prepared. I am just ready to see my family, eat some good food, and relax."

I reached into my Gucci bag and pulled out a stack. I had been planning to give her something extra for her trip, but it totally slipped my mind. I handed it to her. "Take this for a little cushion."

She waved her hands to reject the money. "No, Precious, I'm good. You give me enough already. This job, your kindness . . . That is more than enough." I knew she would not want to take the money. I had thought about sliding it into her purse with a note, but time had slipped up on me and it was too late.

"Aye, take this. I want you to have it. Besides, you can do a little extra shopping. Buy gifts for your family." The hesitation was still apparent on her face, but I'm sure my determination not to take no for an answer was as well. "Come on. Take it." I tried to hand it to her again. Slowly she reached for it.

"I swear, you are too good to me and Samantha. Too good. Thank you." She set her bag down that was draped around her left wrist and reached for a hug.

"Really, it's nothing. I don't mind at all. Have fun."

"I promise I will have too much fun. I will see you when I get back." She picked up her bag and headed toward the door. I followed in step beside her to the door. "Oh, I forgot to tell you. I made you a Greek salad with some garlic bread. Be sure and eat, please don't let me come back to find you skin and bones," she teased me.

I laughed. "I will eat, I promise," I yelled back before shutting the door.

Back inside, I headed toward the kitchen where I would fix a plate of the salad Anna had prepared and have some more wine. I was hungry since I had skipped lunch, so I was glad Anna had made me something. Her Greek salad was like the rest of the food she cooked: divine and perfect for this time of day. It was light, filling, and good. After fixing a plate and cleaning it of all the food, I seized the chocolate ice cream from the freezer and headed straight for the den, with the comfort of my Italian sofa and a movie in mind. Unfortunately for me, I was only able to get two spoonfuls in my mouth before the doorbell rang, ruining my entire comfort zone. I sighed with frustration and a hint of contempt. The one and only thing I sought and planned on doing was watching television and relaxing. Company and/or conversations were definitely not on my radar.

As I swung my front double doors open, I came face-to-face with a short, stout, middle aged white man with glasses sitting almost at the tip of his long nose. The look on my face must have spoken volumes in the direction that I was not in the mood. Him standing at my door was odd as could be, because in a lot of ways he looked like a salesman. He seemed to be a bit uptight and uncomfortable, like most of the salesmen I had encountered in South LA. But in Bel-Air salesmen didn't just show up at your door. It was considered tacky and just a plain no no. Either way I silently prayed for the man, because little did he know that whatever his visit was for, he had better tread lightly after interrupting my quiet time. I was in no mood to be nice or neighborly. I just wanted to be left alone.

Still eyeing him suspiciously I asked, "How can I help you?"

"Oh, yes, hi. I'm Henry Need." He reached his chubby hand out to shake mine, but I never allowed my eyes to leave his face. And I damn sure had no intention of shaking his hand.

"Yeah, Henry." I continued to stare him down. "I think I already asked how I can help you." I wished he would get to the point.

My stare was making him uneasy. I watched him shift his weight from the left foot to the right. He smiled, but I could tell he was forcing it. "Umm . . . like I said before, I'm Henry Need from the bank. Are you Precious Cummings?"

That got my attention because he knew my full name. I didn't understand why anyone from any bank would be standing at my front door, especially citing my full government name like we had previously had a conversation. "How do you know my name and why are you here?" I asked, my lips moving swiftly.

"Well, I have . . . I have these papers for you." He stumbled over his words. It was clear I had made him nervous. He put his hand down into the black duffel bag he carried on his shoulder and wrestled out some papers. The top of his forehead started to form sweat beads. He handed some papers to me. Reluctantly I reached for them. "These are the deeds to your nightclub."

I snatched my eyes away from the papers before I could read a clear word and landed them back onto his face with confusion. The mention of a *nightclub* had my full attention. The man must have been crazy, because I did not own a nightclub. Clearly, he had the wrong Precious Cummings. This was LA, and not that I had ever checked, but I was certain there was another Precious Cummings roaming around the city somewhere. I gazed back down at the papers, and the name of the club that Keisha and Quincy had owned jumped off the page at me. But right next to the word *owner*, my name, Precious Cummings, was listed. There had to be some type of confusion or the guy was on some games.

"Listen, I don't know about any of this. I ain't never been tied up in no business with these two." I handed the papers back to him. "Why are you really here?" I pressed him to be direct.

"I know this may seem like it's all of a sudden, Ms. Cummings, but we have been trying to find you for over a year. It took a lot of time and a private investigator to figure out we had been mailing things to Keisha Greene's address. Honestly, without the private investigator I fear we would have never found you."

The mention of a private investigator had me feeling some type of way. The last thing I needed in my line of work was for some fake-ass wannabe cop without the badge trailing me. It was way too risky. "Wait, so you all been having strangers spying on me? Shit, for over a year?"

"Not really spying, just trying to locate you. I can assure you this was all done in a respectful manner. But we had to clear this matter up."

I really didn't know what was going on, but I knew that with Keisha and Quincy involved, it was some bullshit. They were never legit about anything they did. And I knew I was not in the mood for it. At all. Not to mention this stranger invading my privacy talking about his rent-a-cop following me. And there was no way I was letting a stranger into my home to explain shit to me, because that could have been a recipe for murder, and I was not in the mood to kill anyone. I contemplated slamming my door in his face. But I took a higher road. Instead, I would kick him out nicely, and if and when I decided to talk to him it would be on my terms. "Look, I'm busy. I got to go. You can leave me your card if you would like. I'll come down to the bank and meet with you." My mind was all over the place.

"Uh, sure, sure." He agreed without hesitation but still appeared nervous and reached down in his satchel again, this time pulling out a business card. "And please keep these papers, they belong to you." I took them and the card.

After shutting my door, I rolled up the papers that Henry had handed me. I went to the kitchen and grabbed the rest of my wine from the refrigerator. I revisited my couch, sat down, and finished off the wine, making sure I cursed Keisha and Quincy out with every swallow. Even dead they couldn't seem to stay out of my life fucking with me. Ugh. I rolled my eyes at the thought of them.

Chapter 5

When I woke up, I concluded that I should have taken some Hennessey shots before going to bed. The wine was comforting, but the Hennessey shots probably would have knocked me off my feet. Maybe then I would have slept through the night instead of dreaming about Keisha and Quincy. Those were two people who really bothered me on different levels. But after showering I threw caution to the wind, got dressed, and headed down to the bank to meet Henry. I really didn't feel like talking to the guy, but I needed to know what was really going on. And he had made it clear he could explain this whole fiasco.

The suit he wore looked the same as the one the day before. He really needed to go shopping for a better fit. "Ms. Cummings. I'm glad you could make it." He came from the back to retrieve me after one of the tellers went to fetch him. But he seemed a bit a more confident on his own turf than he did shaking like a leaf at my front door. I guessed being on your own territory gave you balls. The thought tickled me. The day before at my house, he had almost sweated himself into a nervous breakdown. He led me to his office, which didn't fit his appearance. Henry seemed out of touch and down with a plaid couch and a picture of the Beatles hanging on his wall. But instead, he had that new trend Art Deco–styled furniture, with a Jimi Hendrix art piece on the wall. I was surprised.

He offered me a seat, and I sat down anxiously. "So please tell me what's going on?" I wasted no time. I wanted to clear things up and get on with my day.

"I really don't know how to say it but somehow Keisha Greene, aka Precious Cummings, was carrying herself as you. She acquired paperwork claiming to be you. When she came in to finalize all the paperwork, there was a young lady with her who showed identity as her. And she was you. The crazy thing is she used two different Social Security numbers, one of which was hers and one was yours. However, when she was declared as deceased and we were notified, your Social Security number was still listed as active. Now, this sort of thing doesn't happen often, but in this case it did. We apologize for that."

"So what now? I mean, she is dead and I'm alive. And as you have proved, I am Precious Cummings." I still didn't understand so I needed to say it out loud.

"Well, Ms. Cummings, for us it's simple. Even though it was a scam, that nightclub was bought and paid for with a loan that was secured in your name. As far as we are concerned, it belongs to you . . . that is, unless you don't wish to have . . ." He paused and stared at me for a moment. But I was silent. "I guess if that were the case . . . say if you didn't want it, we would try to buy from you. You know, negotiate a good price for it. Seeing as it not your fault that any of this happened."

"Negotiate a price." His words rang in my head like cowbells. "You mean try to get me to sell it to you for less than what she paid for it?"

"Something like that." He smiled and I wanted to roll my eyes at him.

Keisha and Quincy had already fucked me and schemed us both. Now here he was trying to finish the job. I was about to open my mouth and say just that. But a light went off in my head. One thing I knew for sure was that club had been a moneymaker when Keisha was running it. There was no way I was going to sell it back to the bank and take a pay cut. Nah, I was going to bank it. "No, I'm going to keep it." I slightly smiled this time.

Henry returned the smile. "Good choice." He reached down in the drawer to the right of him and pulled out some keys. "Well, these now belong to you. We had the locks changed since we have no idea what happened to the previous ones. These are secure for you."

Taking the keys from his hand, I could hardly believe this was happening. But I didn't have any more questions. I knew all I needed to know. After bidding him goodbye, I headed to my truck and climbed inside. I sat in the parking lot for a minute. I could not believe I had spent months and valuable time trying to figure out a legit business, and just like that one had jumped right in my lap. But was re-opening that club really a good idea? I suddenly questioned myself, as if my conscience wanted to torment me. More than a year had passed, and new clubs had opened in the area and were successful. Suddenly I did not feel so sure. I needed to talk to Promise.

"Hey, girl." Reese greeted me as soon as I stepped inside the salon. Reese was a receptionist. She shared the front desk with Tara, the other receptionist, but in addition to answering the phone and scheduling appointments, Reese was a makeup artist, and she was good at it. She'd even assisted another makeup artist for a special makeover segment on the Fox 11 News and had received many five-star reviews about her work.

"Where my shadow at?" I referred to Promise. Everybody knew how close we were. And the fact that we were twins only added to our connection.

"She is in her office," Reese replied, her phone starting to ring. She reached for it.

I headed toward the back for her office. Dee and Toya both saw me and smiled. I was cool with all the ladies in the salon. Promise had hired a tight team. I could honestly say everybody was great at their craft. They were all motivated and true go-getters with established clientele, not to mention top-notch customer service. Dee and Toya were both hairstylists. Toya specialized in braids but also did regular styles. More than a few of her clients were Instagram famous and bragged on her skills constantly. Dee was bad with cutting and styling. She too had clients who were social media famous in their own right and made sure everyone knew who kept them tight by having her appear in skits. There was also Prel, who did lashes as well as makeup. Her skills got around by word of mouth, and recently she had brought in two celebrity clients. Then you had Promise, who specialized in just about everything. She even braided hair but she only booked styles. I was probably the only person whose hair she braided regularly. She did have a few clients she would braid from time to time that she used to do before she got the salon.

I smiled as I entered Promise's office and witnessed her sitting at her desk. She was the proud owner of her salon, and truth be told she was a natural at it. The salon business was through the roof. In just over a year, she had made back all the money initially invested into the salon and then some. Of course, she wanted to pay me back, but I refused. I had opened that salon for her because she deserved it, and that was that. I would not take a penny.

"What's my one and only beautiful sister doing here?"

Promise greeted me with a huge grin plastered across her face.

I could only grin back at my mirror image. "Ha." I laughed. "I swear you are conceited," I accused her playfully.

"What?" She giggled.

"You always calling me beautiful to signify your own beauty. Since we're the same damn person." I stated facts about us being mirror images. No one could deny either of us of that fact. Light and chocolate, we still matched. I remembered the very first time I saw her, and she confirmed we were sisters. As mad as I was and confused as I was at her showing up out of the blue claiming to be my family, the one thing I knew for sure was she was not lying, because even though I was light, and she was chocolate, we looked exactly the same. Our noses sat the same on our faces, both of our hairlines even started at the same angle. It was crazy. We were undeniable twins.

"Yep." She cosigned. "You are so correct, my dear sister. My, how I love your quickness," she teased me. We both continued to laugh.

"I swear you are something else." I plopped down on the sofa in her office. "So get this . . . I just came from the bank because some banker showed up at my doorstep yesterday raving that I'm the owner of a club. And get this, it's Keisha and Quincy's old club." I dropped the bomb on Promise with no chaser. I had decided not to tell her about it until I knew what was going on, because whenever she heard Keisha's name she wanted to revive her so that she could be killed all over again. Mentioning the girl's name just upset her.

Shock was spread about her face as her jaws fell loose. Her eyes were full of questions and bewilderment. "Wait, what?" she finally managed after glaring at me for a moment. "I mean, how can that be? I know them two fucked-up individuals would not do you any favors. Bitches," she spat out.

"Exactly. You know them all too well. But how about, they schemed their way into the nightclub, and the shit was all in my name. The whole fucking time. Can you believe that shit? I mean, I'm all up in the club shakin' my ass and supportin' her, and it's my club the whole entire time." The more I thought about it, I was really feeling some type of way.

Promise took the palm of her hand and lightly smacked her desk. "You know what, I'm not even shocked. Because those two simply were not shit. There ain't no other way to say it."

When I thought about it, Promise was dead on the head. Those two were calculated and just plain wrong people. There was no good in them at all. But I had to put them behind me and deal with the matter that was at hand. And I was confused. "For a moment when I got the keys from the banker, I was excited. I saw possibility. I figured this could be a shot at me opening up that legit business that I've been talking about. But now I'm not so sure what to do." I had to be honest. "Maybe I should just sell it and get a profit right off the top. You know, get from under it before I lose a dime. I mean, it's been closed since they died. Who's to say it would generate any income?" I was full of apprehension, or just thinking the worst before it came to pass. Who knew, the place could be poisoned before it even started just because Keisha and Quincy were once attached to it.

"Nah, don't sell it. That would be a bad business decision. It's money to be made up in that club. Fuck that. You need to open it up right away. Shit, get that club popping. Keisha's fucked-up ass actually put a lot into it. All you need to do is open the doors and the money will be clean just like you want it. Trust me on this."

I sat in silence and took in everything that Promise had to say. In so many ways what she said made a lot of sense. The last thing I wanted to do was make a bad business decision or, even worse, be a fool. But that could lie in me opening or selling the club. It was almost like being caught between two guns. Promise had put a lot on my mind. But only one thing was for certain: I had to figure things out one way or the other.

Chapter 6

The whole club thing still had my mind all jumbled up. I was overwhelmed with the way I had come by it. The difficult part was if and how I wanted to move forward with it. I took a few more days to think about it while holding my other businesses down. Finally, I decided Promise was right about the club. There was money to be made. Maybe even a gold mine. The first order of business was to get inside and evaluate what needed to be done before I opened the doors. Promise and I both had some time to spare this morning, so we decided to meet up at the club.

I put the key in the lock and opened the double doors that led inside the once-popping spot. I had to blink to adjust my eyes to haze that some might consider light. Stepping inside, the feeling of the music that used to blast out the speakers, and the always energetic, thick crowd came over me. I could hear Keisha yelling my name as I made my way through the crowd. I shook my head to dismiss the thought of Keisha, because she was the last person I wanted to think of. Promise followed close behind me as we navigated our way through, landing directly on the dance floor. In the center of it I stood still and gazed around. Promise did the same thing. The look in her eyes confirmed that she too was having flashbacks of our good times.

"I'll be damned. After all this time this place is still in good shape. I mean, besides the dust, it appears nothing has aged." Promise was in shock at the still good condition of the building that had not been attended to since the doors were closed. I too was amazed.

"Yeah, it's crazy, huh?"

"Mane," she said. "I just can't believe Keisha's psycho ass did such a good job with this place. As much as I hate to, I gotta give the bitch credit." Promise rolled her eyes but smiled.

I looked at her and laughed. She was funny like that. "I can't with you sometimes," I said, then moved closer toward the bar. "So, I'm thinking we get the cleaners in here right away. It definitely needs a good dusting and wash down. I'm going to use that same rehab crew that I use for the dry cleaners. They do a good job."

"Can you believe how good the paint job and the floors look?" Promised shrugged. "You can tell she paid for good quality work. I mean, unless you just wanted to change the colors on the walls, I say leave it like this. I honestly see no reason to change it."

"I was thinking the same thing. I do need to change the name, though, and hire some staff."

"Oh, and don't forget you have to host a grand opening. You know, bring the city out to celebrate with you." Promise was grinning ear to ear. I loved her enthusiasm. "And don't worry, I'm here to help you with everything. We won't leave no stone unturned." That I was glad to hear because I would need her help.

"I'ma hold you to that. So don't go trying to change your mind."

"You know I got you," she assured me.

"Advertising gone have to be huge, sparing no expense. That will definitely bring the people out. You know LA people are a sucker for what they think is hot." That much I could count on.

"Aye, we won't have a problem. When people hear the club is reopening, they will remember the original owners fell off the face of the earth. The mystery of that alone will pack the house. Not only do these LA people like to party, they love a good backdrop of a mystery story."

I looked at Promise and let out a hearty laugh. The girl would say anything. "I swear you are something else. Wicked, wicked, wicked," I joked. "Let's get to work." I could hardly stop laughing thinking of her foolery.

Promise hunched her shoulders and smiled.

Chapter 7

It was early, but I was up and at it. The first thing on my to-do list was to stop by the dry cleaners and pick up the deposits. Before heading over, I stopped by Dunkin' on Olive Street and picked up a dozen doughnuts. I eased into the parking lot of the dry cleaners, turned off the ignition, snatched up the doughnuts, and hopped out of my truck. A few people trolling the neighborhood who were familiar with me said hello. Most were customers of the dry cleaners, some just plain people who had watched me grow up literally since I was a baby.

"Good morning, early bird." Katrina greeted me as soon as I was inside.

"Good morning. Thought I'd shock your world by coming in so early," I kidded. It had been a long time since I was able to stop in right at opening. I used to love coming by early, when the garbage people would be out and other businesses would be preparing to open for the day, cleaning their parking lots and such. It reminded me so much of the old days when Dad was alive. But lately I was just so busy that it made me tired and I'd sleep late. By the time I made it over to the dry cleaners, it would be late afternoon or sometimes late evening.

"Wait, are those doughnuts?" Katrina's face lit up, she winked, and her eyebrows danced up and down.

"Yep. And most of them are your favorite, cake doughnuts. And you better eat them all or else," I playfully threatened. Cake doughnuts had been Katrina's favorite since I could remember. Whenever my dad stopped by Dunkin' he got two cake doughnuts just for Katrina, and the rest glazed. Mainly because we didn't eat cake doughnuts. Katrina always whined that it was not fair that he got all glazed, so he made it his business to get her extra cake doughnuts.

"No worries, I think I got that covered." She reached for the box, set it on the counter, and wasted no time opening it to retrieve her first doughnut of the morning.

"I tell you it's getting hot out there already this morning. I'ma need another shower by noon," I complained. "It feels good in here, though. Good and cold the way I like it."

"Yeah, I make sure to leave the AC on at night just like you said," Katrina chimed before biting off her doughnut. "This is so good." She closed her eyes and chewed with delight.

I smiled. "How the numbers lookin' from yesterday?" I asked.

"Good, numbers still up as usual. I got the reports ready for you and the deposits in the safe ready for you."

"Cool . . . So do you remember the club Keisha and Quincy used to run a while back?"

Katrina nodded. "I remember, I partied there a couple times with you, remember. It was the spot."

"Yep, it was. Well, I'm taking it over. Going to open it

back up." I looked at her closely to see her reaction to the news, good or bad.

The look on her face was kinda like Promise when I told her—just surprised. And maybe a question or two roaming in the back of her mind.

"That's what's up. I didn't even know they were selling that place. Shit, I actually thought Keisha and Quincy would, like, pop back up from the dead. I mean, from what I hear they never found the bodies."

"Yeah, plenty of rumors. But they have been confirmed dead. So, I found out the bank was doing a short sale, so I decided to take it over." Again, I gazed at Katrina to see a reaction. One that might read suspicion. But there was not one. I really hated to lie to Katrina about anything. She was like family, and my dad had made it so. But this, like a lot of other things about me, she could not know. So I had to eat the negative that came with it.

"I still can't believe somebody killed those two. Have you ever heard anything?"

"Nope. I haven't heard anything. And you know Keisha was secretive when it came to Quincy. Everyone knew they had enemies. Just ain't no telling how things could have went down." I continued at being dumb. Nothing good could come of being honest.

"Well, I can't wait to get back in that club to party. So please hurry and open the doors back up." Katrina was clearly amped.

"Absolutely. I got you."

"Oh, and before I forget, you ain't going to believe this. Regina sashayed her little skinny butt up in here this morning with her two weeks' notice. Just out of the blue." Katrina waved her hand as if she was throwing caution to the wind.

"Did she say why?" I asked. I figured I didn't want to

know the answer, but I needed to know, so at any rate, I asked.

Katrina made it a point of rolling her eyes before she answered me, so I knew right away, some bullshit was preparing to fly out of her mouth. I quickly considered retrieving a doughnut from the box to prepare myself for whatever bombshell she was about to share. "She claims she's about to marry that boyfriend of hers. And get this bullshit. She said they are moving to Atlanta for a new start." Katrina twisted the sides of her lips up in a sarcastic manner, so I knew she was bothered by the situation.

Just hearing anything about Regina's boyfriend sent shock waves my way. This ridiculous news was no better. "You talking about the boyfriend who's always forgetting to pick her up from work, and be driving her car?" I had to know.

"That one," Katrina confirmed with attitude.

All I could do was shake my head in disbelief. I did not want to hear or believe that Regina would go up the street with the man, even less leave the state with him. But females were known to do stranger things when they were in love. And no one, I mean no one, could convince them otherwise. Only time would tell the outcome of her strength or weakness. "Well, you tell her I wish her the best on her new adventure. Now, where it concerns the dry cleaners is help. I'm thinking we hire two people, and let's make one of them full-time. The other can fill a part-time slot."

The lift of Katrina's cheeks and slight bulge in her eyes told me she was wondering why two people. "Two people?" Katrina held up two fingers.

I smiled, then shrugged. "Why not. Business is good, and since I am barely here to help you out like I used to. I thought I'd make you the store manager . . . kinda put you in charge. Think you can handle that?" I dropped that bomb on her with a grin. I had been considering it for a while, but my mind was made up. Katrina had worked hard, for my dad and now me. Being a single mother and she had never missed a beat. She had earned it. The tears that streamed down her face in puddles told me she was shocked and excited.

"Are you serious, Precious? Please don't joke around."

"You have earned it, Katrina. I wouldn't want to give it to anybody else." And I meant every word as they rolled off my tongue.

"Thank you so much." Katrina reached out and hugged me and sniffed back tears. She stepped back and wiped at them. "Now, whew." She let out a deep breath. "That good news just overwhelmed me . . . I'm good now." She laughed. "I have just one question, though. For now, can we just hire one full-time person, because I have the feeling Regina won't be gone long and she will be needing her job back. Besides, as new manager, I will be spending a little bit more time here to get my dry cleaners in a manager's zone." She beamed.

As the new manager I now wanted to give her ideas consideration and listen to her opinions. "Tell you what. We will try it for a while and see how it goes. I don't want you spending all your time working. And you never know when you might need that cushion."

"Okay. That's fair." Katrina agreed, still smiling.

"So." I sighed. "I will get the advertisement out there for help wanted. Hopefully, we land someone good before Regina leaves in two weeks. This way you will have time to get them trained."

"Yeah, I'm sure we will fill the spot quickly. People always stopping in to see if we are hiring."

"Alright, it should be a piece of cake, then. Let me grab these deposits and get to the bank. I will get the paperwork together confirming your new position and pay. Then you can sign off officially accepting."

"Aye, you get right on that." Katrina bounced on her toes with excitement.

After grabbing up the deposits I jumped in my truck and headed for the bank. The last thing I wanted to do was stand in a long line. And I knew if I didn't get there early, that would be the outcome. I drove to the bank with a smile in my heart. Being able to show Katrina how much I appreciated her hard work really meant a lot to me. The parking lot looked just how I wished it would. Only a few cars, most of which I knew were employees'. I made my way inside, ready to deposit more of my father's legacy.

Chapter 8

Busy was my new middle name but I juggled it quite well. To be honest it kept my mind occupied, which gave me less time to think about DaVon. I still missed him each day like we were together the day before. I stared out the window as my plane descended on Florida. I was in Miami to meet up with Pablo and Penelope on business, as usual. True to her word, Penelope had stood by my side through my whole transition from regular chick to the hustler I had become. And I appreciated her for that. Keeping her word meant the world to me, and I didn't take it for granted.

My plane landed just in time for me to head straight to the meeting. I picked up the Mercedes I had rented, put the address in the GPS, and directed the vehicle in that direction. Always the perfect gentlemen, Pablo greeted me by kissing my hand and welcoming me to their city once again, as he always did. Penelope kissed both my cheeks and told me I looked beautiful as always. I sat down at the table and assured them both I was glad to be there.

"I tell you, Precious, I hear nothing but good things about you and the business out in LA. I must say you keep me impressed, and that is not an easy job. DaVon would be so proud of you."

"That is my hope," I said with apprehension. I wondered all the time if I handled things the way DaVon would approve. True, he had taught me mostly everything he knew. But he was one of a kind. Everyone in LA said so. I wasn't sure I would ever be able to fill his shoes, but I damn sure gave it my best shot on a daily basis.

"I must say, I love the direction you are taking your operation. The way you can switch it up and still bring in the revenue is phenomenal. You are bringing in lots of money. And you don't have dead bodies all in the streets. Trust me when I say it's not an easy combination. Simply put, you have inspired me."

My senses went into overdrive when he said that last part. What was he about to ask of me? I was sure it was huge. I braced myself for the kill.

He picked up a cigar. "I need you to do me a favor. Not too big. But important." He placed the cigar between two of his fingers. Penelope looked at me and winked with a smile. She knew I was anxious to hear what he would throw at me next. "Precious." He said my name as if a lottery ticket was attached to it. A favor for Pablo, one of the biggest drug distributors in the United States. My heart dropped to the heels of my feet. I waited. "I need you to expand my crews here in Miami. Take some of my team and some of my territory, and make it happen. Miami is a potluck of need right now. Properties selling like hotcakes. People spending money like crazy. But I had to shut down some bosses that grinded for me."

I was surprised to hear that. I wondered if they were six feet under or still snatching breath from above ground. "It's too many hotheads out here right now bringing on too much heat. And it's causing everybody to lose business. I don't take lightly what I ask you to do because I know you have your hands full. But I need you to do this for me. Just spearhead some territory here for me for a while." I was almost speechless for many different reasons, fear and honor, to only name a few. But how could I tell him now was not the time? Silently I cleared my throat to find my voice and prayed my words didn't come out unsteady because never could I let him see my nervousness.

"I will be honored to do this thing for you. But as you mentioned, I have a lot going on right now. And as you know, I lost Clip, who was my right-hand man . . . and I just recently brought on a new one. Not to mention I just gave the okay on opening a nightclub." I tried to stay as calm as I could on the inside. I was so nervous, and I wanted the sweat beads that I was sure would pop up at any moment to stay at bay.

"A boss from day one. That is why it is you who are standing in front of us." Penelope's calm yet controlled voice intervened. And I knew I had a job to do. Nothing else trumped that.

"How much territory is it?" I was ready to be filled in on my duties. I would do this, and I would do it right.

I could see the relief return to Pablo's skin. He lit his cigar and took one puff. "Roughly six blocks or so. But of course, I'm bringing in a team to work under you."

"No," I quickly responded. Pablo took another puff of his cigar. I got to the point. "Look, I know you got your people that you still trust. But I trust my guys and I know how they move. So, if I do this, I want to bring them in." Pablo gazed at Penelope, then sat up in his seat taking his eyes from me for only a moment. He put his cigar out in the gold ashtray that was on his desk. My heart was beating. I had tried him more than once in less than thirty minutes. Who knew what he might do? The guy was Pablo

Alito. A kingpin. He could snuff me out and dare anyone to ask about me. I silently prayed.

Finally, Pablo's eyes came back up and met mine. "That is fine. You have my confidence in your decisions. But I'm going to bring on Marlo. He is a trusted confidant. He will introduce you to the Miami area and help open a few doors." I breathed again. I was cool with that.

"Hold that thought, Pablo." Penelope stood and exited the room. She reentered just as swiftly as she had left. Behind her was this tall, caramel-complexioned man, who looked to be about six feet four inches tall, with a flat top haircut. My eyes went from him, to Penelope, on to Pablo. I wondered who the guy was. I wished someone would fill me in quick.

Penelope must have felt my restless posture. "Precious, this here is Marlo." I had to fight my face muscles to keep my jaws from dropping wide open. No way could the guy who just walked in the room looking he just stepped off Tyra Banks's Fashion Week runway be the guy who would open any door for me in Miami. Unless Pablo meant literally he would open a door for me. When Pablo said someone who would open doors for me, I definitely thought he meant someone who looked a lot tougher.

"You two are going to work together and get the blocks where they need to be." He glanced from Marlo to me. "Precious, you should only have to be here in town a couple times a month. This way you can run your own territories back home and tend to your businesses."

"That is cool. I'm going to fly back to LA—"

Pablo cut me off. "Before you catch your flight out, Marlo is going to show you the spots tomorrow that I have in mind."

"That will work, but my flight leaves at one o'clock, so it will have to be early."

"I can handle that." Marlo jumped in. I couldn't do anything but nod in agreement. I just could not believe this was the guy I was supposed to trust with my life in Miami, while he opened doors. I wondered if I would have to be the one to open doors for him.

"Once I get back to LA I'll meet with the guys, then get back to Miami in a couple days to get started."

"We'll look forward to it." Pablo relit his cigar and leaned back in his seat, and just like that the meeting was over.

I now had a whole territory that I was responsible for in another city. I had to get myself organized to step up in my new position, because working for Pablo and Penelope in their city, on their turf, there was no room for screwups. The pressure was on. I hoped DaVon was looking down on me with support, because I would need it. But to be clear, I was not worried. Like Penelope had said, I was a boss. Even I could attest to that.

Chapter 9

"Hey, I know it's last minute, but we need to meet up in an hour." I was back from Miami and didn't have any time to waste. Plies was my first contact. He would be in charge of contacting the others. "I need you get Mob, Case, and Rob on the line and let them know they need to be there."

"No doubt," Plies replied without hesitation. I gave him the meeting location and ended the call.

My plane had landed only ten minutes prior. I had contacted a car service to pick me up and deliver me home. After the driver deposited my luggage at my front door, I tipped him and hauled it inside. The house was quiet because Anna was off. Leaving my luggage right in the foyer, I grabbed the keys to one of my six vehicles and headed for the garage. It would take me at least twenty minutes to get to the meeting if I drove top speed. The guys had arrived by the time I arrived. I greeted them, then pulled Plies in first to let him know what was going on.

"So, Plies, I know you're just adjusting to your new crew, duties, all that, but we have a new mission. I just left Miami, and while there I was gifted what I consider to be an honor. It's in the form of territory. With that being said, I'm gone need you and some of the guys to back me up."

"Whatever you need, just let me know our position," was his reply. I couldn't find a hint of disinclination in his tone.

"Our position will be solid and airtight. The goal is to get a few blocks in order and increase the sales."

Plies nodded with assurance. "That's nothing. We got that. When do we leave?"

"Soon, that's why I had to bring you in right away. Go ahead and bring the guys in." Opening the door, he gestured the guys inside.

They all took a seat and gave me their undivided attention. Unexpected meetings always seemed to make everyone anxious. "I need you guys to pack your bags. Well, at least a few of you." I figured I'd cut right to the chase. "We're headed to Miami." I added that because I figured maybe the mention of Miami would make the idea seem brighter. "Got some territory out there we need to head up. The usual, you will keep things in order, keep the body count down, and gain the customers' trust so they can spend all their money with us. Same thing we do here, same rules."

"Whatever you need." Mob spoke up first. Case and Rob followed with a co-sign. They made it clear they all had my back.

"Just one thing . . . uh . . . you say keep the body count down. That might not be possible at first, seeing as we might have to open a few doors for ourselves. Which in most cases means bloodshed." Case had a point. But Pablo was a few steps ahead of that.

"Yeah, you know them Miami goons might want to stunt they guns." Rob was matter-of-fact in his description.

"You don't have to worry about that. Doors are being

opened for us as we speak. Nevertheless, make no mistake: We will handle whatever gets in our way. But just like here, make no moves until Plies or me sign off on it. A war will only slow the bag and tip off the law. We need to keep both at the minimum to nonexistent."

"Bet," Case said with a nod.

"Now, this is only temporary, and we still gone have to keep things in order here. Things can't slow down. So we gone have to do a bit of adjusting. Rob and Case, I need you two down in Miami, but I also want to bring in Don P." I'd had my eye on Don P for a while. He was a strong link to the crew who had come up and increased his roles when Clip was alive. And to be honest, I was certain he would be a strong link down in Miami. The kid had heart, and it didn't go unnoticed. "Don P has been standing out making his mark. He has put in major work and I think he will be a good asset down in Miami."

"Yeah, lil homie holds his own." Mob cosigned. "Anytime I'm in a tight squeeze I would pick him to have my back. I'm sure Case and Rob would agree." Case and Rob both cosigned with a *yeah*. That was the confirmation I needed to hear and I knew to be a fact as of late.

"Mob, I'm going to have you reach out to him, and I will meet with him later. Set it up for tomorrow. I'll hit you with the time and the spot."

"I got you." He nodded.

"Mob, your position is gone be here in LA. I need you to hold it down across the board and keep everything smooth. I also need you to personally pick up Case's territory and hold it down while he's away. And I want Ced to pick up in Rob's territory for now. He's being pulled up in rank. His hard work has also not been going unnoticed. Just keep an eye out on his trigger finger. Lil dude be ready to light them up." Ced was a sort of a hothead, but he was quick and smart. Those were good attributes for a hustler and could take them a long way. "This will be a test if he does well. And when Rob returns to reclaim his spot, I might have a small piece of territory for him to claim." I hoped I had made that clear so that he could help Ced understand how important this was. Ced was Mob's little cousin. Mob had taught him everything he knew, and he was making good use of it. After I was done laying out the plan to everyone, they made it clear that it was cool, and I could count on them. We were about to go to Miami and make moves. I was proud to have a team that supported me and knew that I had their back as well.

Chapter 10

With the trip out to Miami, then back home to LA within two days, and straight into a meeting with the crew, to checking on the dry cleaners and progress of the club, I was beat. All I wanted to do was shower, eat, and relax. After my hot shower I felt refreshed. Racing down the stairs to the kitchen, I kinda felt energized. Maybe it was the thought of the wine I had chilled in the refrigerator. Before going to the kitchen, I peeked into the bar area, which was fully stocked. All of that liquor and I hardly ever entered the room unless I had company. Other than that, I had a glass of wine, which I kept in the kitchen, or a bottle of Hennessey that I also kept in the refrigerator. I guess being in the bar area brought back too many memories of DaVon and me, so I avoided it. Just standing in the doorway I almost felt his presence. It was too much. Shutting the door, I continued on to the kitchen.

The wine bottle was just the temperature I liked it. I poured up a glass until it was full. The first taste went straight to my toes and rose to my brain with a tingle that lifted my soul. I was about to go in for my second taste, but the doorbell interrupted that. I almost had my hand on the bottle before it went *ding dong* for the second time in less than a minute.

"I swear, you have the patience of a Sagittarius," I chastised Promise.

"I have the same patience as my sister. Which, I think I have heard you say more times than not, we both inherited from our dad."

I had to smile at that one. She was right. "I can't argue with that, since I made the confession."

I shut the door behind her and followed her into the den. She had called me up and said she was coming with dinner. I was glad for that because on the way home my stomach reminded me that I was hungry. But I was so tired I didn't feel like stopping for dinner or cooking it, so my sister was a godsend.

"Thank you for bringing me something to nourish my tired soul and fill my empty belly."

"Well, it seems that is the only way I get to see you, since you are always busy with this or that."

"I know . . . and I'm so tired. I need a good night's sleep." I reached for my plate that Promise handed me. She had picked up shrimp and filet mignon stir fry from Benihana, and it looked and smelled delicious.

"So how did things go down in Miami?" Promise reached for the remote control and turned on the television.

"Thin—"

Before I could finish my sentence, Promise cut me off with her right hand in the air. "Wait, before you answer that, you need to get some damn wine. I mean, how else you expect me to digest this good food?"

"Right." I stood up. "I'll be right back." In the kitchen I picked up my glass and the bottle of wine that I had already started on. Then I grabbed a glass for Promise.

"Now, as I was saying." I handed her a glass, then polished off what was left in mine before continuing. "Miami was ai'ght. Just turns out I will be spending more time out there than usual."

"More time? What's up?" Promise filled her wineglass and then mine.

"Pablo asked me to run some new territory he's trying to get started up out there for a while."

"Run territory out there?" The surprise was all in her tone. "You already got your own shit going on here. Now you got the club . . . I know you Superwoman, but how you plan on doing all that?" She forked her first bit of stir fry. I followed suit. My stomach was humming.

I chewed and readied myself for her answer. "I got a plan to make it work. In two days, I'm flying back down for a couple days. Then I have Plies and a couple of the guys coming down from my crew here to jump it off. See, I only agreed to do it if I could bring my own crew."

Promise nodded, indicating she agreed with that. "Okay, seems like you got a plan worked out. And I feel you on that part about bringing your own crew. Especially being in a new area you got to have people who you can trust watching your back. Plus you know how they move."

Promise was not in the game with me, but she would be a good backup. The girl thought just like DaVon. Sometimes if I didn't know any better, I would have thought she was a hustler in her past. "Exactly. Get this, though, Pablo put this guy with me who they call Marlo. He's supposed to open doors for me."

"What is he like?"

"I was hoping you would ask that. Let me tell you about this guy. So, we are having our meeting when Pablo tells me how this Marlo will basically open doors for me. You know, hold me down on those unknown Miami streets. I'm thinkin' cool. In walks this six-foot-tall, almost light skin dude, who look like he should be on the cover of *Elle* magazine. No way does he look like a street nigga. And damn sure not like one who could open up doors in the hood. Hell, I would question if he could even get out his whip in the hood." I was still in shock myself when I thought of Marlo.

"Word." Promise laughed. "He can't be that square?"

"Girl, no lies" I held up my right hand as if I was being sworn in. "I'm pressed. I hope he is worth his grain . . . 'cause I'm worried he might get us killed." I sipped my wine.

"Precious, don't say that." Promise continued to laugh. "I'm sure Pablo put you in the hands of the best." I was glad she was hopeful because I was not.

I trusted Pablo and Penelope, so I sighed. "I'm sure." I polished off the rest of the wine in my glass and quickly re-filled it.

"Let's talk about the club. You do realize opening night is in a week," she reminded me. "You can't miss that. You are the owner, remember."

"I know, I know, and I'll be there. I just have to juggle a few things and make it work. It should be a piece of cake." I shrugged my shoulders nonchalantly, but my face had a look of uncertainty.

Promised sighed and smiled at me. "Don't worry, go handle your business in Miami. I got your back. Whatever you need, I got you covered. All you gotta do is show up for opening night."

That warmed my heart, my sister having my back. As I knew she would. "Aww, thank you, Promise."

"Yeah whatever, big head." She giggled. "Now refill my glass. Shit, think I'm just gonna let you drink up all the wine? I did drive all the way out here and bring you dinner."

"That you did. Matter of fact, how about we take a shot of that Henney to really kickstart this good meal."

"And you know I'm wit' that. But you know wit' us, one shot turns into an empty bottle. So, I guess I'll be sleeping in the guest room tonight."

"I guess so." With that I sprinted off to the kitchen for the bottle. A good three to four shots would get me all the laughs that Promise and I could find in that bottle—and the sleep my body begged for.

Chapter 11

I checked into my hotel room and jumped straight in the shower. I swear LA was hot, but Miami was sweltering, I felt as if my clothes were sticking to me. Either that or I just longed to be at the beach like all the other people I had seen on my drive over from the airport to the hotel. Everyone seemed to be on their way to the sand. I saw nothing but surfboards, bare chests, bikinis, and long hair flying out of windows on my drive. I was on my way to meet up with Marlo. I was not sure how I felt about that. Hopefully, this time he would give me a different impression. A safe impression would be nice.

My phone rang just as I slid my right leg into a pair of jeans. I was expecting a call from Marlo that I could not miss, so instead of taking the time to slide my left leg into the other pants leg, I hobbled over to my phone, which I had left on the bathroom counter. I reached for it just before I was sure it was about to be done ringing. And it was in fact Marlo. He gave me the address to the spot where we would meet up. I ended the call, finished getting dressed, jumped in my rented Escalade, and was out.

I noticed Marlo right away standing next to an all-black Ferrari. And he looked the same as he did when we first met, just like he had stepped off a runway. Jeans, a ripped shirt showing a piece of his chest, and a pair of Magnanni loafers. I knew designer shoes because I was into that type of thing. But I swear I did not know one dude from the hood who wore shoes like that. I had to avert my eyes so I didn't stare as I climbed out of the truck.

"Precious." He said my name like we talked every day. I noticed he had that Miami Southern drawl. It wasn't bad, though.

"Marlo," I said, since he wanted to be on a first name basis. He let out a light laugh.

"I see you didn't have any trouble finding the spot." I guessed he was making small talk, because I was sure he knew anyone who possessed a phone could go anywhere.

"Well, we all know the wonders of GPS," I shot back, not sure what else to say.

"Yeah." He kind of looked me up and down. But he seemed to refocus quickly. "Why don't you take a ride with me?" He was supposed to be showing me the blocks that I was assigned to. At first, we rode in silence until he reached the area where certain things would be taking place. "As you can see, the population down here is a little diverse." I could see exactly what he meant as he turned corner after corner. There was all type of people—bombs, the blue-collar types, black, white, Haitian, Hispanics. You name it, they were there. "Gotta stay strapped down here. The gangs aren't that bad. But you gotta watch out for the wannabe quick come-up types. They stay with the stickups." He glanced at me like he was trying to warn me. "Gotta stay sharp. There is no time to sleep out here on these streets. Around here it's more about reputation than money sometimes. They're killing over stupid shit."

I was starting to wonder if he thought I might not be capable. Men were always intimated or apprehensive when it came to females. In any situation, we always had to prove ourselves. "Well, as you already know, I'm from LA. Ain't nothin' I haven't already seen, same streets different state. Me and my crew, we got this." I felt the need to remind him I was not alone, just in case he had forgotten.

"So, when are your guys arriving in the three oh five?"

"They will touch down tomorrow. My right hand had to secure the reup first. Make sure the streets are supplied before he gets in the air. You know, first things first."

He nodded. He was all ears but kept his eyes on the left and right turns he was whipping. "I can understand that. Gotta make sure the home front is straight. So, the shipment for your blocks will be here in two days. And trust, the streets are already ready to rock. Tomorrow I will run a few things down. And that will be that. Everything else is a go."

I assured him we were ready before he dropped me back at my spot to pick up my ride. And more than anything, I was ready to handle this so that I could get back to LA. The club's grand opening was really on my mind. But I kept it at bay so that I could handle this. Pablo and Penelope were counting on me, so I would give it my attention when I was back in LA. Instead of sightseeing like I sometimes did when I was in Miami, I went back to my hotel room, took another shower, ordered room service, and meditated before getting some sleep. I would be energized and have my head on straight for the next day when my crew arrived.

No sooner had Plies's plane landed in Miami than he hit me up. He was as anxious to get started as I was. We met up at a Mexican spot that I had googled and read the five-star reviews. My goal was for us to have a drink and a quick rundown of the day.

"Are you in love with Miami yet?" I asked Plies as he sat down at the table I had secured for us.

"I'm sure if you point me toward the beach I would be." He smiled.

"I figured as much. Maybe another time." I grinned. "How was your flight?"

"Good. I slept the entire way."

"Long night?"

"You can say that."

"Well, I will make this quick so you can get to your hotel and take a nap or something. We will be meeting up with Marlo later to go over some things. Iron out a few details and get on the same page."

"How did things go yesterday when you met up?"

"It was all good. He took me around, showed me the territory, and gave me a little history on it. I assure you it ain't nothin' we can't handle."

"Good. And I should think if something does come up, we can exterminate the issue right off."

"My thoughts exactly." I took a sip of the margarita the waitress brought over to me. We sat and talked for a minute, finished our drinks, and promised to meet up with Marlo later that day.

"Plies this is Marlo, Marlo . . . Plies." I introduced them to each other as soon as we were in speaking distance. I really didn't know how to warn Plies about Marlo's appearance without being somewhat offensive to Marlo or giving off the wrong impression. So I decided the best thing to do was to let him see with his own eyes. And even though he was concealing it quite well, I knew Plies was thinking Marlo was soft.

Like I said, dudes from our hood did not dress or carry themselves like Marlo, so Plies's underlying shock at the sight of him was no surprise to me. In fact, it was a bit funny, but I controlled my urge to laugh. Marlo and Plies shook hands.

"This is Phil." Marlo introduced the guy he had brought along with him. "He is my right hand." Marlo seemed proud to have Phil on his side.

"Glad to have y'all in my city." Phil's drawl was a bit deeper than Marlo's and his appearance was that of a hood nigga. Exactly what Plies and I were used to. Phil had a mouth full of gold. His bottom teeth had diamond studs in them and were bling blinging right out his mouth. He had on Timbs, a pair of blue jean True Religion shorts, and a white tee. He and Marlo were like night and day. It was crazy.

"Phil gone have your back out here in these Miami streets. Together he and I are going to open up these Miami doors while you take control of the block."

"Fo' sho. And y'all ain't got shit to worry about. While you in the city, make yourselves right at home. Because Phil said so." Phil looked to be only about five feet six inches tall with a medium muscle build and a head full of thick dreads. And there was no doubt in my mind that his bark was as big as his bite. I was glad to meet him.

"I think that meeting went well. But what's up wit' yo man Marlo?" Plies and I met up at the bar close to my hotel to chop it up. I figured questions about Marlo would come up. "Ya man look like he kinda soft. Not trying to be funny but that nigga gone get us killed out here in these Miami streets." A smirk spread across Plies's face.

I had to laugh; I could no longer hold it in. "It's likely," I joked. Then I wiped the grin off my face. "But that's why you got to be on your shit out here. The guys gotta be focused. You in charge just like back home when I'm not here. I will be back and forth between Miami and LA, and so will you. Your duties in LA are going to be the same, so you got to hold them both down."

"I got it. As long as Marlo opens these doors up, him and that nigga Phil, we should be straight. Real talk, I ain't underestimating no nigga. The guys fly in later tonight. I'ma meet wit' them so we can be ready in the morning."

"Yep, make sure everyone on the same page. Marlo gone hit you up in the morning to meet you and the guys with the product."

"Then it's game time." Plies downed the shot that was sitting in front of him. I followed suit. I was just ready for it to jump off. The sooner everything got started, the better. I would feel much better when I had some results. But I was leaving it all up to Plies because my flight was leaving early in the morning. I had to get back to LA.

Chapter 12

"So are all you ladies coming out tonight?" I asked as I sat in Promise's chair getting my hair styled. It was the day of the grand reopening for the club, and I had to look my best. Who was I kidding? I always looked my best, tonight would be no different. Promise had put a lot of energy into putting the finishing touches on everything, from picking the new DJ to making sure the event planner brought my vision to life. The most difficult was obtaining the liquor license. She had been a huge help reaching out to some connects that help rushed the application through. I really appreciated her and was glad it was almost show time. With all the advertising that was done, I was really hoping to bring the city out. Tonight, would show and tell.

"Dang, Precious, I'm not going to be able to attend. I agreed to go to this party with Dell," Toya shared. Dell was her boyfriend. And no one in the room was a fan of him.

Promise sighed with agitation and I was pretty sure she rolled her eyes, but I was not facing the mirror. And since she was behind me styling my hair, I could not see her face. "So, you actually going to go out with that clown?"

"And watch that ignorant nigga gone get stupid in front of a crowd. Just mark my words." Dee threw her two cents in but vowed they were facts. "Trust me, you would have more fun at the grand opening."

"I know I would. And I really want to be there. That's why I'm going to try my best to still slide through later. But Dell had this planned months ago, and I don't feel like arguing wit' him about it. Y'all know how it gets."

"Hmm," Dee replied, her lips twisted up full of sarcasm. "I know he is a whole asshole." Toya looked at her, defeated. She knew Dee would say nothing different and could care less what she thought about it.

"It's cool if you can't make it. The club will be popping all the time now, so there will be other times." I let her off the hook. Promise was done with my hair. She wasted no time jumping in Dee's chair to get her own wig did up.

"Are you ready?" Reese asked as she approached me. She was going to do my makeup.

"Yeah." I stood and walked over to Reese's booth.

"Well, for those of you who are attending, I'm having a driving service pick each of you up, because no one is walking away sober tonight."

"I'm wit' all of that. It's been a minute since I stepped out." Dee was hyped. "I can't wait to be drunk and lit."

"Me too. I'ma be sure to have double of everything," Promise added. "I already picked me up a bottle of Extra Strength Excedrin for that headache I plan on having tomorrow."

"Right," Dee cosigned. "Shit, I might just spend a night at your crib so I can share that bottle."

"Reese, are you sure you don't want me to send them to pick you up?" I asked one last time. I had tried to convince her twice already.

"No, I'm just going to come later. My babysitter gone

be running a little late, so I'll just drive." That was the first time she had given me the reason why. Now I understood.

After Reese was done with my makeup I shot out of the salon and drove straight home. I had to get dressed. My plan was to take a good long bubble bath to relax before going out. I knew my night would be long, and a shower would not be relaxing enough, it would be quick and impersonal. At the moment a relaxed mind would do me good.

I had a driver pick me up in a private Bentley. The ride over was quiet, just the way I wanted it. The driver pulled up to the club and got out to open the door for me. Just as I stepped out of the car, Promise pulled in. I had ordered her a private Bentley as well. She stepped out and we smiled at each other.

"Damn, Sis, I guess you dressed to kill tonight. That dress is hitting every curve just right."

"I hope so. I was trying to show this body off." I hunched my shoulders and grinned. I had picked out a metallic bodycon dress by Alexandre Vauthier. I couldn't front, the dress was expensive but comfortable. Even though it was tight, it fit every curve like Promise had declared. It would move with my body like the perfect silk. I was dressed to party. And Promise didn't disappoint with her one-sleeve mini-dress with a low back cut-out. "And I see I taught you really good taste. That Valentino go hard."

"Well, you know. I'm a quick study. Shall we?" Promise let out her arm and we locked elbow to elbow. Security seemed to gracefully move the ropes as we stepped through like the bosses we were.

As we entered, I could see my security throughout. That I didn't spare any expense on safety was a must. The DJ was already mixing some Cardi B and Bruno Mars, and the dance floor was in full swing. People were quickly arriving, and that made me feel good.

"I told you this was a moneymaker." The grin Promise wore was stretched from ear to ear.

"You did. And it looks as though you were right. And it looks so nice in here. Thank you so much, Promise, for stepping in and making sure the last-minute things were handled so that the doors could open tonight. Especially getting the papers to secure the liquor license. That was huge. You really came through."

"No thanks needed. I always got your back. Now, let's walk through this crowd so you can shake a few hands, and thank some of these paying people." Promise chuckled and sniffed back tears that were coming on. She was such an emotional version of me.

"Come on, crybaby," I teased. I shook a few hands before we headed to our VIP area. I had made sure to reserve one of the biggest VIP areas we had. We had three big VIP areas which I called Suites VIP, and two regular size VIP rooms. Our Suite VIP area was stocked with all the luxuries we would need.

"That shit is nice." Promise gushed over the VIP spot. The plush couches and ottomans were of the best quality and brands.

I had replaced the furniture that Keisha had inside. Her stuff had been nice, but I didn't want to actually sit on anything she or Quincy had sat on.

"Aye, aye." Dee stepped into the VIP area chanting and twerking as Megan Thee Stallion's "Hot Girl Summer" blasted out of the speakers. "This is what I'm talking about. Party over here." Promise rushed over right next to her and they both started twerking.

"I swear you two gone get me started." I was ready to dance but chilled. Promise and Dee walked back over to where I was standing.

"Precious, this club poppin', period," Dee said. "Definitely my new party spot."

"No doubt. And be sure to bring all your friends and family." I laughed at my shameless promotion as one of the waitresses came over to take our orders for drinks.

"Katrina, I thought you might not make it." I was glad to see her finally show up.

"Not make it? Nah, I wouldn't miss this for the world. I went home to take a nap and slept a little longer than expected. Besides, I would be pissed if I missed all this." She glanced around the VIP room.

"I know, right?" I signaled for one of the waitresses. When she came over, I had her bring Katrina a drink.

"It's on point up in here, Precious. Girl, you are doing it big," Katrina said.

"Thank you," I replied from where I was standing. I could see a few guys that I recognized as ballers around the way. They were speaking to my security.

One of the security guys, Chad, came inside. "Hey, it's a few neighborhood ballers tryin' to get inside. Say they want to congratulate you on your new spot."

I pretty much recognized them all; there was only one who I was not familiar with. "Have they been through security outside?" I knew the answer to that already but wanted to double-check for my own nerves.

"Yeah, and they are clean," Chad confirmed.

"Okay, send them in, then. Just keep a close watch." I wasn't really scared of anything, but I was who I was, and some people knew what I looked like. That meant I had to take extra precautions even when I didn't want to. Because I never took my safety for granted.

Promise walked over to me as the guys came inside. "You said they could come in here?" she asked, her eyes darting from me to the three guys that were headed straight for us. She had stepped closer to the bar and turned her back for moment, talking to Dee, when I had given security the okay.

"Yep, why not?"

"I guess it's cool. They all fine." Promise's eyes were glued to them.

"Ain't that the truth." Dee had moved in beside her and agreed.

The first guy, who seemed to be the leader of whatever they had going on, moved in first.

"Hey, Precious, is it?" He talked over the music. I glared at him. No answer came out of my mouth.

Promise burst out laughing. "Wait, did you not just ask to come up in here?"

The guy looked at me then her and smiled. "I did." His answer came out as unsure.

"So, my guess is you know her name. Why the guessing game?" Promise still wore her grin.

"You right. My bad." The unknown guy seemed intrigued by Promise. "I'm Quan aka Q." It was clear that he thought now was as good a time as any to come out from under Promise's crossfire.

"Hi, Quan, I'm Promise, and this is my sister Precious." Promise's introduction was comical. She extended her hand to him and they shook hands.

"It's nice meeting you, Promise. And Precious." Quan reached out to shake my hand. I wasn't in the habit of shaking hands with strangers, but I was in a good mood and Promise had aced the entertainment for me. I shook his waiting hand. He seemed pleased. "I just wanted to come up here and congratulate on your new spot. It's really nice. Besides that, I love supporting business that have faces like ours. I own a barbershop not far from here. We welcome you to the area."

"Thank you, I can appreciate that." I kept it simple, but

I did sincerely appreciate the support, especially if it was coming from the community.

"And here is a welcome gift." The tall, dark-skin guy standing next to Quan passed him a bottle. Quan passed it right off to me.

"A bottle?" I was surprised. "You didn't have to do that." I mean, the money was good for business, but he had gone all out just to welcome us.

"It was nothing. Like I said, welcome. Now, I'll let you ladies get back to it."

"Well, you and your crew are cool to hang out in here and have some drinks," I offered. He accepted and they walked off toward the VIP area's private bar.

Promise reached for the bottle he had given me. "Dang Precious, this a bottle of that Armand de Brignac. That shit like nine thousand a fucking bottle." Promise looked at the bottle again as if she was trying to be sure of the name. "Damn . . . who that nigga say he is?"

I almost laughed at her reaction, but I was little curious too. "He says his name Quan." I tried to appear nonchalant.

"Dude say he own a barbershop." Dee hunched her shoulders. "I don't know, maybe business good and shit. He fine, though." She smiled. "Not to mention he was eating you up with those eyes of his, Promise."

"Ha. No, he was not. But let's crack this bottle. If Ms. Precious here don't mind."

"Do whatever you want with it." I could care less. I was ready to get back to the party.

"In that case pour up, bitch," Dee chanted.

"Sho' nuff," Promise yelled, then popped the bottle.

I held out my glass to be filled up. Promise wasted no time obliging. "Let's toast, ladies. To the new club and success." I held up my glass first and they followed.

After our toast we went into full party mode. We danced, finished off the bottle that Quan gifted, and took shots all night. The club turnout was all that I had hoped it would be. I had gone down to check on the numbers. The bar was selling out, not to mention the bottle that Quan had purchased was huge, and it was clear from the crowd and all booked VIP's that we had done well. I was thankful. And it was clear that everyone was having a good time, especially Promise. She was turned all the way up.

I had tried to ignore it, but it was clear that Quan was fond of Promise just as Dee had declared. He kept his eyes on her all night, and before he left, I watched him slip Promise a note. As we left the club, she confirmed that he had given her his phone number because she refused to give him hers. I only laughed as my driver opened the door to the Bentley and I climbed inside.

Chapter 13

"I meant to come by yesterday but I got held up at the club waiting on a new order. But I really wanted to get by here to check on the new girls." Katrina and I had decided that it was best to go ahead with the original plan and hire two workers, one part-time, the other full. This week had been their first week, and as usual, I just didn't have time to get by there to check on them. That is why I knew without a doubt bringing Katrina in full-time was for the best. Plus, she was a good, dependable, hard worker. I really counted on her.

"They are doing okay except for that part-time girl." Katrina silently rolled her eyes. "She was supposed to be here this morning. Long story short, she ain't here nor has she bothered to call." It was clear Katrina was pissed. If her body language didn't spell it out, it was all in her tone. Katrina rarely ever missed work and was always prompt. So, I knew as a manager she didn't play with others doing the opposite. "I think she should be fired." She was matter of fact. Another reason why I hired her. "It has only been a week, and already I wasn't feeling her work vibe anyway. Ain't much else I need to see from her, it ain't worth it. My training time is valuable and not to be wasted on the ungrateful." Katrina was just not having it.

"Well, as the manager, if that is your observation of her, then I'm fine with it." I wanted her to know that I supported her decision. The girl was passionate about her position. I could respect that on a lot of different levels. "But you will need to get someone soon to fill her spot. So you have to set them interviews right back up."

"For now, I think we are cool with just Dominique, since she is the full-time person anyway. That is, if it is okay with you? I mean honestly, we got it. The part-time position was just a filler anyway. You know, breaks and in betweens, as we discussed. And for now, I got that." Katrina seemed sure of herself to handle it.

"I'm okay with it. But if and when you start to feel like it's too much, you need to set up interviews to get someone else in here. I don't want you getting overwhelmed."

"I know. Maybe in a couple months I'll look into hiring someone and getting them trained. Don't worry, it'll be fine."

"I trust your judgment." I sighed. "Now let me go in this office and check these numbers." It seemed that was all I did lately, the club, the dry cleaners, or the crew. That was all I knew. I had started to wonder if I should have gone to school for accounting if this was all my life was going to be.

Chapter 14

The water from the pool felt so good on my feet, I thought long and hard about jumping in for a swim, but I decided against it. Instead, I let my head fall back and allowed the sun to soothe my face with my eyes closed. I could sit here all day and just relax. But Promise and I had plans for spa facials, full body massages, and all that. And I was thrilled. Only I didn't want to pull myself from my poolside to go. Sighing, I slowly pulled my feet from the water, stood up, dried my feet off, and made my way inside the house.

"It is a beautiful day outside." Anna walked past me when I was back inside.

"It is. And that is why I'm going to enjoy it. No work for me." It felt so good to say. And I hoped it came true. I had instructed Plies and Katrina to only call me for flood, fire, or blood, nothing less. The club was closed, so I was good there. "And I want you to get out of here early today. No matter what you have to do," I ordered Anna. But I could only hope that she listened to me as well.

"Today I promise I will. Samantha and I made plans to go to the beach." She sounded really happy.

"That sounds fun. Tell her I said hi."

"I sure will."

"Well, I'm going to put on my shoes and I'm out." I talked and walked at the same time. I was in such a hurry to get to the relaxation that awaited me, I almost tripped over myself.

I had made us reservations at the Hotel Bel-Air spa. It was a popular spot in LA where the celebrities or just the well-off hung out to be pampered. Promise and I made it our business sometimes to have a spa day there. We also made sure to support the spas in the hood, but today, the Bel-Air spa was the pick. I pulled into the parking lot and had to keep from running inside. I was truly amped to be pampered.

"Hey, you." Promise was standing in the lobby. I could tell she too had just arrived.

"Hey." We hugged. We were always ecstatic to see each other.

"Come on, let's get checked in. I can't wait to get started." It was clear Promise shared my enthusiasm. We both worked too much.

We stepped to the counter to check in and I gave my name for our reservation. I always made this my treat. Promise used to try to argue to pay, but I made it clear. I was the rich one. There was no need to argue. We had laughed and she'd agreed. The hostess took us back to undress, then first up was mani-pedis. Soon as we sat down, they started with the drinks.

"Ooh, chile, I been waitin' on this drink since I rolled out the bed this morning." Promise sipped from her wineglass as soon as it was placed in her hand. I grinned.

"I feel you." I sipped mine. "It's on point too." We talked about the club and drank probably a whole bottle of wine before our feet were done. By the time we were headed back for the facials, we were both relaxed.

"So you gone make me ask?" I said as we sat down.

"Ask about what?" Promise played dumb, but I knew she knew what I was asking.

"About Quan, or wait—aka Q?" I repeated how he had introduced himself to me. I knew something was up with them, but Promise had been closemouthed about it.

"Oh, that." She tried to downplay it.

"No, don't do that. I ain't stupid." It had been a couple months since they had started dating.

She laughed. "He cool. Just like us, he stays busy with work. You know he owns two barbershops?" she said, her eyebrows raised. "When we first met, I thought he only owned one."

"Two, huh?" I repeated. "Yeah, you already know I checked up on him."

"Mm-hmm. This I know. Because I know you. So what you dig up?"

"Well, if I dug up any bad shit by now, I think you already know you would have an earful." I gave her a quick side-eye with a grin. "His reputation still pretty clean in the streets. But I still want to meet him." She had yet to allow that by never mentioning him.

"You already met him twice. Remember?"

"True, but that was at the club. There's a million other people in there, so that does not count. I'm talking about personally. Besides, you never really bring him over to talk to me when you at the club."

"Well, how personal can it get when the dude introduced himself to you? As I remember it, he went out of his way to do that. Even buying you a nine-thousand-dollar bottle of champagne. What else could there be?" She shrugged.

"Don't even play with me. Now you trying it. You know exactly what I mean."

"So you ain't buying that either?" I shook my head while the aesthetician tried to apply cream to my face. "Okay, well, at least it was worth a try."

"If you say so." I smiled. "No, for real. How about I take you two out for dinner when I get back from Miami next week?" It was time for me to head back out there to check on things again.

"I guess. I will talk to Q and get his schedule so we can set it up. Like I said earlier, the man owns two barbershops. He stays busy. But I will let you know."

"Ai'ght. Just give me the time and the day that works for you busy businesspeople," I teased.

Once our facial cream masks were applied, the massage therapist came in to get us so that our massages could begin while the masks set. I was so relaxed that I was on cloud nine. And from the beam on Promise's face, she was on the same cloud. By the end of our retreat, we agreed to make this spa day more often than once every two months or so. We would see if our schedules permitted. We both laughed that we doubted it.

Chapter 15

"It's like I told you the last time you were out here, everything running smooth. Rob and Case holding this shit down," Plies said.

"And I don't expect no less. I knew from day one y'all would hold it down. Our rep is on the line," I replied.

"And it will be intact when this run is over. Besides, ain't neither Rob nor Case caught a body since we been here, which is a plus considering they are manning new territory. And they got the rookies walking in a straight. Plus, we been on the reup damn near three times a week. Shit booming. And LA still on top. I come home twice a week, I do a double reup right before I leave and soon as I get back."

"That's what's up. And you know that new product that just came through will be shipping out to us in two days. So you gotta be back in LA to distribute. Mob been catching the back on the straights. I gotta say everything is on schedule and business is still a success."

"No doubt. I wouldn't have it any other way.

"You, Rob, and Case ain't out here falling in love wit'

the three oh five, are you?" I joked. "You know Miami is the mecca of tourists for pretty shit."

"Mane, hell no." Plies boasted, but was all smiles. "Listen, the view nice and all, but me and the fellas all agree that this country-ass heat ain't it. It's a different hot out here. We ain't fuckin' wit' that on the long term." He chuckled.

"I have to agree with y'all on that."

"But yo, what's up with your boy, Marlo?"

"What you mean? I thought everything was cool wit' him. Clearly, he been opening up them doors." I gladly repeated Pablo's promise.

"No doubt, that he has, but I just can't feel the dude out, though, you know?"

"Well, I guess that's the mystery of him. Don't let that get you shook, and you lose focus. I just want you to keep your nose clean and make sure Rob and Case are straight. Hopefully, in a few months we'll be up outta here and back in LA for good." I could feel his unease about Marlo. His appearance and his role just didn't seem to match. I knew a lot of people that would say that didn't matter, but it did raise questions. None of that mattered, though. We had a job to do, and it would get done. Plies assured me once again he had everything under control. I told him I had to get going. I had a meeting with Penelope, and it was a bit of a drive.

"Precious, let me apologize for keeping you waiting." Penelope greeted me with open arms, and we hugged. One of their dozen housekeepers had brought me outside to wait by the pool for her. We were meeting up to chat as usual, business and pleasure. "I missed you the last few times you were in town, but I just couldn't get away. You know this or that."

"No need to apologize, it's fine." A waitress approached us with a tray of wine-filled glasses, and a waiter behind her held a tray of shrimp cocktail. Penelope and I reached for both. "How is Pablo?" I asked.

"He's good. You know him, all business and a cigar." We both laughed.

"I'm sure he is getting daily reports from Marlo. So I'm hoping everything is to his liking."

"And it is. Sales are phenomenal, the body count is down, and the customers continue to increase. This is where we needed to be."

"I'm glad to hear he is content. My guys are honored to be able to bring value to the area."

"Listen, I know you still got important business in LA that you need to get back to quick as possible. And I wanted to assure you that Pablo approved the new product as we discussed. It is a hundred percent pure. I know there was some worry with the hit in the Bay Area that there might be a delay, but it's already through customs and will still arrive as you had wished. So I hope your guys are ready."

That was music to my ears. Some knuckleheads in the Bay Area had been targeted by the feds because of some money laundering accusations. A few shipments were being monitored really closely to be sure everything was straight. "We look forward to the network."

"Good to hear. I trust this will continue to boost where needed. On that note, how is the dry cleaners going? Oh, wait, and the new club? I don't want to forget about that."

"They both are doing good; business couldn't be better. The club is definitely poppin'. Next time you in LA you got to come party with us."

"And I will as soon as I can travel to the West Coast, and I really need to get out there. Lately, I have been only using my passport. And frankly, I'm sick of those long-ass flights."

"Well, how is the store in Saint-Tropez?"

"Great. Business is booming. That's why I need to get out to the West Coast, or at least another reason I have to get out there. I want to hunt for a good location so I can open a shoe store out there. I'm even considering doing one out in Hollywood."

"Oh, for real? That would be dope. Well, let me know when you're coming. I actually know a few spots that you might be interested in for the one out in LA."

"Cool. I figure why not expand to Cali if we can do a takeover in Saint-Tropez. LA and Hollywood piece of cake." She snapped her fingers. "Soon as I can get away, I'm on it. You've been back and forth to LA like you agreed to. And I know business comes before pleasure, but what's up? How is your personal life going? As in the dating department? I mean, it's been a while since I had time to pry." She grinned. "But you never mention anyone, so . . ."

I sighed. This question was becoming too common. "I swear if it ain't you, it's Promise. You two always bugging me about that."

"And for good reason. All work and no play is a horrible combination: frustration and endless drought."

"Well, since you put it like that, dang. But honestly, I don't even think about that. Between my business here and LA, the only thing I have time to think about is the hustle. And I know you understand that."

Penelope looked over her beautiful pool and seemed to think over my words. "Real talk. And trust me, I get it. But listen, Precious, you are young, things can be balanced. And yes, even with this cryptic lifestyle we lead."

I shook my head and sipped my wine. Penelope seemed to think some more. I could tell she wanted to get through to me. "I know the game is all heart, no real sleep, and full throttle to end. But you got to make room for needs, or trust me, you will lose sight of the other three."

"And that is where those Don Julio shots come into play," I teased. We both laughed.

"Ain't that it?" she agreed. "I consult with Don at least twice a week." She held up her hand and we both laughed.

"Ladies." We both turned to see Marlo approaching. I had to shut my mouth to conceal my surprise. Penelope had not mentioned he would be stopping by.

"Marlo." Penelope smiled as Marlo bent down and kissed her gently on the cheek.

"Hi." I stared at him. I didn't know about Penelope, but it was burning my soul to ask him if he was hot and crazy. He was dressed in a full-length red coat that stopped just below his knees. The guy was just peculiar, but Penelope acted as if he were normal. I had to admit, though, he had manners. It was clear that somebody had set him on the path to respect. It appeared that he had been raised right.

"So I guess you been waiting on this eighty-degree day to pull that coat out, huh?" Penelope teased him, but I was glad she asked.

"It comes around once in a while," he joked, revealing a set of perfect white teeth. But nothing to explain the craziness of him wearing that coat.

"Would you like a drink?" Penelope offered him.

"No, I'm good. Just received word on the south side, three blocks that I had put claim on were cleared for takeover. They will be ready in a week. I will have them supplied with workers and product."

"Good. And I need you to have the ward swept. No bodies would be ideal but make the point."

"Done." He turned to me. "Precious, will you take another ride with me?"

That also caught me by surprise, just like his hot-ass coat. For one, I had no idea he was coming over; two, he asked me to take a ride with him. I looked from him to Penelope, whose facial expression said *take the ride.* "Um, well, I drove here." My voice had a hesitant tone to it.

"That is quite alright. Your car will be fine. I'll watch it with both of my eyes." Penelope smiled at me. I got the feeling she was enjoying this.

Soon, Marlo and I were pulling into a location that was full of land, trees, and a building that looked to be newly built. It appeared to be some of kind of factory, except there was no real parking lot, just dirt and gravel, and only three other cars parked out front.

I felt Marlo's eyes on me, so I looked him straight in the face.

"Are you strapped?" he asked me, out of the blue.

"Of course," I answered him, but the look on my face read his question was a dumb one. I would never be caught in an unknown city in my line of work without being strapped. Hell, I didn't even ride around LA without being strapped. That was one of the first things DaVon taught me about this life.

Without another word, he climbed out of the car, and I took that as my cue to follow. Once he reached the door, he knocked twice real fast, then waited a minute and knocked only once. I glanced around at the area while we waited. The door opened.

When we were inside, the guy who opened the door led us to a room that appeared to be the office of the building. I stepped in behind Marlo and noticed two guys standing in the far right corner. My eyes quickly scouted the room. One of the guys started talking to Marlo, and he responded instantly. The other guy in a white wifebeater jumped into the conversation, and suddenly, the conversation was heated. It went from zero to one hundred real quick. I saw an unfamiliar guy come from out of nowhere.

Marlo's coat seemed to blow open. Two guns came up, one in each hand, and he fired, shooting the unfamiliar guy and the other two men. Another tried to sneak up from the opposite side. I turned just enough to aim and shoot him, the bullet landing evenly between his eyes.

A few quick steps backward and we were out of the building, inside Marlo's car and speeding away from the messy scene. Finally, we were back onto a main road of nothing but highway, heading back the same way we had come.

"Thank you for having my back." Marlo broke the silence.

"How about you tell me what that was all about."

"Fair question. The two brothers in the corner were thieves trying to steal blocks that did not belong to them. They both had been warned by Penelope herself." I knew that meant there was nothing else to be done.

"Next time, I would like a heads-up."

"In this line of business there is not always a heads-up." He glanced at me and smirked. "Besides, I thought this hot-ass coat and me asking if you were strapped was heads-up enough."

My eyes went back to the coat, and suddenly it all made sense. The big coat to hide the big guns that he shook the room with. I started to say something else—the words were on the tip of my tongue—but I chilled. Because he was right, and I would tell somebody else the exact same thing.

"We almost back in the city. Would you like to stop for a drink?" Talk about unpredictable, I was beginning to think this guy was it. He had shown up out of nowhere, taken me on an unwarranted drive, put me in a line of crossfire, and now, he was offering me a night out on the town in form of a drink. I was done.

"No. My flight leaves early." He nodded and with his eyes glued to the highway he smiled.

Back at Penelope's, I jumped in my rental and headed straight to my hotel for a shower and drink. I sat back and realized that I had now been introduced to the real Marlo. I had to admit his aim was on point and he was clever. Penelope and Pablo had not made a mistake with him on their team. At least at this point I didn't think so.

Chapter 16

Setting the elliptical to match my speed, I felt rejuvenated. It had been a week since I had been to the gym, and I was not happy about it. I tried my best to get in there several times a week, but between all the businesses and meetings I had going on, I sometimes just could not squeeze it into my tight schedule. I did manage to go for a run twice during the week, but I still wanted to hit the gym. And even though I had a full gym at the house, for some reason I couldn't motivate myself get in there and sweat off my calories.

Not one drop of sweat had attempted to penetrate my skin, but I could feel the burn coming on as one leg followed by the other, glided back and forth. With R. Kelly beating my eardrums through my Beats by Dre, crying his heart out on "Forever," I attempted to keep my stride to the beat. My speed was top notch, and nothing could slow me down. Except my intuition that told me something, or someone, was trying to get my attention. Slowly, I allowed my eyes to open, then pulled out the wireless bud that was in my left ear.

"Well, I was wondering when you were going to open

those eyes of yours or if I was going to happen to scare you straight when I snatched those Beats out of your ears. That for sure would get your attention." Promise grinned. Stepping on the elliptical right next to me, she adjusted her speed.

"I swear I will kick your butt if you try rattle me like that. Just evil." I smiled. "And why are you late? I have lost a whole two pounds waiting on you." I continued to move at top speed, never breaking my stride.

"You know me, I needed one of those cinnamon toasted bagels with some cream cheese before I came up in here. So basically, Panera Bread became the focal point of my morning. Shit, because one thing I knew for sure. This devil-ass elliptical was not going anywhere."

I couldn't help but giggle at her. "Get your crazy butt started on that run, then, because you gone need an extra five miles to burn the fat from that sinful bagel off."

"Sho' you right. As soon as I gobbled up the last bite I hated myself." She wasted no time falling into step. "I tried calling you last night before I went to bed. It was still pretty early, I figured you might still be up catching up on one of your reality shows."

"Nope, not last night. I was not feeling it. I was crazy tired. I showered and went to sleep early. I didn't even have any dinner."

"Tired, huh?"

"Yep. And that hot shower didn't help matters. Once I was fresh and clean, it was a wrap. My body fell into that bed and there was no getting out."

"Trust I understand. I been feeling like that some nights getting in from the salon. Some nights I'm too busy to have a nightcap. Now, you know I gotta be tired for that."

"I know, right?" I agreed. "I could have stood to have two shots last night before I went to bed. But it's all good."

"Can't be nothing but all good when exhaustion knocks

you on your butt. So how was Miami? Things good out that way?"

"Things are on the right track. Flowing the way they should, thankfully."

"Plies, holding it down, huh? With his fine self." She looked over at me and winked.

"Shut up, Ms. Thirsty," I joked.

"Damn, sure am thirsty. On God, if it wasn't for him and Clip being friends, I would have took his ass down a long time ago."

"I swear you something else. Just plain crazy."

"Something like that. But only Tuesday through Saturday. Sunday and Monday, I clean 'em up and send them home." She giggled and increased her speed.

"My sister the player. No nigga ain't cuffin'." I laughed.

"You about got it right. Hell, name one of them that's worth it. Games, games is all they play. I just happen' to be wit' it."

"Do you." I kept it real.

"Hey, come to think of it, I been meaning to ask you about that dude out there in Miami. But every time you come back, I forget. You remember?" She snapped her fingers. "The weird one you were talking about?" Without a doubt, I knew exactly who she was referring to.

"Marlo." I said his name as if to confirm her curiosity. I had no clue what made her think of him.

"Yeah, Marlo. That's his name." She grinned, looking at me as if a light went off in her head. "What's up with Mr. Softy?" she teased.

Her description of him was funny, and I would have laughed, but the picture of Marlo pulling those two guns from under his coat was no laughing matter. He had handled those guns like a professional hit man. I would have been impressed if I could be easily impressed. "Actually, he is not as soft as I originally thought." I decided to keep it real again.

"Wait . . . what?" Promise's eyebrows raised. All the signs read *do tell*. I couldn't do nothing but shake my head at her nosy gesture.

"I hate to be the one to break it to you, but Marlo actually does have balls. Yeah, turns out they were bigger than I gave him credit for."

"Aww, hell naw. And actually, you didn't give that brother no credit. You stamped him as a square and left it at that. But spill it. And you better not be withholding juicy details like you slept with him."

That threw me off. My left leg almost missed its glide on the beat. I had no idea she would jump to a conclusion like that. But this was Promise—her mind was wild. "Whoa, slow down." I held up my right hand in a stopping motion while keeping up with the beat. "Let's be clear, them are not the balls I'm talking about, Ms. Nasty."

Promise shook her head in an up and down motion. "Ohhh, my bad." She giggled.

"You and that one-track mind. Just nasty."

"Aye, I thought where there is smoke, there is hot steamy sex." She continued to giggle.

"Uh, no." I playfully rolled my eyes at her. "Now, if you calm down and give me a chance to tell my story, maybe I can get it right. Damn, you done jumped the gun. Sex. I swear you trippin'." I was still in awe of her quick conclusion.

"Okay, go ahead. I'm all ears."

I filled her in on Marlo and his moment. Promise listened and sped up even faster on her elliptical. I was sure that Panera Bread was her motivation. She had eaten that delicious bagel, with her favorite cream cheese, and now she felt guilty. We ran on the ellipticals for another half hour before bringing the machines to a halt. No sooner had we stopped and I took a drink from my water bottle than my bladder alerted me that it was full to the top. I excused myself and rushed off to the bathroom.

"I am so sorry." The average-height, brown-toned guy that stood in front of me apologized. We had almost bumped into each other as I rounded the corner from the bathroom.

"It's fine." I said. I looked him in the eyes. Sweat beads were on his forehead and a towel was wrapped around his neck.

"I'm Austin . . . Austin Payne." He extended his well-groomed right hand out to me.

"Nice bumping into you, Austin," I replied, not offering up my name and flat out ignoring the hand he had extended to me. I was more interested in stepping around him and continuing on.

I started to do just that so that I could get back to Promise, but he asked, "Do you work out here at this location a lot?"

"I get it in when possible," was my evasive reply. There was no way I was telling a stranger my consistent moves. Who was this guy?

"This my workout partner." Promise stepped in. I hadn't even seen her approach us. "Hi," she added.

"Hi, I'm Austin Payne." He reintroduced himself without any hesitation.

I watched Promise's moves as a familiar look came over her face. "Hey, you are the guy that spoke at that seminar about brand building I attended a few months back. The professor from the university. I remember because you were the only professor there."

"Yes, I did speak at a seminar. As of late, I've been speaking at them all over LA."

"Well, you were very informative." Her eyes reverted

from him to me, where she delivered a smile, then focused back on Austin. "How rude of me. I'm Promise, and this is my sister. But I guess you can see the resemblance."

Austin's lips spread across his face in a huge smile. My iPhone pinged and they both looked at me. It was business as usual, that seemed the only time my phone received a call or text. And at this moment I considered it to be right on time.

I ended the conversation. "Austin, it really was nice to meet you, but Promise and I have to get going." Promise's smile dropped. She turned and looked at me, her face a huge question mark. I knew she was not ready to go, she wanted to stay and chat. But I had to leave, so it was not up for debate. Without another word I turned and walked away. She followed, then sped up beside me.

"Why do we have to get going? I wanted to stay and talk to him. Shit, I was just getting started." Her long legs moved just as fast as mine. But the burn from the elliptical was definitely kicking in. I fought the urge to slow down, because if I could, I would jump right back on the elliptical. While I may have wanted to escape Austin, I was not by far ready to leave the gym, but I had to meet up with Plies, and that trumped my workout.

"I have business, Promise. And I thought you might not want me to leave you with the guy. Or should I say stranger."

"I swear, you are so paranoid." She chuckled at me.

I headed straight for the locker room to grab my keys. I never brought along a gym bag because I made it a rule to never shower at the gym. There were too many germs floating around. And even though it was one of the top fitness places in LA, I trusted no one.

"So did you see the way Austin gawked at you? He was eating you up with his eyes. Those beautiful brown eyes," she added.

"No he was not. Don't do that." I shut her down with that instantly.

"And ain't he just fine?" She jumped to the next thing without arguing her case. I wouldn't be surprised if she didn't hear a thing I said. She had her mind made up.

"He ai'ght," I responded. "Nothing special."

"I swear you woke with your eyes wide shut," she accused, with a chuckle in her tone. Then sucked her teeth.

"Maybe." I didn't deny it.

"All you can say is 'maybe'? Yep, it's official, you are woke with your eyes shut, because that man fine as hell, my dear sister. Every bitch up in here would say that."

"I'm sure they would. Most of them probably thirsty." I looked at her and smiled as we reached the exit. "Look, I will hit you up later after I handle this business."

"Cool. I'm going back to finish my run on the elliptical since you are leaving me hanging. So, you can run off and work. Or whatever." She pouted.

"I know and I'm sorry. But I promise to make it up to you. Now bye." I gave her a quick hug, then I headed for the exit. I had to get home and take a shower before meeting up with Plies.

Chapter 17

"Katrina, the numbers just get better and better week after week. I'm really considering opening up another location for the dry cleaners. It's a no-brainer."

"Really? I mean, I don't think it's a bad idea. Ain't that what Mr. Larry dreamed of? A chain of these all over LA."

"Yeah, he talked about it all the time when I was really young. But as you know, he just couldn't get this one to get the numbers that he needed to produce. And with the equipment being old and constantly breaking down . . . he just never got the chance." I could picture the smile my dad would have on his face just to hear me have a conversation about expanding his beloved business. He would have been overwhelmed with excitement.

"I remember when things were going bad with the equipment. It was tough for him. He would sit in his office with his head in his hand." Katrina's voice broke off like she would tear up. I knew how she felt about my dad. "Mane, I wish he were here. You think he would be shocked that you brought me back to work here?"

"Nah, he always knew how you felt about the dry cleaners. And you always been family. He would just be glad to know you came back." Katrina nodded in agreement. I decided to go ahead and drop the other bomb I had considered, but already knew my answer. "Well, I would like to open this new location. And I would like for you to be the general manager of that location, as well. I will increase your salary even more, of course." I had to add that so she knew just how serious I was.

Tears flooded Katrina's face as the words left my mouth. "Precious, I really don't know what to say. You have been being so good to me. Everything that I have been praying for is just coming out of nowhere. I can't thank you enough."

"Like I have told you a million times before, you deserve it. You work so hard here, giving this place one hundred percent of your time. And again, you are like family, you and Lalah. I'm just glad to be in a position to offer you these opportunities."

"And I am thankful for each and every one. Now, I can pay you back all of the money I have borrowed from you over time."

"Don't start that, Katrina." I played at scolding her but wanted to be clear as I had always tried to be in the past when she started this conversation. "You owe me nothing. Anything you have ever asked me for, I was glad to give it. For the last time, you owe me nothing. Not a dime. That's the end of that." I really hoped this time I was clear. "Now, I got some ideas for the new spot. I will be meeting with a realtor soon to look at some options . . . Excuse me, I gotta take this." The ringing of my phone interrupted us. The number was unknown, but the realtor had told me he might be replacing his phone. I answered.

His voice was familiar, but until he actually said his name I was unsure. "Austin?" I repeated his name with a surprised tone that I was unable to hide. Mainly because I had no idea why the man was on the other end of my cell phone. I was at a loss for words.

"Um . . . I know this is a quite a surprise . . . but Promise, your sister," he added as if I didn't know who Promise was, "gave me your number." He was definitely nervous or playing a square.

Either way, once I had heard Promise's name it all made sense. I should have known from the time he announced himself on the phone that she was behind this.

"I'm not sure if you are busy at the moment?" His hesitation was a bit annoying.

Not that it mattered either way. I wasted no time answering his question. "Actually I am in the middle of something."

"Well, I will make this quick. I was wondering if you would mind going out with me?"

I blinked hard and swallowed. Nothing was in my mouth, but I think the pure shock of his question was bit much. I didn't even know him. His words came out nervous, but his actions seemed bold. "Um, Austin. I'm going to have to say no. I have a lot going on." I wasn't even sure why I added more than the word no, but the guy had me caught me off guard.

A whimper of words tried to come but he paused and cleared his throat. "I know this is out of the ordinary and I understand." He paused again and cleared his throat. I wished he would spit it out. Had he not heard me say I was busy? "It's just the other day when I met you at the gym, I instantly wanted the chance to get to know you. But you left in a hurry."

"Yeah, like I said then, I had to go. Same as now." I threw that out there again. I really was trying hard not be rude. But the brother was pushing me.

"I see, and I promise not to hold you up." What the hell

did he call his continued talking? Shit. I rolled my eyes. "When Promise gave me your number, I honestly didn't have the nerve to call you." He chuckled lightly. I remained silent. "But I just finished up this seminar, and right in the middle of my speech, it occurred to me that surely if I can talk to a room full of two hundred people, I could call you up and ask you out to dinner. So here I am."

"Two hundred is a lot." Somehow and for some reason I did not know, I agreed with him.

"I was thinking something simple, nothing fancy. Just dinner and mutual conversation."

"Tell you what. Just text me the restaurant, date, and time. But I really gotta go." I ended the call before he could respond. For one, I could not believe I had agreed to go. And two, I was not in the mood for questions. All he had to do was follow my directions if he intended to see me at his dinner.

I wasted no time getting back up front to continue my conversation with Katrina. She was with a customer, and she finished up with them first. "I have to say, Precious, I'm just too excited. I can't wait for the new location to open."

"I'm excited too. You know we have a lot of work cut out for us. Once I meet up with the realtor, hopefully a spot is found right away. You know my patience is short. But I will keep you in the loop on everything."

"Okay. Please let me know what you need me to help with. You already know I'm down for the long hours, so please hit me up, anytime," she assured me.

"No doubt you will be involved every step of the way." I looked at the time on my phone. "Listen, I gotta drop this deposit off at the bank. I'll call you later, though." I all but ran to my car. I had to call Promise right away. I opened the door to my Mercedes truck, slid inside, and said her name into my Bluetooth.

"What were you thinking giving that strange dude my number?" I asked Promise right away. I didn't even give her a chance to say hello.

She didn't seem deterred in the least. She screamed through the phone with so much exhilaration, I had to hit on my brakes as I pulled out of the dry cleaners parking lot. Her scream startled the shit out of me.

"Girl, he called. I mean damn, I was beginning to worry. I gave him that number a week ago. And as hard as it has been, I have been patiently waiting to get this call from you."

"First off, if you don't stop all that screaming before you make me wreck out. You scared the hell outta me."

"Aww, I'm sorry. Please be careful, my dear sister, I did not realize you were driving. I was just excited to get this news. I thought he had changed his mind or given up." She quickly jumped right back on the subject of Austin.

I rolled my eyes. "No, he didn't give up. Maybe procrastinated a bit, but he called. And for that I'm going to kill you. Murder you real slow . . ." I playfully threatened her. "You of all people know better than to give my number to anybody. Especially a man who says he tryin' to take me out."

"Precious, dude is a professor at a college, not some gangster over in Jordan Downs. Stop trippin'. Not to mention he fine as hell, regardless of what you say or try to downplay."

"I swear I don't know about you sometimes." Again, I rolled my eyes as if she could see me.

"Just continue to love me, things will work out." I could hear the humor in her tone and I knew her lips were stretched from cheekbone to cheekbone into a smile. "Now, tell me, did he actually ask you out? What was his exact question? Just run it down to me, and please don't leave anything out." She pressed me for information, still amped.

There was no way I was going back over the whole conversation that had transpired between us. I would keep it short and simple. I didn't want to talk about him any more than I needed to. "Listen, the answer to yo' question is yeah, he asked me out . . . and I said yes." I sighed with frustration.

"You did? Aw, I am so proud of you." If I didn't know any better, I would think she was jumping up and down. The phone was vibrating, and the sound was going in and out.

"Whatever just know it was against my better judgment. And I'm going to tell you now, do not bug me about this date. You better not bother me about what I'm going to wear, my hair, or nothin'. Got it?" I threw a warning finger up as if she was in front of me and could see it. But even I knew it was no guarantee she would honor my request. Promise did what she wanted. A blind man could see that.

"I won't, I won't," she chanted. Or should I say lied. "I would go so far as to say I promise . . ." She popped her mouth. "But that might be a lie, sooo . . ."

I couldn't help but laugh. "My thoughts exactly." With that I hung up on her because I knew she was telling the truth. I would just be glad when the whole fiasco was over with.

Chapter 18

The oven timer went off just as I entered the kitchen, so I was right on time. I slid oven mitts onto both hands before I retrieved the casserole dish from the heat that awaited as soon as I opened the oven door. I set the dish on the countertop and looked it over. It looked delicious and smelled even better. I looked around the kitchen. Everything was finally ready. This was the night I had invited Promise and Quan over for dinner, with all intents and purposes of getting a better read on him. I had spent time with him at the club a few times, but I wanted to see him without the hype and the rush of the atmosphere that the club possessed. Originally, I had planned to have a chef come in and cook the food. But at the last minute, I wanted to do something simple, quick, and tasty. So I decided to jump in the kitchen. I had thrown together lasagna, Greek salad, garlic bread, and butter rolls. For dessert I had made a homemade peach cobbler, and I had vanilla ice cream in the freezer. Even my mouth watered just thinking about it.

I wanted the mood to be as down to earth and comfortable as can be, so I decided we would eat at the kitchen table. The doorbell rang just as I started to fill a glass with ice from the ice maker.

"Coming," I yelled, as I made my way down the massive foyer that led to my front door. Promise had a key but never used it unless I took too long to answer the door. She wouldn't use it if she was bringing company either. We had discussed this because we never wanted outsiders to know we had access to each other's homes.

"Hey," Promise sang as soon as I pulled the double doors open. She wore a smile that was wider than the Mississippi. I could also read the *don't kill the guy* look in her eyes that she blinked back.

"Hey, you two. Come on in." I stepped to the side so they could enter. Quan looked the way he normally did. Cool, calm, and collected.

Inside he turned to face me. "Hey." He was full of confidence. "I know you invited me as your guest, but I don't like to show up empty-handed." He handed me a bottle of wine. Again, I noted that it was Armand de Brignac. The same bottle as the one he had purchased at the club to "welcome us to the community," as he had put it. From the looks of it, my inviting him over was already paying off, because the one thing I was learning quickly was he liked to spend his money. If he was a show-off or conceited I wasn't quite sure yet, but I was sure I would figure it out.

"Thank you." I accepted the bottle.

Promise started making sniffing sounds with her nose. "Damn, Precious, you got it smelling good up in here. Whatever you cooked must gone be really good."

"You know how I can get down when I want to," I playfully bragged with a wink. "I hope you two brought your appetites because I cooked way too much."

"I can always eat." Quan had the nerve to rub his stomach. I knew he was just trying to be a part of the conversation and I was probably being petty. But there was something about him rubbing his hand across his stomach that annoyed me. I played it off and smiled. He hadn't been there long, I had to get a grip on my petty before he ended up back outside and in his car before another word came out of his mouth.

"Well, everything is ready if you two would like to eat now while it's hot?"

"Heck yeah, let's do it." Promise had caught my annoyance. We were twins, we pretty much sensed everything about each other, so it just wasn't much I could hide from her.

"Promise, you can lead Quan to the kitchen and I'll make a quick stop to add this bottle to my collection."

Promise had already retrieved the lasagna dish from the counter and set it on the table when I entered the kitchen. I went to the refrigerator, grabbed the salad, and set it on the table. I then seized a bottle of wine I had chilling. I told Promise to get the garlic bread and rolls.

"Everything looks good." Quan observed the table once everything was set.

"Yep, you did your thing." Promise nodded with approval. "See, Quan, my sister a baddy and she can cook."

"Oh, stop." I shot Promise a serious look. I hated being the center of attention. "Alright, don't be shy, dig in." I reached for the salad first. I had cut the lasagna up into decent-sized squares. Quan reached for that dish first and put two squares onto his plate. Clearly he could eat. I guessed he didn't lie about that.

Promise reached for the garlic bread and wasted no time biting into her piece. "Bread of any kind is my guilty pleasure." She talked and chewed at the same time. I just smiled at her.

"So, you are from LA, right?" I started the conversation once everyone had a full plate, and they were obviously satisfied as they stuffed their faces. I was enjoying my food as well. My lasagna was so cheesy, juicy, and full of seasoning. I was certain it could be boxed and sold at any retail store. I patted my own self on the back.

"Yep, born and raised. Deep in the hood too. Lost two brothers to the streets before I was eighteen." He shared that part without being asked.

"Dang, baby. Sorry to hear that," Promise said. I was surprised to see that he had shared that since obviously he had not told Promise about it beforehand.

"It's cool, sweetheart." He gazed at Promise.

"Yeah, these LA streets ain't no joke." Unfortunately, I knew it all too well. But I was not in the mood to share my story. "Kinda sink or swim situation out here."

"No doubt. That's why I had to do something different. See, they were older than me. They were tied to the gangs even before they had the mind to try and get money. But me . . . I saw things different. Talent, if one wanted to put it into words. I knew how to fade somebody up by the time I was twelve. I was so good that instead of trying to get me to join a gang, everybody in the hood wanted me to cut their head. That became my ticket."

"That's what's up. Gotta set yo' self apart from them streets."

"Exactly. I'm glad I learned early. I hear you own a dry cleaners."

I glanced at Promise. She had been telling him my business.

"Quan was telling me about his journey to opening up his barbershop business. You know the pros and cons. He wondered about your process with the new club and all. But I told him that you owned a dry cleaners first, you were kinda experienced. How you stepped up and groomed me with the salon too." Her tone and the apologetic look on her face told me she was trying to explain. Because she knew better. I trusted her because I knew she would never tell him about my other life, but I didn't like the fact that he was questioning her about me running a business. The next thing I was learning about him was that he was nosy, and that I did not fuck with at all.

"Yeah, I see you opened the club and it seemed like you were seasoned at it and you own another business. So, I was thinking you could give me some advice. Because I've been thinking about opening up another business. But the memories from opening up the barbershops kinda make me apprehensive."

"Why apprehensive? How is business?"

"Business good at both, I can't lie. I have been very successful in the barber business, plus it's my passion. At first, I struggled. I knew how to cut heads, I ain't have no business sense, though. I just don't want to hit some of them same ugly hurdles that I dealt with in the beginning. But I really think it's time I try something else. You know, add another stream of revenue. Just wanted some fresh advice from someone who might save me a headache." He gave a little laugh.

I nodded, indicating that I understood. We talked for a bit longer, eating dessert along the way. I threw out a few pointers about starting up a business, a few things to avoid and such. I really encouraged him to get a business consultant because I wouldn't be giving out any more advice. Before long, it was time for me to go. I had told Promise the day before that I had plans, so she reminded me of the time. Quan asked if he could use the bathroom before they left.

"So, where you about to go anyway?" Promise was being nosy.

I had not told her that I was meeting up with Austin because I didn't want her to bug me about it. But since it was about to happen, I figured why not. "I guess you'll be happy to hear this. I'm meeting up with Austin for drinks." I playfully rolled my eyes at her.

"Hell yes, I'm happy. Finally. And don't you ruin it." She gave me a playful threatening nudge on the shoulder. "I'll know if you do."

"I'm sure you probably got a wire on me," I joked. "I really don't want to go. I should have never accepted when he asked." I sighed. "I almost used this dinner with you and Quan as my excuse not to go, this was my only free day for a minute . . . But I figure fuck it, he will only ask again. Guess I will go ahead and get it over wit'."

"Would you stop pouting and just enjoy yourself?" she said, just as Quan reentered the kitchen. I walked them to the door with Promise grinning from ear to ear. Then, reluctantly, I grabbed the keys to my Mercedes truck, headed out to the garage, jumped in, and hit the interstate. I could not believe that I was actually driving to meet a guy as in *going on a date*. That just sounded like too much, which is why I had only agreed to drinks and no dinner. That was too formal. Ugh, that damn Promise and her meddling. I turned up the radio and allowed Young Dolph featuring T.I. with "Foreva" to entertain me and busy my mind, 'cause any small thought would encourage me to turn around and go home.

Chapter 19

"Wait, is that Starbucks?" Dee turned around from her station to face me. When I opened my eyes before climbing out of bed, I had decided to make the salon my first stop of the day. Then on the drive over I had the idea of bringing coffee and bagels along for everyone.

"It sure is." I set one of the two drink carriers I was armed with down on the closest counter to me. "And I got bagels. Reese went out to my car to grab them."

"Ah damn, you really wanted to make my morning. I drove here half asleep. Coffee will do me good," Dee said as she perked up.

Reese's footsteps could be heard right before she entered the room. "These bagels smell so fresh and good. Make me want to bite right through the box to get to them." She came in carrying the dozen mixed bagels I handpicked.

"Sit those right here. And just pass me a tub of cream cheese. I went to bed last night without dinner." Dee sipped her first taste of her coffee.

"Well, I guess my first thought to bring all these goodies was correct." I smiled at both of them.

"Sure was. I am a true believer of following your first mind." Dee reached down in the box and retrieved a bagel. "Toya gone be so happy about these bagels. I literally just hung with her and she said she was starving."

"Eat up, then. But please, save Toya one of them cinnamon bagels. You know she love those. Or be prepared to throw down," I teased. "Where is Promise?"

"In her office." Reese sat down at her makeup station, bagel in one hand and coffee in the other.

I walked to the back and tapped on Promise's door. She had it pulled shut, but it was still cracked a little. I could smell the lemon bar wax she was burning.

"It's open," she announced. I opened the door to her sitting at her desk going over what appeared to be her weekly report.

"Oh, so you in here faking like you working?" I teased.

"Ha, whatever. You know I'm the busiest woman in show business. Well, that's besides my big sister. She's a badass." We both giggled. "What you are doing here this early in the morning?"

"Out and about, got shit to do. You know how it go . . . these streets stay poppin'. But I thought I'd stop in and see you before my day got crazy busy. Here is your morning fix." I handed her a cup of coffee. "And I got bagels out there."

"I swear you love me." Closing the documents she had been going through, she reached for the cup with wide, smiling eyes. "Thank you so much, I needed this." She took a sip without hesitation. "But I feel ya. My day about to be insane. I got like eight clients today. Shit, I need a break, a quick shot of Hennessey, and I ain't even started yet."

"Hey, you know I was thinking the same thing. Maybe we can get that shot later."

"No doubt." Promise pushed her report back to look at me. "So, it's been a couple days since the dinner at your crib. We ain't talked but I'm tryin' to see what's up. What you thinkin' about Quan? Your real thoughts?" I knew this was coming sooner or later.

I sat down on a chair at her desk facing her. I sucked on my teeth for a minute and flashed back to the dinner. "I'll say he's ai'ght." I had decided that for the moment, but my mind was not 100 percent made up yet. "But my eyes gone stay on him. You know my motto: I don't trust shit. No matter who the nigga might be. I stay woke."

A smile spread across Promise's face. "Of course you do." Her tone was joking. Promise knew I never sugar coated anything. I said what I thought. I would never be the type to eat dinner, share stories, and fall for the first impressions presented to me. It would take a lot more than a hard knock story, expensive wine, and few good manners to win me over. Promise was my one and only family member that was close and dear to me. Quan could never understand what that meant. But he would know firsthand what it meant if he ever crossed my sister.

"Hey, this LA. The school of hard knocks. In more ways than one."

"I'm still learning. But you right. Enough about me and Quan, though. Let's get down to the juicy stuff."

I raised my right eyebrow with confusion. "Juicy . . . what you talkin' about?" I played dumb. There could be one thing and one thing only she would call juicy. And I had known from the time I walked through the front door that this line of interrogation was on the menu.

"Precious, do not antagonize me with your games. I want to know how the date with Austin went? Don't you think you have made me wait long enough?"

I had not called her on purpose just to avoid this as long as I could. "First off, it was not a date. Let's be clear on that." I went in for the denial.

"Whatever. Just get to the point." She was on the edge

of the Italian chair that she'd ordered for her desk. She said it made her feel like a queen on her throne.

"Like I said, it was not a date." I refused to allow her to rush me. "It was drinks." She playfully rolled her eyes at me. "Everything was cool, you know. He was nice and all, but . . ."

"But what?" She sighed with frustration. "Come on, what's the 'but,' Precious? You're making me crazy."

"Promise, I know you don't want to hear this. But I can't right now with the dating and stuff." Again she rolled her eyes at me and bit her bottom lip. I knew she was thinking of what to say, how she could counter my reluctance. So I tried to explain. "Listen, I have to focus on the business right now. DaVon's business needs me. I have to put my energy into it and in order to do that I have to stay focused. Non-focus is no good in my line of business."

"Precious." She said my name but I held up my hand to cut her off. I had to make the rest of my point.

"Plus, you know I'm trying to open up the new dry cleaners. I got to find a new spot for that. I'm working with a realtor on that now and it's squeezing up my free time. Realistically, I'm just too busy. I don't have the time."

"When it comes to business I get it, but . . ."

"Ain't no buts—" A tap on the on the door interrupted me.

"It's unlocked," Promise announced.

Dee stuck her head inside. "The delivery is here, they just need your signature."

"We are coming out now." She stood and I followed. Promise walked over to the delivery guy who was waiting patiently with an iPad so that she could sign.

"Thank you so much for the bagels and coffee, Precious," Toya said when I stepped in the booth area. "I was hungry, and plus I didn't go no damn sleep last night." She sighed and wiped down her station.

"Why you ain't get no sleep last night? Shit, I talked to you around eight and you said you was going to bed," Dee reminded her.

"Well, that was the plan. I took a shower, then dozed off for about an hour. I woke up to use the bathroom and couldn't get back to sleep. Just tossed and turned until it was light out."

"Bitch you shoulda had a drink, then. You too grown to be beating the covers." Dee laughed. "Couple shots of that Hennessey and I promise you would have been back out like a light. Works for me every time. I can't stand to toss and turn. That shit will drive me crazy faster than a cheating-ass nigga."

Reese, Toya, and I burst out laughing at Dee's antics. "Bitch, I swear sometimes you are too funny." Reese held on to her stomach trying to control her laugh. "Let me get back up front, clients are about to start arriving." Reese exited the room.

"The shit that comes out of your mouth. Tiffany Haddish ain't got nothin' on you." I continued laughing. My gut ached, I had laughed so long and hard.

"Y'all know she is crazy." Toya chuckled one last time but her face seemed to turn hard. "But nah, I wasn't in the mood. Well, at least not at first. Soo . . ." She stopped and gave a long sigh. We all looked at her. Something was going on, and we were about to be front row and center to find out. I reached down in the box for a bagel and waited. "Dell didn't bring his black ass home last night. And he would not answer his phone. As of this morning before I came in to work, he still had not answered his phone. Matter of fact it's not even on, it goes straight to voicemail. What y'all think he is doing?"

I looked straight at Promise. My facial expression was

bewilderment. She had just walked in the room and went straight for the bagels, busying herself with spreading cream cheese. She gazed up at me for a second, then bit down into her bagel.

"Precious, what does that look mean?" Toya shot at me.

"It means don't ask dumb shit." Dee's voice boomed across the room. "I told you to put his bomb ass out. Nigga stay on some shit. And you stay tripping off him."

"I know, but . . ." Toya paused.

We all tuned in on Reese yelling. "Yeah, she is here but we are not yet open? Plus, you don't have an appointment."

"Who gives a fuck?" an unfamiliar voice yelled. We all spilled out toward the front.

"Brandy, why are you here?" Promise asked. I looked from Promise to the unknown female. Suddenly, I realized she was Quan's ex-girlfriend. Promise had mentioned to me a few days before the dinner that she had been tripping.

"Why you think I'm here? I'm tired of you coming between me and Quan. My man." She threw both her hands in the air with force.

Promise chuckled out loud. "Hold up. I'm coming between y'all?"

"That's what the fuck I said. I ain't stutter up in this motherfucker." Brandy threw her right hand on her hip and stood back on her legs.

"Nah, but I think you got some wrong information. One, I ain't coming between shit. I don't break up happy homes. So kill that with the ridiculous shit you spittin'. Two, Quan is not your man, we both know that. Saying dumb shit make you look desperate."

Brandy started laughing, then spun around with her hands in the air, stopped, and glared at Promise. "Ha, and that's what you think, huh? Bitch, you are just dumb as hell," she accused. "I ain't got to be desperate for shit. I know what the fuck belongs to me. Stupid-ass bitches always think . . ."

It was my turn. I'd had enough. "Aye, you need to get yo' disrespectful ass—" I stepped toward Brandy. I was going to choke her quiet if she didn't shut up. Promise stepped in front of me and Toya followed.

"Don't do it, Precious, I got it. She ain't worth it," Promise whispered to me. "Brandy, sweetie, all that dramatic shit you are doing is too much. Now you need to leave. This is my place of business, not some street corner. I know it ain't your fault that you don't know the difference." Promise remained calm, which was a surprise to me because my blood was boiling.

"Bitch, fuck you and this piece of shit you claim as a business. Fuckin' trash dump." Brandy seemed to get angrier as she glanced around. Clearly Promise's look of success was starting to bother her.

Dee suddenly pushed past us. "Bitch, you better get yo' stupid ass out of here, before I beat the shit outta you." Promise and I grabbed her just before she reached Brandy. Reese and Toya pulled Brandy out of the salon and into the parking lot. "I hate stupid-ass hoes like that girl. Bitch can't see that the man done wit' her simple ass. Promise, don't believe nothin' out that thot's mouth. She just thirsty," Dee spat. Reese and Toya both walked back inside.

"Whew, chile. That chick crazy." Toya was breathing hard, her loose tie-dye shirt now hanging off her right shoulder. "Hoe got me all tired." She attempted to shift her shirt back into place.

"I swear LA got the craziest bitches ever when it comes to a nigga." Dee turned to head toward the stations area. Reese and Toya followed without saying a word.

"Hey, that bitch might be crazy. That is true. But you need to check Quan about this shit. It's unacceptable." I looked at Promise.

"Oh, trust me, I am. Got this hood rat running up in here? What if clients would have been in here? I done worked too hard to have my shop classified as the love and hip-hop drama stop."

"Damn right. So tell that nigga to check his bitch. Ex-bitch, whoever she is." I sucked my teeth to fight back my agitation. I looked at the Rolex watch on my wrist that I had thrown on that morning. "I gotta get going, though. I'll call you later if I have time to grab that shot." I made the door my destination. I had things to do. Quan and his past were already about to make me catch a body before noon. I had zero time for it. I carried a gun to protect myself from real crime in the streets, not to fight off jealous ex-girlfriends.

Chapter 20

"This area will be perfect for your machinery," Christopher said. He was the realtor that I had chosen to help me find a new spot for the new dry cleaners. He had come highly recommended to me, so I wasted no time calling him. So far he had been pleasant, not to mention easy on the eyes. Christopher was tall and had a light complexion, full lips, and curly hair. From the looks of it he was probably mixed. And Promise was enjoying every minute of his presence. She had tagged along with me to look at the property.

"Yeah, I really like the space. The last two places were a nice size, but the electrical plugins in both places were not enough to accommodate the machinery we require. And I would really prefer not to have to deal with rewiring if it can be avoided."

"Yes, that can be a pain, and it will take a bit more time if you have to do that," Christopher agreed. "Not to mention the cost could be immense."

"Aye, what's up, y'all." Plies greeted us from behind. He had come by to meet up with me for a quick minute. We needed to talk numbers.

"Welp, Plies, what you think about this spot?" I asked him.

"The location is on point. I don't know much about a dry cleaners needs. But it's huge in here, so space shouldn't be an issue."

I nodded in agreement. "Hey, Christopher, give me a minute."

"No problem take your time. How about we continue to look around, Promise?" He smiled at her and they walked away.

Plies and I ducked off closer toward the front door. He had just got back into town but had to leave first thing in the morning. My schedule was so busy I couldn't squeeze him in, so I had told him to come by to meet up with me. "I know it's crazy having you come by here. But I got a full day of meetings with this realtor, and the club. Booked," I added.

"I feel ya. But you'll be glad to know everything is good here in LA and Miami. Especially here, we are stronger than ever. Product this week was through the roof like you predicted at the meeting."

I nodded. I had known sales would be up. One of my revivals was doing extra madness when dealing with his customers. And the word was on the street. Those customers were coming to us now as I figured they would. They could have gone to another supplier who was cheaper, but we were quality, so we won the bid. But I had no doubt that would be the outcome.

"Miami on point too. We might be able to get back here permanently, sooner than originally expected. Marlo is doing a good job strengthening the teams. The guys that they have brought on have all come a long way. Rob and Case are showing them how to keep things tight and still build revenue. A few of 'em were trigger happy in the beginning, but you know how that adds up." I nodded in agreement. That was most of the time the story in any crew.

The constant good reports from Plies confirmed what I too believed to be true, though. Pablo would feel comfortable with us out of the picture once and only once he could see full potential in his crew. "Well, I'll be back down in about two weeks. Hopefully, it's all good news. Maybe bring y'all home back from Miami."

"No doubt. I'm sure it will be. I'm getting out of here tomorrow evening and heading back."

"Make sure you take care of the shipment that will be in first thing in the morning. Secure the blocks and collect for the week before you fly out."

"You know I'm on it."

"I'll verify the count in a couple days. Mob can do your follow-up until then."

"Fo' sho."

"Cool. Now I gotta get back to the realtor. Don't want him to think I don't respect his time." Plies chuckled at my little joke before saluting me goodbye.

I rejoined Promise and Christopher, but from the looks of it they didn't miss me the least little bit. I was sure if Promise smiled any harder, the corners of her lips would pop. And Christopher's eyes were glued so hard to her face they would have to be surgically removed.

I broke into their conversation, for which I was certain they both cursed me out in their heads. "Well, Christopher, I think I'm going to take the place." I glanced around. "Now there will be an offer that I can't refuse, correct?" I teased him.

"Of course. I'll get you those numbers in about an hour. No worries." I knew he would fight like hell to get me the best numbers. His goal was to impress Promise, who had him wrapped around her finger. And they had known each other for less than an hour. So I wasn't worried.

"Good. I'll wait for your call." I reached my hand out and shook his waiting hand.

We all exited the building but Promise and Christopher had managed to get side by side. For a minute I thought I might have to pry them apart. It appeared to be reluctantly, but they both finally said their goodbyes.

"So, what do you really think about the place?" I asked Promise.

"I think it's great. And when I think about the dry cleaners you already own, I say thumbs up. This place is bigger, which means you will be able to do more with the space. Which financially means more revenue. And the area seems in need of a dry cleaners. All points toward success."

"Good observation." Everything she said I agreed with. I trusted her judgment.

"Now, what did you think of Christopher?" she asked. I should have figured that was coming.

"No, I think I should be asking you that question. Seeing as you two were getting to know each other's anatomy."

"Hmm. And ain't his anatomy good." She smiled at me. I could only smile back. "Well, you know I think he fine as hell. But . . ." I wondered what her *but* was. "He just seems a little too square for me."

"In that case he is a keeper." I laughed. While I had dated DaVon, who turned out to be a drug dealer, he had been the first guy of his kind to ever catch my interest. Promise, on the other hand, seemed to be attracted to bad guys. She was a magnet to their persona.

"You would say that." She smiled. "I rebuke squares, remember? It's our secret." She playfully shushed me.

"Whatever." I grinned. "So what's up with Quan? Your boyfriend." I emphasized *boyfriend* to tease her. "What did he have to say about his ex-girlfriend's behavior?"

"Ugh, Brandy? That stank bitch." She rolled her eyes and wrinkled her nose if as she had a whiff of a bad order. "That bitch is lying. Every word out of her mouth. Lies."

"Do you believe him?"

She looked at me, sucked her teeth, and rolled her eyes again. "I don't know." She folded her arms across her chest. "I just really don't, to be honest with you. But I do wish I had beat that hoe ass. That unnecessary disrespect she brought to me and my business."

"Yep. I wanted to smack her ill-mannered ass too. It was really hard not to. But she looks like the police type for sure. And I don't need that heat. I would have had to body that simple bitch."

"Slut," Promise added for good measure. We both laughed at Brandy's expense. Like I said, I never trusted shit, and the truth was most times somewhere few and far between. But just like in most cases, if the accusations she made about Quan were true, when the time was right it would reveal itself. That much I was sure of.

Chapter 21

"I guess I should never doubt you. I mean, not that I did doubt. But damn, you were on point when you said she would be back," I said. Katrina's prediction had been spot on.

"Aye. I won't say I told you so. I mean, I hate to be right because I don't wish no ill fate on her and shit. But that nigga ain't worth the garbage can he crawled out of. He a bomb," Katrina spat.

I was at the dry cleaners to meet up with her so that we could talk to Regina, who was back in town from Atlanta asking for her job back. She had actually been back for almost two weeks, but between me traveling back and forth to Miami, and all my businesses, I had been too busy to meet her. Today I had a minute, so Katrina set up the meeting.

"Hey, you know how we are when we in love. No matter how people try to warn us or even if we see the signs ourselves, we have to learn the hard way."

Before Katrina could pick up where I left off, Regina strolled in. She had a sorry look written all over her face.

I smiled at her in spite of her dumb decision. "So, you made it back from the country," I joked, to break the ice.

"Just barely. But we all fall on some kind of bad luck sometimes." She laughed, lightly.

"Yeah, then we search for grace. I have needed some a few times," Katrina added.

"Thank you for seeing me today, Precious, I know how busy you be . . . and . . ." Before she could say another word, tears started falling down her face. "Aye, listen. I'm not gone bullshit you, Precious. I know you gave me this chance at the dry cleaners and you worked with me, paid bills for me, when I needed extra help. And I appreciate you so much for that. I know I should have never left with that dumb-ass boyfriend of mine. Katrina, I know you tried to talk me out of it . . ." She sniffed back tears. "But I just wouldn't listen and . . ." I held up my hand and stopped her.

"Listen, Regina. Real talk, you are a grown-ass woman. Whatever decisions you make in your life are yours to make. So you don't owe me no apology or explanation about why you did what you did." I wanted to be clear on that. The sob story and the tears were too much for me and not that deep.

"I know, but—"

"Ain't no buts. Your life, your decisions. Period. The only time I will ever be tripping is if it affects my business in a negative situation. Now, when you left you gave two weeks' notice, and that's what I would ask for. So you good. However, this dry cleaners do not have a revolving door for employees to keep leaving and coming back. With that said I'm gone let you come back again. Right now, though, it will just be part-time, so I hope that's good for you."

"Oh, that works. I'm cool with that. Thank you, Precious."

"Katrina said she told you about the new dry cleaners opening up soon. When that location does open up, I will be able to offer you full-time if you interested."

"You already know I want that position."

"Aye, it's all good, then. Just so as we understand each other. This the last time."

"Trust me. I'm staying until I finish with school this time."

"Well, I'm glad to have your big-headed butt back," Katrina joked, and playfully nudged her shoulder.

"Girl, I'm glad to be back from the South. Oh my God, I have nothing against Atlanta, there is much fun to be had out there. But damn, it's hot as hell out there. Shit, I think I baked like a potato the whole time I was there. That Southern life is not for me. And not to mention they have the nerve not to have a beach."

"I swear LA got your ass spoiled." I laughed. "Well, welcome back to civilization."

"Thank God." She smiled. "But they need those beaches for more than just fun. Hell, they need them just so people can take a dip to beat that sweltering-ass heat." She wiped at her forehead as if it was sweating. We all giggled.

"Well, listen, I'm going to call you tonight once I go over this schedule and let you know when to come in," Katrina added.

"Cool, I'll wait for your call. I'll catch you both later, though." With that Regina rushed out into the heat. The smile spread across her face was a mile long.

"That went well," Katrina said, then sighed. She reached over by the register and fished out the schedule she had been working on when I came in.

"Hey, y'all." Lisa said, as she strolled through the door

with a smoothie in her right hand. Her shift was about to start.

"Hey." Katrina spoke.

"What's up?" I replied. "I see you are still showing up. Guess that means you like it here?" I asked. I didn't get to see her much because I was normally in early on Katrina's shift.

"Oh yes. I love the hours and the people. I'm hanging in here." She smiled, and I noticed her right tooth was brown. She was light skinned, short, and a bit chubby but still cute.

"Well, I'm glad to hear that. Some of these customers are originals. Been coming in here since I was a baby." Saying that part almost made me emotional, but I kept it under control.

"That's what's up." Lisa sat her smoothie down on the counter under the register.

"Remember I was telling you about Regina, a past employee?" Katrina asked her.

"Yeah. You said she might be returning."

"Yes, well, we just met with her and she will be returning, so you will get to meet her, soon."

"Cool. I look forward to it." Lisa turned and headed toward the back to put her purse away.

"So . . . more good news," I announced. I rubbed my hands together and gazed at Katrina. "I picked a spot for the new location." I was all teeth and gum.

"Aww, snap. Where is it?"

"Tell you what, since Lisa is here, why don't you come take a ride with me?" I suggested. Lisa strolled back into the room toward us.

"You ain't said nothing but a word. Let me grab my purse." Katrina was excited. "Lisa, I'm going to take a ride with Precious. I'll be back shortly."

We pulled into the parking lot of the new spot. This was the first time I had returned since I had said yes to the offer, a week ago. But just from approaching it, I saw it in a different light than I had the first day I saw it. I had hope for it then, but now observing it, I was even more certain I had made the right decision. There was a vision of my dad in my head, him standing out front, viewing the place, and nodding with approval. That made all the difference for me.

I glanced over at Katrina just as I put my truck into Park. She wore a huge grin and a look of approval. We got out and made our way up to the entrance. I used the keys I had received from Christopher two days prior to unlock the glass double doors.

"Oh yes, this is it, Precious." Katrina's eyes seemed to dance around in her head as they roamed the place. "It's huge in here. The building doesn't seem that old either. Oh, the potential," she all but sang.

"The building is fairly new, the realtor says it was built like fifteen years ago."

"This is perfect." Katrina's eyes continued to eat the place up.

"The remodeling starts tomorrow."

"Tomorrow?" Her eyes grew big with her question.

"Yep. I don't want to waste no time. They will be replacing the floors, and painting, of course. I'm meeting with a commercial company tomorrow to get the machinery ordered, and supplies. The alarm system will be installed in the next few weeks. I'm ready to get this show on the road."

"I guess we got our work cut out for us, then."

"Yep. I'm going to run the ad for help the day after tomorrow. I paid for that two days ago. The plan is to hire only two people part-time, and they can float between both dry cleaners. I want Regina to be full-time at the new location, and Lisa can remain full-time at the old location. And you of course will be floating between both locations, managing. I'm sure you can handle that."

"You know I can. I can't wait. I will not let you down."

"I already know." I smiled. "You can start setting those interviews up for a week from now. People gone start blowing you up soon as that ad hits the papers. The pay gone be seventeen fifty an hour. And once Regina get to full-time, bring her pay from the eighteen seventy-five, she getting twenty-one seventy-five."

"Cool. I'm sure she will be happy with that."

"I'm sure she will. Like I said, if we can make the business work with the few people we hire, I can keep pay rates at a decent amount."

"Right. Luckily, so far it's been all good."

I continued to look around, imagining the look of the place once it was complete. Another milestone on this long journey of being a successful business owner, all the while picking up the torch of my father's dream.

Chapter 22

I reached for my cell phone and sighed with annoyance. It was ruining my plans to sleep at least an extra hour. I had no meetings and no plans to be anywhere early, which was rare, but ignoring my calls was never an option. And seeing Promise's name on the screen gave me hope that I probably wouldn't have to move out of bed right away. If it were Plies or Mob it might be quite different.

"I know you are not still in the bed? Get up."

"Promise, it's only ten o'clock. And on a Saturday at that."

"I know that. All of my clocks work and I keep up with my days of the week. Now get up." I knew she was not about to let up. She could be bossy that way at times. "We still have to go shopping for something to wear. And I need a bad outfit, so I'm up and ready." Our birthday had been two days before, and we both worked all day and me most of the night. But tonight, we had plans to celebrate at the club, and we had to be on point. So I could only agree with her, as much as I hated to get out of bed.

Slowly I sat up on my right elbow. "All of this is true. I just thought I might get an extra hour this morning."

"No, ma'am, we should have been in traffic two hours ago. You know it's Saturday and the whole LA gone be in traffic."

"Ai'ght, ai'ght. Let me jump in the shower and throw on something. What's the first stop? I'll meet you."

"Neiman Marcus, no doubt," she confirmed matter-of-factly, then hung up before I could reply. I yawned and kicked the covers off in my last attempt at being combative for not wanting to give up my bed. I showered, dressed, threw on a pair of Tom Ford sunglasses, and headed out. And just as Promise had predicted, the whole of LA was out. The interstate was bumper to bumper. And not one person had patience. Annoyed, I finally pulled up to Neiman Marcus and hustled my way to the entrance.

"Hey, hottie," Promised teased me once I arrived.

"Good morning, my beautiful, annoying sister." We hugged and went inside. The air-conditioned store met us with open arms. It was scorching outside.

"Good morning, ladies. Can I help you with anything?" A tall, thin white sales associate approached us.

"Not at the moment," I replied. I was not in the mood to be prompted and probed. I just wanted to grab something cute and be out. Maybe I could catch a good nap before the party.

"This is cute." Promise felt the fabric of a silk minidress with spaghetti straps.

"Yes, that material is the best," I complimented, as I browsed another rack. "Glides up and down your skin."

"Just like a man with good solid hands."

"You're crazy." I chuckled.

She laughed. "No, real talk, though. That's what I need for tonight. Something that will slide up and down my ass all night while I bounce it up and down."

"Don't start. I can see already I'm gone have to keep

you from that Don Julio tonight," I joked. "Your ass can't wait to clown."

"You know me like a book. I can't wait to celebrate. I could barely sleep last night. I'm geeked."

"Me too," I had to admit. "But I can't lie. I slept all night and had plans on getting extra sleep this morning, until you jacked that up."

"My bad. But I couldn't help it. What kind of fit you got in mind?"

"Ah, something cute and simple. I don't need nothing sliding up and down my ass like you," I teased.

"Oh, hell yes you do. Twerking is all we are doing tonight."

"I'm wit' that." I laughed. "But what I really want is some badass shoes. The more inches on them, the better."

"I feel you. Mane, the DJ better be on fire too, 'cause I don't plan on sitting down all night."

"You already know he gone be lit'. He got strick orders. No worries on that end," I assured her. I had one of the hottest DJ's in the area. He was well known and charged his worth, so I wasn't concerned. "So is Quan coming through tonight?"

Promise stopped gawking at another dress she had set her attention on and glared at me. "Do that nigga look stupid? Of course, he gone be there." I shook my head at her in amazement. She was always in control. "He came through the other night on our birthday and dropped ten stacks. Oh, and this." She extended her wrist to me.

"Damn, a Rolex. My dude be showing out, huh?" I examined the watch that was sitting so pretty on my twin's wrist. I remembered when DaVon had bought me my first Rolex. I'd felt like new money.

Promise nodded with a grin on her face. "Girl, he don't mind spending that money. And you know I say no to nothing."

"Well, he had better got you something nice or we was gone have to flatten his tires," I joked.

"Right. Oh, and we going out of town next month."

"Where to?" I asked.

"Miami. He already got the tickets and everything. I'ma shop till I drop. Nigga better take at least sixty thousand. I'm going to visit this art gallery out there. This painting I want cost about forty thousand."

"Okay, okay. I see you." I smiled.

"He wanted to go to the Dominican Republic. But I told his ass I ain't leaving the country with no nigga I just met. Period."

I laughed. "You are something else, Promise. Aye, but I would have said the same thing. If anything were to pop off, you want to be on American soil."

"Damn right. I ain't no fool. And I got to have that painting. But listen, I'm gone need you to look out on the shop for me while I'm away. Dee and Toya can hold the customers down. I just need you to handle the financials and just keep an eye out."

"You know I got you. Whatever you need. All you need to worry about is having fun down in Miami and picking up that painting. Trust there is fun to be had there."

"Well, you should know since it's your second home."

"Hopefully, not for too much longer. I mean, Miami's cool and all, but I could stand to have few less trips out there. Besides, I never get to have any real fun when I'm out there."

"And why is that? Can't you go have some fun when your work is done? Maybe have that Marlo character show you the town."

I had to snap my head in her direction. Why would she even suggest that I hang out with Marlo? Did he even sound like someone I would hang out with on a personal level? "Why would I hang out with Marlo?"

"Why not? Ain't he from Miami? Hell, I'm sure he knows all the hangouts."

I thought about her questions for a second. I guessed she had a point, but never once had I thought about Marlo and fun. To keep it real, I didn't see him as the fun type of guy. He had once asked me to go out for a drink. But that was right after we had bodied some fools. I had to politely shut that drink down. But Promise was right. "Yeah, he is from the city, shit, he might even have the key to the city. But I'm sure his fun is not mine. Meaning we have nothing in common."

"Hmm, so says my twin. Sometimes you perplex me, my dear sister. But I urge you to see some of Miami when you get the chance."

"I mean, I've been a few places with Penelope, but . . ."

"Well, clearly she ain't showed you Miami. You just said that. So since Marlo ain't allowed to show you shit because of your damn hang-ups," she smacked her lips and sarcastically rolled her neck, "maybe venture out on your own and see the city on your own. With your Glock, of course." She winked at me.

I shook my head with a smile. I was over the whole conversation. "So what time is Dee and Toya showing up at my house to do our hair and makeup?"

Promise gazed at her Rolex. "I told them around six thirtyish. Dee said she might be running about a half hour behind. She has to run an errand for her mom."

"Cool, that gives us a little extra time. We should have time to grab something to eat when we leave here. I'm starved." The rumbling noise in my gut kept reminding me.

"I'm wit' that. I ain't had nothin' this morning but a banana."

"And I know exactly where we should go." I looked at

Promise and we both smiled. We had the same idea. One of our favorites when we were in the area. The Cheesecake Factory. We finished up our shopping and headed straight over and grabbed some fish tacos, then made our way back to my house where Dee and Toya would be coming to doll us up for our party.

Chapter 23

Dee and Toya had hooked us both up. Our faces were beat to the gods and our hair was on point. After Toya and Dee left, Promise and I had a shot of Hennessey and retired to our rooms to get dressed. We had showered before we did hair and makeup, as we didn't want to risk messing either up. I looked myself over in the mirror. I liked my outfit. It was simple but popping. I had chosen a pair of high rise tweed shorts with a silk camisole, and just as I had wished for, I had gotten a pair of shoes to die for. I had chosen a pair of Rene Caovilla metallic leather booties with crystals. They were sparkly, and the heels thin and high. My legs looked gorgeous in them.

"Yeah," I said, to answer the tap on my door.

"The car is here. Are you ready?" Promise asked from the other side of it.

"Yes, let's bounce." I smiled at my image in the mirror. I had ordered us a driver and one of my favorite cars to be chauffeured in, a Maybach, with a fully stocked bar.

"Ai'ght, grab that bottle for our second drink of the night." Promise pointed at the unopened bottle of Hennessey.

"At your service," I joked, then opened the bottle and poured us both a shot as I had been instructed. "Now, let's toast to a fun-filled night, and that by his grace that I can dance in these shoes all night without producing bunions on my beautiful toes," I kidded.

"I know that's right. Those bitches bad, though. I'm gone have to get a pair."

"Fo' sho." We both raised our glasses, then downed our shot followed by a second. With our chests on fire from the shots and the good mellow feeling that followed, we arrived at the club in no time flat.

The club was jam-packed as we made our way inside. Just as I had promised, the DJ was on fire. "March Madness" by Future was blasting out of the speakers. Making our way through the crowds of people, we headed straight to our VIP area. A few people noticed me and greeted me with high fives and handshakes.

"Aye, aye." Katrina and Regina were already dancing in the VIP area when we strolled in.

"That's what I'm talking about." Promise joined them. Bending over, she started bouncing her booty.

Promise and Katrina sang along with Future, "We balling like it's March Madness."

"Happy birthday, ladies," Regina said, hugging us both. Katrina followed suit.

"I'm glad y'all made it. Precious, your bodyguards outside of VIP was tripping about letting us in. I thought we was gone get kicked out before we even got in."

"Ah, shit, what happened? I know y'all on the list I made sure of it." I was confused. I had checked more than once to be sure everyone I invited was on the list just to avoid what they were saying.

"They didn't have the list out at first when we got to the door," Regina said. "I guess we was a little early."

"I don't why they didn't have the damn list ready." I

sighed with frustration. "My bad. But they have to use that list before allowing anyone up in here. Gotta make sure squatters ain't trying to get up in my VIP." I smiled but was serious. "Nah, for real, though, I made it clear to them to always use the list. Guess they ass just slow about getting it out."

"We feel you." Regina laughed. "Mane, and they ain't playin'. They had this bitch on lockdown like you is a queenpin." Promise's eyes caught mine quickly, and we all busted out laughing. "It was all worth it, though. I just love your DJ, he lit'. I swear he lit'. I been twerking since I hit the entrance door."

"Shit, me too," Promise added.

"Yeah, he hot in the city. He came highly recommended." I was glad they were having a good time. "Regina, I can't help but notice that you lookin' stress free." I was glad to see it. The girl was too young to be looking like she carried the weight of the world on her shoulders.

"I'm working on it. Getting back into my old routine and, of course, fun like this helps."

"No doubt. And you be sure to have plenty of it while you here."

"Shit, if your DJ keep this up I won't have no issues." Regina got hyped as Gucci Mane featuring Drake's "Both" blasted out of the speakers. "Aye, aye," she sang out with a drink in her hand.

Dee and Toya both stepped into the VIP area soon after. I had the waitress hand them a drink and we all turned up off Drake. We repeated after him with our drinks in the air and booties bouncing. The song finally ended, and we all sat down, out of breath.

I waved the waitress closest to us over. "Can you bring us all a Don Julio shot?"

"Damn, Sis, you are starting early." Promise chuckled.

"Damn right. We are celebrating tonight, it's our night.

Ain't no turning back, you bitches gone drink up or shut up," I said, laughing.

"I'm wit' it." Dee chimed in. "But if I pass out, you bitches better carry me up outta here. And I better wake up in my bed with both my eyelashes attached."

"You know I got you," I assured her, still laughing. The waitress approached with our shots. "Let's toast to my twin and sister. I love her more than life itself." I raised my glass.

"And I her," Promised concurred. "Before my sister, I was lost. There is no love like a twin love." Tears ran down both our cheeks as we all clinked glasses, then swallowed.

I smiled to keep from crying. It was occasions like this that I missed DaVon the most. He would have gone all out for me on my birthday. And Promise too, because she was my sister. He would be so happy to know that I had a sister, a twin at that. Yeah, DaVon would have spoiled us both rotten.

All of our VIP guests we had invited started to arrive, and our VIP area was packed to maximum capacity. There was so much fun to be had, and every guest seemed to be having it. People greeted Promise and me with happy birthday over and over and were generous with gifts. We were given envelope after envelope.

I excused myself to make a bathroom run and signaled one of the security guys to walk with me. Whenever I was in the club, I kept security close by. With there being so many people inside, I never trusted if an enemy could be nearby. Even though I kept a low profile, some people knew who I was or thought they knew who I was. And when the crowd was deep, I felt more exposed, so I took a little extra precaution. And tonight the crowd was thick, but I finally made it to the bathroom. On the way back I stopped by the bar. It was almost time to do a formal toast with everyone at the club. I wanted to make sure the sparkling cake and champagne I had ordered arrived to our VIP area on time. Everything seemed on schedule, so I headed back. Once again, more people who noticed me as the owner shook my hand and spoke to me as I made my way back through the thick crowd.

"Precious, what's up, girl?" Chantel, a girl who use to buy hair from Keisha appeared from the crowd.

The look on my face, I was certain, was a surprised one. "What's up?" I spoke back in spite of it.

"I was wondering when I would run into you. I heard you own this place now. I done partied here a few times already. And, girl, I got to say it is poppin'."

"Thank you. It's good to see you." I truly was shocked to see her out. Chantel always looked good—she wore the best hair, clothes, drove the hottest whip, you name it. But according to Keisha, her boyfriend, who owned two fitness clubs in LA, was abusive and kept her on lock down. And I believed because in the past every time I saw her, I saw him. But she was out and there was no sign of a guy lurking.

"Listen, I have a birthday coming up soon and I would really like to rent out at least two of your VIP areas. It's gone be huge. Girl, I done finally broke free, you know, single and shit. So it's gone be my coming out of freedom slash birthday bash." She was all but screaming over the music.

"Hey, we can make that happen. Just stop by the bar before you leave and get the info."

"Cool, cool. I'll do that."

"Ai'ght, well, it was nice seeing you." I turned to walk away but the force of another body against mine stalled the process. "Hey, I'm so . . ." I started to apologize but the familiar face in front of me stunned me.

"We have got to stop running into each other like this."

Austin smiled. And he was right. Once again, we were bumping into one another. Out of all the people in LA, the guy was drawn to me like a magnet.

I took one step backward to put some space between us. "I agree with you on that. Who knew LA was so small?" I gave a little chuckle. I looked over his shoulder as if I was looking for something, then put my eyes back on him. "But look, I'm sorry and I hope I didn't step on your toes. This club is packed from wall to wall, as you can see."

"It's cool. No worries," he assured me. "I didn't know you hung out here." The two guys standing behind him glared at me. It was clear they were all together.

A smile spread across my lips that I was unable to control. For a quick second my eyes again wandered toward the VIP area, then back to Austin. "Promise and I have a VIP area, you and your friends are welcome to come up." I invited them without hesitation. I didn't want to be rude and I had to get going. The toast we were supposed to give was growing nearer.

Austin turned sideways and glanced at his friends, who both smiled, Austin turned to me and accepted. The crowed was thick but somehow, I managed to lead the way back to the VIP area and not lose them. I breathed a sigh of relief when I arrived. I could also see the relief on my security's face. He was a big guy, so whenever I stopped to speak or shake hands, he was left trying to fit in between the thick crowd. In VIP there was space, and he could breathe.

Promise's face lit up when she caught a glimpse of Austin behind me. She rushed over as I made my way in her direction. She was ready to be on one, there was no doubt. "Hey, Austin," she said, then extended to her hand to him.

"Hey. I see you are having a good time."

"Shit, better than most. I love a good party, and good shit." She kept it real. "Who is this you got with you?" Promise never wasted any time beating around the bush. Austin introduced the two dudes with him as coworkers. I was not surprised. They looked like college professors, really smart and nerdy. Austin looked keen but he had a hint of swag. He didn't look nerdy like his partners. I offered them the full use of the VIP area and told them to drink up. They stepped away to get a drink just as Quan swooped in and grabbed Promise by the waist.

"Damn, baby, you look so good. And you smell delicious." Quan hugged her tight, shoving his lips down the crease of her neck. He came up for air with a grin. "Hey, Ms. Precious," he said over her shoulder.

"Hey, Quan." For some reason I felt as if I really didn't want to speak. Maybe I wasn't getting a good vibe, or maybe I was waiting for a real explanation about his exbitch and her dramatics. Either way I kept my cool. Tonight was about fun.

Quan released Promise from his embrace and stood in front of us to grab both our attention. "Now you both know I couldn't show up without bringing y'all a bottle of that bubbly. My man right here got 'em." A tall, skinny dark-skinned guy that I had seen with him several times produced two bottles of fancy champagne. "Happy birthday to both you beautiful ladies."

"Aww, thank you, baby." Promise kissed him on the cheek. I simply moved my lips to say thank you.

Suddenly the music stopped. "Mic, mic, check." The DJ interrupted, then fake cleared his throat. "Now, I know y'all came here to party tonight. And most of you know tonight is special. So I want all y'all to join in as we wish two special women a very happy birthday, Precious and Promise." People started cheering and clapping. Finally, the sparkling cake fizzing all over the place came through the door with two top-model-type guys carrying it. It was so pretty. "On the count of three, everybody sing 'Happy Birthday.' I'll count it off." The DJ started counting. "One, Two, Three. Happy birthday!" Everyone seemed to scream. Confetti fell from the ceiling, Champagne bottles all over the club started to pop just as I had planned. Promise and I popped our own bottles the waitress had handed us. The moment was magic. "Cheers." Promise lifted her bottle of champagne in the air. "Mask Off" by Future blasted out of the speakers just as Promise and I drank from our bottles.

"Aye," I yelled. I felt good all over. I started dancing with my bottle in my hand and singing along with Future. Promised reached out and hugged me just as the song ended, and we giggled, both tired from all the dancing and balancing the heavy bottles.

"So, I guess it's safe to wish you ladies a more formal happy birthday." Austin was now standing in front of us.

"Yes, thank you," Promise said, breathing hard from all the dancing we had done.

"Yes, thank you." My breathing was just as heavy. "Whew." I took in a deep breath and set the champagne bottle down on a table next to me. I was done with it.

"So that's what this whole extravaganza is all about. You two have the whole club celebrating your birthday, shouting you out. I guess you got it like that." He continued to smile at me. He seemed impressed.

"Yep, we the queens up in this bitch tonight. Oh, and your girl here owns the place. So we kinda special up in here." Promise laughed, then walked away, leaving us alone.

"Oh, so you the owner up in here?" He glanced around. "Well, this place is nice, really impressive. You really know how to shock a guy." He glanced around the room as if he was admiring the place and seeing it for the first time.

"Seems like it, huh?" I returned his smile. "Really, it's nothing, though. Just a little something to keep LA on the map."

"You have a pretty good crowd. I would say you're doing a good job."

"Yeah, it seems that way. They keep showing up, we keep supplying the atmosphere and the drink." I really didn't know what else to say. Dee was over in a corner talking to one of the guys who had come in with Quan. I silently prayed for the guy all while laughing inside. Dee could be a handful. She was straightforward with the guys—if he was a softy, he was in trouble. Toya, Katrina, and Regina were busy dancing and giggling. And Promise was off entertaining Quan. I had no chance of being saved. Or at least I thought so until Promise suddenly headed my way.

"I hate to interrupt, but Quan has to leave." She eyed me. "I'ma walk him to the door, but I'll be right back."

I wanted to grab her by the arm and beg her not to leave me, but the twinkle in her eyes confirmed for me that nothing could stop her. She bounced off and twirled her arm into Quan's. He signaled for the two guys that had come in with him to follow him. I thought Dee might come my way, but instead she wasted no time joining Katrina, Regina, and Toya. Lisa had come in but was booed up with some unknown guy. I gave up. No one was coming to rescue me.

My eyes had drifted off into the room, but I could feel Austin's eyes all over me. I guess he was waiting for me to give him my attention. "I know running into you here was a coincidence, but I really wanted to tell you that I enjoyed the drinks we had together."

"Yeah," was my dry response. I really didn't know what to say to him.

KeKe Wyatt and Avant's "You and I" blasted out the speakers and I felt it move through me.

"Can I have this dance?"

"Yes" slid off my tongue so fast my heart skipped a beat. The song had taken control of me, if only for a second. I was no position to tell him no.

Austin pulled me into his arms, and I fell in step to the beat of KeKe and Avant's crooning tones. I loved them together on this song. It was like a battle of love and war between them, and they made it sound so good. DaVon and I had slow-danced to this song countless times. With my eyes closed, I pictured the full length of his face and could feel my face gravitate toward his jawline. He was there with me, but the song ended and I opened my eyes to Austin smiling at me.

"So you think I can get you to go out for another drink with me? Maybe even add some food to the equation this time?" He chuckled, and I followed suit. I'm sure he thought I was softening. But I wasn't, nor were the shots or champagne speaking for me. I just felt different in the moment. So I nodded in agreement to his invite.

"But listen, I'm going to sit down for a little. I been on my feet for a minute." I was starting feel the strength of my Rene Caovillas.

"I'll join you if it's cool?" he asked.

"Hey, it's whatever." I shrugged and headed for one of the couches. My main focus was to sit, and I didn't care who joined me. Just as I reached my destination I looked down from the window in VIP, and there was Promise. Her head seemed to be bouncing up and down in an aggressive manner. It appeared from where I was standing that she was arguing. Her movements were aggressive.

I paused and turned to Austin, who was standing on my heels. Had he been any closer he would have been on my ass. "Um, I have to go check on my sister." I stepped around him and made my way out of the VIP area, through the crowd toward Promise. As I got closer, it was clear that Promise was yelling.

Then I saw Brandy's face. Once again Quan's ex-girlfriend was at the root of the bullshit. Just as I approached Promise, she plunged her fist toward Brandy, and it landed in the middle of her right jaw right above a dimple she had. Unable to reach Promise, I watched as she plunged blow after blow into Brandy, with people just standing around watching, basically, giving them room to fight it out. Just as I got in reaching distance of them, two of my security guards rushed past me and pulled them apart.

Now free of Promise's punches and stranglehold, Brandy kicked and screamed, trying to get back to Promise, and Promise continued kicking and screaming, trying to get back at Brandy. Security used all their might trying to hold them both back.

"You fuckin' nasty slut. Nasty ass-hoe," Brandy shouted. "Ugly-ass hoe."

"Shut the fuck up, you thirsty bitch. Fuck you . . . Let me go so I can finish whooping this hoe ass." Promise tussled hard to get loose.

"Stop it. Just calm down." I tried to talk to Promise.

"Bitch, you too tall anyway. Quan don't want you. He like short women like me." Brandy smirked. But pain was written all over her face.

"You are pitiful, just plain jealous of me. But I'm gone shut that mouth tonight. Let me go. This bitch done disrespected me too many times." Promise almost broke free, and I almost fell backward as her force pushed me back. I stumbled to catch my balance in my heels.

This shit was wearing me out. I was over it. "Aye, get her out of here, now. Take her outside and don't let her back in," I yelled at security. The poor guys were sweating like they had run a marathon trying to control the two of them.

Brandy continued to fight, trying to get away from the security men's grasp. "You know what? You can keep Quan's snitch ass. I don't want his ass anyhow." She sounded winded. I was glad to hear she was getting tired. Maybe then she would calm down.

But that word *snitch* had my undivided attention. What did she mean by that?

"Bitch, dumb bitch," Promise continued to yell and tried to push toward Brandy's direction. But security blocked her way.

I turned my attention back to her, still trying to calm her down. "Take her to back to VIP," I instructed them. Following behind security, I paused for a second and glanced back in Brandy's direction as she was being pulled toward the door exit. Her words hit my thoughts one more time. But I needed to deal with the issue at hand. I brought my attention back to Promise and blew it off. Getting my sister calmed down and under control was my priority.

Dee, Toya, Katrina, Regina, and Lisa all appeared in the crowd ahead of us. It was clear they had been trying to break through. As soon as they were in earshot of me they started asking what happened. I ushered them back toward the VIP area. Once inside I had Promise sit down. She immediately started to fill us in on what happened. I glanced down at the rest of the club and noticed the party was still going strong, the DJ was back on fire, and it appeared no one had missed a beat. All they cared about was drinks, music, and having a good time. The turn-up for them was real. But I needed a drink.

I waved a waitress over. "Please bring another round of Don Julio shots for all of us. And make them all a double."

"Fuck that. Make mine a triple," Promise added, with a

huff. She looked ready to kill. But she didn't have to do that. All she had to do was say the word and I would handle that for her. Brandy didn't know who she really was messing wit'. Bringing her drama around was starting to affect me. With the life I led, the last thing I needed was petty fights over a nigga in my circle. Fights brings cops, violence catches cops' eyes. The last thing I needed was my club getting a bad rep, then cops wanting to hang around. I didn't deal with cops at all. Zero. Brandy was making unnecessary risk. I wasn't heartless, I didn't take the girl's life for petty, but no way was that bitch gone cost me shit. I hoped for her sake that was her last attempt at bringing drama into my business, and to my sister. Anything else and I would handle it. Or, if I wanted to be blunt, dead it.

Chapter 24

"I hate that I missed your birthday. I really planned on getting out there to celebrate with you." Penelope apologized for the second time. "Besides, I been wanting to get out there to party at your club. I hear good things." Penelope may have lived in Miami, but her eyes and ears were states wide.

"And you hear good truth," I confirmed with a smile. "I promise you would enjoy yourself. So far we been bringing LA to its knees when the doors open." I continued to smile as I thought about business the club was bringing in. My club was becoming the talk of the city. "But I'll be out there in a couple weeks for your bash. I know it's gone be lit'. So I'm excited." I was talking to her as I balled down the interstate headed to a winery to meet up with Austin.

"Yes, you know we aim to please. Why don't you bring Promise with you? I mean, I know you have business while you're here, but she would enjoy the party."

"Yeah, she would love that. Bet. I'll let her know she is invited." I ended the call as I pulled into the winery parking lot. Just as I found a parking spot, my phone rang again.

"Hi, Precious, got a minute?"

"Sure, what's up?"

"I just wanted to let you know that everything on the list for the grand opening has been completed," Evett, my lead planner for the new dry cleaners opening event, informed me. "And I know you worried if Chef Roblé could attend at such short notice. And the answer is yes, he is on board. He and his staff will be there. Good news, huh?"

"Yes. Very good news." I sighed with relief. I had really wanted to get him. It had been hard with his busy schedule but Evett had pulled it off. She had come highly recommended, and she was bad. "Thank you so much, Evett."

"No problem. This is what I do. Now, don't forget we meet in the morning with the cake decorator to finalize the cake. It should take about half an hour or so."

"I'll be there." I turned off my ignition and ended the call. Finally, I could relax. My grand opening would rock, I was sure of it. I made my way inside, ready to drink and eat some cheese. Austin had hoped we could get something to eat, but the closest I would agree to eating with him was the cheese. I simply was not ready to go on what he wanted to call a date. A drink was still enough—at least, enough for me, and in my opinion only what I wanted mattered. He could take it or leave it. Either way I was good.

The hostess led me to him. He greeted me with a huge grin, then stood to up to pull my chair out for me. I really would have preferred if he did not do that, but he was so focused on trying to be a gentleman. I told myself to forget about it and I let him.

"I was starting to think you might not show up."

I almost rolled my eyes and told him he was starting to sound insecure. Instead, I settled on, "I'm a person of my word."

"I'm glad to hear it. You look nice." He ate me up with his eyes. I wasn't comfortable with it. I decided to ignore it. "So, have you ever been here?"

"Actually, I haven't."

"Well, trust me when I say they have the best wine."

"Then I'm ready to try some." The waitress came over. Austin ordered three different wines and some cheeses with fancy names. He looked like he knew what he was doing, so I rolled with it. I just hoped it hurried up. I had skipped breakfast, so I was hungry.

"I was really surprised to run into you at the club. But I gotta say I'm glad that I did."

"Yeah, I was a bit surprised to see you there too. But I guess LA is as small as we've heard." I chuckled.

He laughed. "I think I've heard that once or twice. It's either that or we are drawn to each other."

Now he was getting mushy. But not on my watch. "Nah, I think it's the first one." I corrected him.

He laughed again. He could tell I was reverting. "Why didn't you tell me you owned a nightclub?"

"It's a pretty new business venture. I've been dabbling in a few. Trying to get my footing."

The wine and cheese arrived. We both watched the waiter set it up on the table.

"Sweet or dry?" Austin asked.

"Let me try the dry first." I reached for some cheese and took a bite. "Mmm." I savored the taste as I chewed. "This is good."

"That is Jersey Blue. Exquisite." He smiled.

"I guess you do know your cheeses," I complimented him while wearing a smile.

"Some might say so." He laughed, then sipped his wine.

For the next hour we sat and ate cheese, sipped wine, and joked some. Austin walked me through fine cheeses and wine like he had taught the class himself. I got the feeling he was trying to impress me.

"I must say. I really enjoyed myself," I told him as he walked me to my car.

"As did I. I know it seems the LA tide has been with us, and we have managed to run into each on more than one occasion, but I really don't want to chance the universe making it happen again . . . so I must ask now. Can I take you out again?" He shoved his right hand into his pocket. He seemed worried about my answer.

I hit the remote start on my car. "I see you like to take things fast. One request after the other." I teased him, but I was also serious.

"Precious, this might sound lame. But it's not often in LA that you meet a woman with confidence and no intention. It's something about you." Now that part I thought was lame. I laughed. It sounded like a pickup line for sure, but he looked so sincere when he said it.

"Confidence, you say? Now that's laying it on thick. It's hard for a girl to deny that." I continued to laugh.

Austin playfully pretended that he was grabbing his heart. "Oh, she laughs at game. My broken heart will never be the same." We both laughed at his antics.

My laugh faded, though. I was not one to beat around the bush. My serious face took hold. "Listen, I'm a busy person. Spare time is a luxury I don't have a lot of. And the spare time that I do manage to carve out, I use wisely. And to be honest, I'm not sure I want to spend that time dating. Not even a man who tells me I have confidence." Coming out of my mouth, that probably sounded harsh.

This life had made me blunt. A man would have to have thick skin to try and pull up on me.

He opened his mouth to speak, but I knew what he wanted to say. And it would be a waste of his breath. I decided to help him out. I gently held up a finger and placed it over my lips in a shush manner. "Never say never." With that said, I opened the door to my two-door Porsche and climbed inside.

Chapter 25

"I tell you, the humidity out here is kind of thick, but it feels good against my skin. Too bad this chocolate can't catch no tan." Promise giggled. She slid her Burberry sunglasses on as we scurried toward Christian Louboutin in Miami. I wanted to be out of the heat as fast as my legs would take me. Our plane had landed the evening before but as soon as I got off the plane, I had some business to attend to. By the time I got back to the hotel and Promise, I had a couple drinks. So instead of going out, she decided to call the front desk and scheduled massages for us. And I was gang for that. But today after an early morning workout in the hotel fitness room, followed by a breakfast filled with nothing but fruit and coffee, we decided to get some retail therapy before the bash. And Christian Louboutin was on our list. The goal was to spend no less than twenty stacks inside. I loved shoes, so I was geeked.

"Consider yourself lucky, I hate when my damn skin burn. Shit, I wished all my life I was Daddy's skin tone. Not to mention that pure chocolate you and Daddy were blessed with won't ever crack."

"It is smooth, huh?" Promise softly ran her fingers up and down her forearm to tease me.

"Get yo' ass in this store and stop showing out." I playfully chastised her. I pulled one of the double doors open that led us inside. We both just glanced around, took in the breathtaking sight, and smiled at one another.

"This shit is just beautiful," Promise whispered to me. Her eyes danced with excitement.

"Ain't it." I slowly traced my way toward all the glitter and glamour. "I feel like I died and went to dazzle heaven," I joked. "Look at these, Promise." I picked up a pair of Grotika ted pumps. They were silver with spikes. "Talk about badass."

"Damn, look at the spikes on them. They go so hard, Precious. Make me want to sing 'Bitch Better Have My Money,'" Promise joked.

"I know, right? You sing and I'll twerk." I smiled, holding the shoe. I twirled it around in my hand as if it was on display. The shoe and its beauty teased me. "I got to have these. Let's get matching sets." I observed she shoe closely, never taking my eyes from it. The thirteen-hundred-dollar tag on the shoe meant absolutely nothing. I was just getting started.

"Hell, yeah, you know I want a pair." Promise's eyes were already fixated on the next pair of shoes. I signaled for one of the salesladies to get two pair of those. And I followed Promise over to our next victim. The saleslady just beamed. She could probably smell the money on us, which meant commission for her. Which meant she would stick to us like flies to shit until we exited the store. We'd probably have to fight her off to keep her from trying to carry our bags out to the car.

"Those are cute too," Promise said. We admired a pair of lemon-yellow pumps. "I think I'm going to enjoy Miami.

These shoes match Miami, spelled out in fun and badass shoes."

"That they do," I agreed, picking up another pair of shoes.

"I needed this getaway. I almost thought I wasn't going to be able to make it. I've been so busy at the salon."

"Well, I'm glad you are here." I looked at her and thought about bringing up Quan and that whole shit show with Brandy. But I decided it was not the right time. I didn't want to be angry, and I didn't want to make Promise angry. I would wait.

"So what happened on your little drink outing with Austin?" She dug in. "I mean, since you always make me ask instead of just spilling the tea."

"That's because you be so damn anxious. You never give me time to share."

Promise playfully rolled her eyes, then sighed. "Just spill, Ms. Debbie Downer," she teased, shaking her head.

I rolled my eyes at her while sizing up another heel I was falling in love with. "As much as I would like to not admit this, especially to you, hanging out with him was cool. I'm glad I went."

"Wait, what?" Promise got excited, just as I predicted she would. Being dramatic, she set the shoe down that she was examining. She turned to me and pretended to be giving me her undivided attention. "Now, please say that loud and clear."

"I said I'm glad I went," I repeated. "I swear, you play too much. Real talk, though, the wine tasting, and cheese was good. I mean really good. I ain't never tasted cheeses like that before. Hell, I ain't never set out to taste different cheeses before, as a so called date."

"So are you saying you enjoyed the food but not the man?" I glared at her with a *stop it* stare. "Well, I'm glad you even took the time out to go. So I'll leave it at that."

"Yeah. Now you talking. Leave it at that." But I knew her, and she would not be leaving it at that.

"Are you at least thinking about dating him?"

"Wait, I thought you would be leaving it alone. That took all of five seconds for you to change your mind," I teased her.

"Oh, just shut up."

"For real, though. Why does it have to be all that? Why can't we just grab some wine, cheese, a little conversation, and be cool?" I elaborated, because I knew no one could find anything wrong with that.

"Don't kid yourself, Precious. You need more. Anyone would."

I thought about the last part of her statement. Maybe I needed to break some reality down to her. She knew my lifestyle, but maybe she never thought about it. I stood directly in front of her, blocking her space. "Look at me, Promise, I mean really look at me. Do you know who I am?" I asked but answered the question right away. "Yes, you know, the real me. What I do. So you know firsthand that my life is complicated, and not at all safe. Now think about your boy Austin. He is a model citizen. A professor at a legit university." I hoped I was getting through to her. "That man has no idea who I really am, and he can never, ever know. You know, and I know that. Right?"

"Yes," Promise answered. The look on her face was one of reluctance. "But that's not all you are, Precious. You are a good person. Kind at heart, caring, and giving. My one and only sister. And I love you . . . believe me when I say you deserve a good man."

"Yeah, and Austin might be that. Maybe he is or maybe he ain't. But he is a different man from a different world."

"That doesn't matter, though, Precious. I mean, it doesn't have to." She decided to remain stubborn. No matter what.

"It does matter. Don't lie to yourself. Because I won't."

"Fuck all that, it's time you think for yourself and go for happiness while you are still young." I could see the pain all over Promise's face. She really wanted that for me, and I was glad that she cared. But I didn't see how it could be helped.

I smiled at her. "You know I never think about my age. Maybe I should. And I love you too and I hear you . . . Oh, you will be happy to know I invited Austin to the dry cleaners grand opening."

The grin that took over Promise's face told me she was happy and hopeful. "Sooo, you'll continue to date him . . . maybe even consider having a relationship with him?" I guessed that reality I had hoped to get her to see was out the window. Nothing I had said stuck, it went in one ear and out the other.

"Hold up. You are moving too fast, Sis. Let's grab a few more of these shoes and get out of here before we be late to the bash."

"You ain't said nothin' but a word. And the last thing I want to do is be rude to Penelope by being late to her bash. That she invited me to . . . Ooh, I want these and those over there." Promise pointed to her next shoe victims. The saleslady nodded and recruited her other sales partners in to help out.

Like I said, I dropped them twenty stacks plus ten more as a tip and we blew that spot. We still had one more store to hit before getting dressed.

Promise's face wore the same anxiousness, excitement, and just plain awe that mine had the very first time I saw Penelope and Pablo's house. One of the five security guards dressed in Armani suits led us up to the door. Then another security guard slash butler led us inside. Promise's mouth dropped open and she stood and admired the mansion.

"Oh my God, Precious. It is just amazing." Her eyes darted so fast and wide I was sure they might pop out of the sockets. "I love it here. If I was to never leave here, I would be happy."

I chuckled at her enthusiasm to see more. I could tell it was eating her up inside. "I would have told you what to expect but it's hard to explain. Get this, they have an elevator, and I know you thinking people have elevators in Bel-Air where I live. But they have not one but two elevators."

"Mane, I'm moving in. Do you think they might object? Because the one thing I'm sure of is they have enough space for me."

I could only giggle. "You and me and several of the people here could move in and never see them or each other in years."

"Precious, my favorite." Penelope came from behind. She greeted us with hugs and smooches. "Promise, it's a pleasure to meet you. I swear you two are just beautiful. You should be like model twins or something."

"Oh, stop it. You are the one that belongs on the cover of *Elle*," Promise said.

"Who am I kidding? You're probably right." Penelope's accent was strong. She was truly stunning. "Promise, I'm so glad you could make it. I still can't believe this is your first time in Miami."

"Yep, my Miami cherry was popped yesterday when the plane skidded down the runway. And I'm glad to be here. Miami has been good to me thus far, no complaints."

"They better or I will shut the city down," Penelope threatened with a giggle. I looked up to see Pablo headed for us. "Ohh, Pablo, come over here." Penelope waved him over.

"Precious, how are you?" Pablo reached for my hand and kissed it. He was suave that way. A kingpin but a gentleman.

"And this is Promise, Precious's twin." Penelope introduced us. Pablo had never met Promise before. I was glad they were finally meeting.

"I guess you can't be denied, you two are identical." Pablo smiled. "It's nice to meet you." He then reached for Promise's hand and kissed it. "I've heard nothing but good things about you," he added.

"It's nice to meet you as well. I have to say I adore this house." Promise's eyes were still dancing around in her head, for as far as they could see.

"It's too big." Penelope smiled. "Pablo likes big, but I prefer one room, in and out." We all laughed. A short, stocky Hispanic guy approached us. He wanted to speak with Pablo and Penelope. Pablo excused himself and walked away.

Penelope turned to us. "Ladies grab a drink and mingle. And Promise, please get a look at the house. Make yourself at home."

"Precious, I thought that was you." Marlo stepped in beside me. I was not surprised that he was at the bash, but I felt odd with the way he approached me.

"Oh, hi." I'm sure my tone gave me away. He stared at Promise, who was standing next to me, and the question was all over his face. It was obvious that we were family, the same person, to be exact. "Marlo, this is my sister, Promise." I decided to go ahead and put him out of his misery.

"Aye, I knew something was going on here. Twins or the Twilight Zone." He chuckled. "Hi, Promise. Welcome to Miami." He extended his hand to her.

Promise stared at his hand for a brief second. She had to catch herself, I could tell her mouth almost flew wide open. She was indeed mystified about him. The things I had told her. "Hi." She managed to keep it together and not show face.

"So, is this your first time in Miami?" The smile on Marlo's face had still not worn off.

"Yes, it is."

"Are you enjoying yourself so far?"

"Yes, actually I am," Promise said. Then her eyes along with mine fell to the lady that landed on the heels of Marlo. She lightly tapped him on the shoulder.

"Pablo will see you now," were her only words. She smiled at us and stepped away just as abruptly as she had appeared.

"Well, ladies. Guess I'll catch up to you later. That is, if you are still around. And it was nice meeting you, Promise." He smiled at us both, with a nod.

Promise and I watched as he strolled off toward wherever he was meeting Pablo. I turned to face Promise. Her eyes lit up without words and she lifted her wineglass to her lips and emptied it. Then she seized a fresh glass off the tray of a tall waiter as he swooped by. "Precious." She said my name as if it I was being accused of some wrongdoing. "You never, not even once said that Marlo was fine. Girl . . . he fine as FUCK!"

"Fine?" I questioned, then sipped my drink. "He ai'ght. I mean, he is not all that." I was calm.

"Bitch, I'm not gone even have this conversation with you. You can be coy about a lot of things. But not this. That man body . . . hell, face. You know what? Fuck it. He is a GOD!"

I couldn't help but laugh. I looked around to be sure no one heard me. Promise was being so dramatic. "I simply do not know what I'm going to do with you and your antics." We both smiled.

Penelope approached us with an unfamiliar woman.

"Precious, we need to talk for a minute." She touched the arm of the girl standing next to her. "Promise, this is Asha. She is going to show you this entire mansion."

Asha smiled. "Promise, this place is huge. Let's not waste any time."

"Well, lead the way." Promise held on to her glass.

Penelope and I watched as they walked away, then I followed Penelope as she led the way to the meeting room. I knew it was time to talk business. These bashes or parties were never completely about fun. Business was in most cases the focal point, but it looked better sometimes when you entertained. I recalled the times DaVon met with Pablo and Penelope. There was almost always business involved, but back then I was able to enjoy the festivities without the pressure. That seemed like a lifetime ago.

Penelope opened the door that led to a room that resembled a casino hall. As many times as I had been inside their home, it still amazed me that I hadn't seen half of it. Inside Pablo was sitting at a card table smoking a cigar. Marlo stood at the other end. They both turned their attention to Penelope and me.

"Pablo, baby, not another cigar. Come on, Papi, put it out."

Pablo always seemed to have stars in his eyes when he looked at Penelope. The love they shared was clear. "Right away, my love." He took one last puff, then smashed it in the ashtray next to him. "Precious." He stood. "Come on in. I hope your sister is enjoying the party."

"She is. But I think she loves this house more." I grinned.

"Good. Make sure she has a tour."

"Asha is on it," Penelope said.

Pablo nodded. "Precious, I'm glad you made it out to party with us again. It's always a pleasure. I wanted to bring you in and let you know that I appreciate everything your crew has done while they were here. I couldn't have asked for a better one. They sold all the product expected plus more. They keep the blocks that are assigned to them in line without leaving a host of bodies. Dead bodies always equal shortage. Not good for business." I knew this to be true. I could hear DaVon in the back of my mind making that point.

"We were impressed." Penelope chimed in. "Marlo here was even impressed and that does not happen often." Marlo nodded in agreement in my direction. "He's like Pablo. You have to make a firm believer out of them. Action is wise when it comes to them. Nothing else suffices."

"Always." Pablo reached for his cigar but quickly withdrew his hand with a smile. I was sure Penelope's presence reminded him. "So now the day has come for me to let you know that your crew can return home to LA."

The words out of his mouth were music to my ears. I wanted to jump for joy, but cool points were on the table, so I chilled. "Listen, thanks for giving us the opportunity to prove our loyalty to you."

"Hey, we're going to miss seeing you so often. I was getting used to you being here so much," Penelope said, her lips twisted in a pout.

I smiled. "Look at it this way, now you can get out to LA," I reminded her.

"Yeah, I have to make that happen. I really must."

Marlo stood off listening. I thought about telling him bye, but we were not on that level.

Penelope turned to Pablo, "Well, Papi, if you are done, Precious and I are going to rejoin the party. We don't want miss out on the drinks and fun."

"Please. I can use another drink." I prepared to fall into step with Penelope.

"It was nice meeting you, Precious. And working alongside you," Marlo, spoke up. I was surprised that he said anything. He had been quiet since I walked in the room, only nodding when Penelope had referred to him.

"Likewise," I replied. I really had no clue what to say to him. Penelope smiled at Pablo then led the way back to the party. With my back turned I could tell Pablo had already relit his cigar.

Penelope walked a few steps up the hallway, then stopped and looked behind us. She gestured for me to keep walking alongside her. She whispered, "You know he is sweet on you."

"Who?" I played dumb, but I knew exactly who she was referring to. And to be honest I was shocked to hear her say it.

"Now, don't you even do it, I know you see the look in that man's eyes. Marlo is smitten by you. He has been since the first time he laid eyes on you."

"Penelope, no." I shook my head, disagreeing with her observation. "No way." I was truly shocked to hear her suggest it. "Dude and I are like coworkers." I tried to make her understand how ridiculous what she was suggesting sounded.

Penelope turned to me and laughed. "Yeah, coworkers." She used her best sarcastic tone.

Off in the distance I saw Promise headed in our direction. "Listen, I have to chat to these two coming my way." Penelope waved at two women approaching us. Both had this anxious look about them. I excused myself without hesitation and parted ways with Penelope. I continued toward Promise.

"Precious, this house is even more spectacular than I ever could have thought!" She boasted a mile a minute, then she fished out another drink from a passing waiter.

"I know, right?" I agreed with her. "Hey, the day has been long. I'm getting tired," I announced. The meeting with Pablo. Then Penelope's wild accusations of Marlo's interest in me had made it even longer.

"Actually, I am too." I was surprised to hear Promise say she was tired. "Besides, these shots are starting to wear my legs down. I think I might be drunk." And I had to agree with her, she was tore up. "But I refuse to admit it." Promise covered her mouth and giggled. We decided it was time for us to go. Just as we made our way down the corridor, Marlo approached us.

"Wait, I know you ladies are not leaving for the night?" he asked. I wondered if he really cared or was simply trying to be nosy.

"You guessed right," I replied. "It has been a long day."

"Aye, I know how it is. Been up since five a.m.," he added. I wasn't sure if he was looking to have a conversation, but I did not add or take anything away from what he stated. "Well, I guess this is the last time we might run into each other."

"That could be facts." I kept walking. Marlo's presence could be strong at times, but for some reason I felt like stopping and giving him my undivided attention.

He must have been thinking the same thing. He stopped and I followed suit. Promise had kind of fallen behind us a bit, almost stumbling on the back of my heels. Marlo saw it and chuckled but quickly put his attention back to our conversation. "Tell you what. How about the next time I'm in LA I give you a call?"

I wasn't sure if he wanted an answer that would be an invite or just an okay. I decided on the latter. "That is where I will be. Just hit me up and let me know when you touch down." I felt stupid for the nonchalant answer.

"I'll do that. Have a safe flight back," he added, then continued on past us. I couldn't help but wonder if that brief look on his face was disappointment. If it was, I was clueless as to why he would be disappointed. But I didn't dare ask. Without looking back any longer, Promise and I headed for the exit. The valet drivers retrieved our vehicle.

"Miami don't owe me nothin'," Promise said, as she slid inside the SUV I had rented. I was glad to hear she had enjoyed herself. But I had known she would. Truth be told, I had enjoyed the city better with her being there. We would have to hit Miami up again.

Chapter 26

I was not surprised but grateful that everyone I had invited had turned out for the grand opening. This meant a lot to me because my dad's dream was riding on it, and that I did not take for granted. I knew without a doubt that if he were looking down on me, he was proud. People told me all the time how proud he would be of me, especially his friends. The ones that had shown up tonight had tightened their lips and repeated it over and over. But if only I could see that approving smile on his face, or hear the elated tone in his voice, I would be more convinced. Since that would not be happening, I settled for everyone else's words.

"This is nice, Precious." Promise glanced around. Her eyes were full of approval. "Being here, I almost feel his presence. Just makes me wish I had met him," she said, referring to Dad.

I could see the sadness on her face when she mentioned him. And I felt her pain because I felt the same way when I thought of our mother. I just wanted to comfort her as much as I could. "I'm sure his presence is here. Besides, I can't think of any place else it could be: all his hopes and dreams in the place he loved. The dry cleaners was his happy place even when business sucked, machines barely working, and clientele down. He smiled. So, trust he up in here." I joked a little to hopefully ease her pain.

Promised smiled. "You are so silly." And just like that my joke had worked.

"Precious, this food is good." Katrina approached.

"It better be. I only have the best chef that money can buy." I sipped my wine.

Promise's eyes grew wide as if she had just remembered. "Wait, you did say you were getting Chef Roblé from TV?"

"Yep, the one and only. I had to. Besides him being on TV, I heard good things from other people he catered for. So I figured why not. It was not easy getting him, though. Not only was he expensive, which I would expect, but he was booked up for months. Nevertheless, Evett my event planner pulled it off. She bad," I bragged. And knew it was true. Evett came through, held it down, and got shit done. Like a true boss. If I was looking for a female to be my right hand, I would definitely recruit her.

"She has done a good job, hands down. This grand opening is on point. Oh, before I forget, Dee and Toya wanted me to apologize for not being able to be here tonight. They are getting ready for that hair show," Promise reminded me.

"Yeah, that hair show is going to be huge. Half of LA gone be up in there." I started to elaborate but the sudden change on Promise's face got my attention. I watched her eyes light up as they landed on the entrance door.

Austin's eyes did the same as he headed straight to us. "Ladies." He addressed all three of us.

As if on cue we all dished out a *hey* at the same time.

"Thanks for coming," I said.

"Y'all, excuse me." Promise walked off without any explanation. Regina motioned Katrina over and she stepped away too. Just like that I was left to entertain him alone. I would remember to curse Promise out later for her little stunt. I was sure she had excused herself just for that reason.

"I see you have a nice turnout." Austin observed the room.

"I'm just grateful to see everyone turn out. So since you came, does that mean we have your dry cleaning business from now on?" I joked.

"Of course. But only if I can get the discounted rate," he teased in return.

I was almost relieved to see Promise walking back toward us, but I had a sudden urge to roll my eyes when I noticed Quan on her trail. I wasn't sure when he had made his grand entrance, but I should have known if Promise was in the building, he was coming. "Precious, congratulations on your newest venture," he said no sooner than he was in speaking distance of me. I had not seen him since Promise's and my birthday party. It almost felt odd with him so close.

"Thank you." I kept it dry and simple. Promise burned a hole in me with her hard stare, but I knew she was not surprised at my tone. I had made it known I was not happy with him.

"Why don't you all make yourself comfortable, maybe have a drink or two?" I suggested to Austin. "I have to mingle with some of my guests." I excused myself. The way I was feeling about Quan, I thought it was best I kept my distance.

I walked around and shook some hands to be sure everyone felt welcome and comfortable. Promise was on my heels in no time flat. "So Austin did show up." Her excitement became apparent.

"I told you I invited him." I kept my response casual. Anything else would only encourage her.

"Yeah, I know. But I was afraid you might call him up and uninvite him."

"Oh ye' of little faith." I smiled. She was being dramatic. "But to be honest, I have been so busy I forgot about him and the invite. So even if I didn't want him to come, I would have forgotten to uninvite him."

Promise's mouth dropped open with shock. "My cold-hearted sister." She chuckled.

"Perhaps." I smiled. "I see he," I nodded in Quan's direction, "came through to see you."

"He . . . ? So is that what you call him now?"

"Hmmph, I thought you might prefer that than b—"

Promise held her hand up and started to giggle. "Don't you dare. Are you still mad at him about that bitch Brandy acting up at the club? Say it ain't so."

"I'm not mad at him, I just need to keep my distance from him. And he needs to check his *bitch because she is running amok.*" I spat that part out. And I meant every word.

"Agreed. And trust me, he has." Promise smiled at a guest who kept eyeing her.

We had not talked about the situation or Quan. I just didn't bring it up because the very thought of it made me want to spit fire. And to be honest with myself, I still didn't want to discuss it, because I never trusted shit. I just gave her an *it's cool* nod. I was done with it. "Never mind the bullshit. Let's get back to the guests."

Katrina stopped in front of me. She sounded as if she had been running a marathon. "Hey, a big order of roses just came in. I'm talking about huge. That expensive stuff." She placed a card in my hand. I looked on the back to see who had sent it, but it was blank. I opened it. *Congratulations,* it read. It was signed P & P and I knew it was from Pablo and Penelope. The dry cleaners had nothing to do with the business we had in common, but they knew what it meant to me personally. So the fact they acknowledged it meant a lot to me, I really appreciated their support.

"It's time to head outside for the ribbon cutting," Evett whispered in my ear as I slid the card back into its envelope. Evett gestured for me to follow her. I handed Promise the card, then gestured her to follow me outside.

Everyone gathered around outside for the big moment. I pulled Promise in close to me and gazed up at the sky for just a brief second. The day was beautiful, the sun was shining, but there was a cool breeze in the wind. It was just perfect. The last thing I wanted was for it to be scorching hot out, then everyone would be huffing and puffing to get back inside before they broke a sweat. Instead, when I looked up toward the sky it felt like I had been kissed by the sun. I couldn't block the smile that took over my face. It was confirmation that Daddy was there with me for this big moment. The grand reopening for the old spot had been special, but this one was an honor. Now we had a chain, or at least the beginning of one. I had done it.

Evett motioned for me to start. I wasn't nervous, but I really didn't like speaking to crowds. At my other grand openings I had merely thanked everyone for being there and cut the ribbon. But today my heart was set on something a bit more.

"Well, I don't have a speech planned. But as always, I want to thank all of you for taking time to come out and support me on this big day. As most of you know, this dry cleaners is my legacy from my dad, Larry Cummings. He put his life into this business . . . and he lost his life in this business, literally." A tear escaped my eye before I could stop it. I paused and took a deep breath before going on. Promise rubbed my back to help calm me, but tears were running down her face as well. "Okay. Sorry. I didn't mean to tear up. This is not a sad occasion but a happy one. Now, what I was trying to say was. . . . this dry cleaning business was my dad's blood, sweat, and tears. And I feel his presence here today as me and my sister Promise contin . . ." I reached for Promise's right hand. "Continue on his dream, his legacy, and continue to grow while producing job opportunities and servicing our communities. With that said, we are going to cut this ribbon in honor of him." Evett passed the scissors to me. Promise and I both held on to them as we had discussed and cut the ribbon. Everyone applauded while Promise and I hugged, cried, and cheered along with them.

The night before I had invited her out to the house and popped open a bottle of champagne. Then I presented her a deed tied in a red bow making her part owner of the new dry cleaners. I made it clear that I wanted us to share equal partnership in our father's legacy, which I knew he would have wanted. Just a year prior, while having the garage at Dad's old house redone and all the old junk removed, the contractors had found an old rusty box buried beneath some broken concrete. It had taken me six months to open that box out of fear of what I might find. To my shock and surprise I found a letter that he had written to himself about Promise. Inside he tried to explain how his stubbornness and willingness to hide behind his shame for allowing us to be separated ate at him and tore his heart apart. How he didn't have the courage to fix all that he had destroyed. How he loved her beyond measure. How he had prayed every day that one day, he would wake up and be able to face me, and tell me the truth, in hopes that I could forgive him. That he could find her in hopes that she could forgive him too. How when the day he did try to find her at the last address her mother had given him, they were gone. But he promised that soon as he got his business back on track, he would hire a private investigator to find them. The sad part was the letter was dated about two months before he was murdered, so he never had the chance.

The letter really explained a lot to me. So when I submitted the deed to her, I figured it was the perfect time to share how my father really felt. Promise and I both drank wine and cried most of the night. But it was from happiness. That's how I knew our dad was in heaven rejoicing. Because of his letter, I knew he would have wanted Promise to have a piece of his legacy, and I knew it without a doubt.

Chapter 27

I answered the phone on the first ring. "What's up?"

"Dang, I wasn't expecting you to answer that fast. Girl, you sound like you are wide awake this a.m.," Promise said. The background sounded as if she was rummaging around or something.

"Actually, I am. I went to bed early last night without eating, I was so tired. I woke about an hour ago and couldn't go back to sleep. My stomach started to growl, so I figured I'd make me some pancakes. And consequently, not only am I awake, I'm full of energy. Oh, and did I mention, full," I added, then rubbed my stomach. My stomach was so tight it felt as though it could burst.

"Good, both should be to my benefit, a full stomach and lots of energy. So this should be a good time for me to ask you for a favor, my dear sister."

"I don't like the sound of this," I teased her. "Lay it on me before my breakfast wears off."

"Well, I was wondering if you could go by and open the salon up for me this morning. I have a shipment coming in, in about two hours. And I have an appointment coming in about that time, also. And as long as my appointment can get in until I get there, she will be straight. Reese and I both are running late this morning, and we were the only two who could be scheduled this early. Everybody else has something to do. But Reese should beat me there and then she can take over." She ran on and on without taking a breath.

"Promise, first off, calm down. Now, you know I got you. I can be there in about an hour give or take."

"Ahh, thank you so much." She sighed in relief. "I know this is last minute and all. And you keep a tight schedule. And I really don't want to inconvenience you."

"Like I said, I got this. Handle you and I'll see you when you get there. Unless Reese beats you there, of course."

"Cool." She hung up.

Traffic on the interstate was moderate, so I arrived right around the time I had predicted. I pulled into a parking space and headed inside.

"Arrrrr." I shook from the chill. I figured the AC was on high, it was so cold inside. I made the thermostat, which was in the booths area, my destination. Had it not been insane I would have turned on the heat just to warm up. Instead, I adjusted the temperature to a higher range. The AC shut off immediately. I breathed a sigh of relief.

I headed back toward the front so I could see the delivery guy once he arrived. "Quan," I mouthed. I was startled to see him standing at the front desk. He must have been quiet when he came in. Or he was on some sneak shit.

"Sorry, I didn't mean to alarm you." He seemed a little surprised to see me just as I was to see him.

"No problem, but next time say something so someone can know you are here. You know, a small courtesy warning." I wanted to curse him out. Sneaking up on people could get you shot, especially in LA. I was sure he knew that.

"No doubt. For real my bad." He apologized again. "Is Promise in the back?"

"Nah, she ain't here yet."

"Oh, snap, she's normally here this early. Guess I'll have to slide back through." He turned to leave but stopped in his tracks. He turned back to face me. I wasn't in the mood to talk to him, so I gave him the *what the fuck you want* stare.

"Hey, Precious." He said my name as if I was not looking dead at him and as if I had given him permission to. It annoyed me. I sighed, then stood back on my legs to hear whatever he wanted to say.

"Listen, I just want to apologize to you for the way things went down at the club with my ex Brandy. I want you to know that I spoke to her about her behavior. I made it clear that what she did was not cool. That it was fucked up on some next level bullshit."

I really didn't want to discuss this with him, but I couldn't help it. Besides, he had brought it up. Not me. "Aye, real talk. She needs to calm down and stop blowing up spots. Because the shit she does reflects on you. And the message she is sending is all wrong. Especially wit' you out here tryin' to date my sister. Promise is a grown-ass woman with a business and a promising future. She can't be mixed up with all this drama bullshit." I eyed him matter-of-factly.

He shook his head in agreement. "Aye, and I feel you on everything. And I really care for Promise. I ain't never met a woman like her, and I would never put her in a position like this on purpose." The look on his face seemed sincere, but that could have been a part of his act. I continued to eye him. I'm sure my eyes were burning holes in him, or at least that's probably how he felt. "I ain't expected none of this type of bullshit to jump off. I'm just as shocked as y'all are at Brandy. Mane, I don't know with her sometimes. She out here acting like she jealous about me moving on with my life." I took this as his attempt to try to explain her actions. But I really didn't give a fuck about her reasons. "I never knew she would act like that toward me. But you know how people can turn on you . . ." He cast his eyes downward for a brief second, then back on me. "Like your old friend Keisha."

The mention of Keisha stalled my comeback that I had ready for him. Instead, I quickly replayed what he had said in my head to be sure I heard him right. Just as I started to address him, the delivery guy opened the door and strolled inside pulling a dolly. The delivery guy looked at me and seemed a bit startled. It hit me that he probably thought I was Promise, but the light skin was throwing him off. I wished he would not stare. I was occupied with my thoughts and not in the mood for his roaming eyes. He briefly eyed Quan, then set his sights back on me. Clearly, he had a lot of time to blow.

He finally opened his mouth. "Um. Good morning." He still seemed unsure. But I was starting to think that maybe he was just nosy.

"Yes?" I responded. I was annoyed that he was becoming too familiar too fast.

"I have the delivery order here." I guessed he thought I was blind and could not see the packages on my own.

"Precious, again I apologize, but I gotta run," Quan said, then quickly turned to leave.

I returned my focus to the delivery guy. "Yes, bring them back here and I'll sign for them," I instructed. Reese opened the door and stepped inside.

"Good morning, Precious." Reese sang my name almost. It was clear she was in a good mood.

"Good morning," I said back. Keisha's name was still ringing in my head. "Um, I have to get going. Can you check this order and sign for it? Promise should be here any minute now." I exited the salon.

Inside my car I sat in the quiet and again replayed Quan saying Keisha's name. I considered his reasoning for bringing her up. More importantly, I wondered how he knew about her in any way that pertained to me. I knew people in LA knew we had been friends, and especially that she used to run the club I now owned. He had wanted to know about me being a successful business owner, according to Promise. I guessed that it was possible that in talking about that, Promise had mentioned Keisha. Or maybe I was jumping the gun. My phone rang and grabbed my attention. I again brushed Quan off.

Chapter 28

I pulled up to Starbucks and rolled my eyes at the crowd that had already formed inside. I was so not in the mood to stand anywhere near a bunch of coffee-craving freaks who acted as if their life depended on caffeine. But instead of backing up and speeding out of the parking lot, an option I really considered, I turned off my ignition, sighed with frustration, and made my way inside. Only for Promise would I actually go inside a place that at the moment I dreaded to go. She had called me about an hour ago requesting that I pick her up a cup of coffee from Starbucks. Now, I was a fan of Starbucks, but I didn't make it a habit, and whenever I arrived at one and they were packed, I was out.

"You better enjoy this coffee that I stood on a loaded cafeteria line to get." I handed the hot cup to Promise.

"You are such a godsend this morning. I really need this." She sat down in her styling chair.

"If you say so. And why a regular coffee? You normally want a latte."

"No, not this morning. I need real coffee. My head is spinning, and or banging. Pick one. Either way I'm miserable." For the first time I realized she looked a little frazzled. She sipped from the coffee cup. "I hung out with Quan and some of his friends and their girlfriends last night, and I think it's safe to say I had one too many Don Julio shots. I swear it seems like you are moving side to side." She rubbed her forehead.

"Oh, so you out here going up on a Wednesday," I teased her.

"I would laugh if I could." She drank from her cup again.

"You of all people know that Don is for the weekend. Now, if you must have a shot during the week, I say keep it at a taste only. I mean, unless of course you can hang with the big dogs."

"At this very moment I agree with you one hundred and seventy percent. Right before you strolled in here, I ate three Extra Strength Excedrin like they were candy."

"That might help. What was the occasion, anyway?"

"Occasion? What occasion?" Promise seemed confused by my question, as she continued to rub her forehead.

"Quan and his friends on a Wednesday? I mean, why go so hard with the Don Julio shots?"

"Oh, that. There was no occasion, it was just 'the night,' nothing special." She shrugged, but it was a weak one. "He wanted to hang with some friends. I'm overworked and bored, so his idea was all good."

"Well, I hope he had a good time. I mean, it's clear you did."

"Hmm, tell me about it. Quan left my house so messed up this morning he forgot his cell phone. When he realized he left it, he made an illegal U-turn to come back and ended up getting a ticket. Thankfully, they didn't test him for alcohol, because I'm more than certain he would have gotten a DUI. I told his ass he got lucky." Promise attempted to chuckle but grabbed at her forehead yet again.

"Shit, you already know." I agreed with her. The LAPD was not known for giving anybody a break, especially a young black man. There were actual horror stories with videos to boot in some cases of how some of them had been treated when they were pulled over. Quan must have had angels sitting on his left and right shoulders. An illegal U-turn should have at least gotten him a black eye, or worse, several busted ribs. "Quan must have done something good in his life. Somebody watching out for him. Because you know the LAPD normally would have gotten in that ass. You should have been taking that cell phone to check on him at the ER before he was handcuffed and taken off to jail." I was being sarcastic but realistic.

"I told him. Listen, I'd go see about him in the ER, but I ain't signing no bond to get no nigga out of jail. I don't like nobody that much. He better call up his people for that one."

I smiled. Even with a hangover and a headache, Promise never changed. "You know he apologized to me about the Brandy situation when he stopped by the salon last week?" I had been meaning to bring it up to her, but I had been busy. And the few times we had talked, it kept slipping my mind.

Promise looked at me, cradling her cup in both hands. "Oh, I didn't even realize he had stopped by the salon." I was surprised that he hadn't mentioned it.

"Yeah, he came in looking for you. I told him you wasn't there yet. Then before he left, he stopped and just apologized. He claimed that Brandy was just bitter."

"Hey, that much I agree with him on. That bitch is crazy. But she must want to get fucked up like Keisha's hoe ass because I'm done playing games with her. The club incident is the very last disrespect I'm gone take from that hoe." The mention of Keisha's name sparked my curiosity about Quan bringing her up to me.

"It's funny that you used Keisha as an example." I thought back to exactly the point Quan had said her name. "Have you brought her up to Quan before in conversation?"

Frown lines instantly formed from Promise's eyebrows. "Hell naw, I hate that bitch. I would never waste my spit on bringing her up, especially talking to Quan. Unless maybe I was drunk and not in my right mind."

Now I was curious. Quan had mentioned Keisha's name to me, and Brandy called Quan a snitch. Something was odd. "Promise, how much exactly do you know about Quan?"

Sipping from her coffee cup again, Promise bit down on her bottom lip, deep in thought. It was clear she was seriously contemplating my question. She looked at me and slightly shrugged her shoulders. "To be honest, nothing but what he told me. He was born and raised in Compton." I could tell she was reluctant to admit to me that, that was all she knew about him. "But he is cool." She instantly followed up.

My cell phone rang. It was the club. I answered. "Aww shit, I forgot all about that. I'm on the way." I ended the call. "Damn, I got to run. I forgot today is the day for my alcohol delivery at the club. You gone be good?"

"I'm cool, those pain pills have kicked in and this coffee doing its part."

"Good. I'll hit you up later."

"But what about lunch?" she asked. I was on a roll for forgetting things.

"Shit, I forgot all about we was about to smash."

"Uh, yeah, and Reese should be here soon with the wings."

"As much as I hate to, I'm gone have to take a rain check. By the time I drive over to the club and get back, the wings will be long cold. Besides, I have an appoint-ment with my guys in about three hours."

"Ai'ght, your loss."

"I'll hit you up, though." I rushed out of the salon. One of my workers at the club had just informed me the driver was en route. I had to hurry. But Quan was still on my mind. I filed him as one to continue to watch—now even closer.

Chapter 29

I was sure I was not the only one, but I swear every time I watched *The Players Club* I wanted to play Diamond just so I could be the one that beat that Ronnie hoe down. In my opinion it took Diamond way too long to beat her up. No way. The very time she tricked me and drugged me, I would have beat that ass and good. And no matter how many times I watched it, I harbored the exact same anger as if it was real life and I was the one being wronged.

"There you go, Diamond. Check that skank," I yelled at the television as if she could actually hear me. "Get her." I was excited as she delivered one of my favorite lines in the movie. I stalled with the gunshot as if I was right in the room with them. *I want everybody out the muthafucking dressing room, please!* I laughed and popped a handful of popcorn into my mouth. I was enjoying the movie and my free time.

Just as Diamond's fist connected the first blow to Ronnie's cheek, my cell phone rang. "Aww, hell naw." I smacked the sofa with my free hand—the other held on tight to the popcorn bowl. "Not tonight. Please." I rolled my eyes, reluctant to get the phone. "Ugh," I moaned as I reached for it.

"Hello," I answered, not hiding my annoyed tone of voice. The crying on the other end of the phone mellowed my attitude. "Wait, what?" I had to ask again.

"Precious, my apartment caught on fire tonight." Katrina cried harder.

"Oh my God. Are you and Lalah okay?" I asked, referring to her daughter.

Katrina sniffed and paused for a minute. It was clear she was shook up. "Yes, we are okay. Ummm . . . I'm here at the hospital. The doctors are checking over Lalah again. But they say everything for the both of us appears to be okay."

I sighed with relief at hearing they were fine. "Thank God," I replied.

"I'm scheduled to open at the old location in the morning, and Dominique and Regina both have appointments tomorrow."

"Are you kidding me? Don't be worried about that. That will be handled. Now, what hospital are you at?" Katrina gave me the hospital information. I wasted no time getting dressed and heading over.

"Hey." Katrina slowly raised her head and looked up as I entered the room. They were still in the emergency room area in the back. I walked over and hugged her. Lalah was knocked-out asleep.

"Thank you for coming, Precious. I can't believe they let you back here. I've been hearing people argue with nurses all night trying to see a friend."

"Girl, you know I lied and told them I was your sister." We both chuckled. "Are they gone release you guys tonight?"

"Yeah, we just waiting on our release paperwork."

"Cool. So, what happened? How the fire start?"

"Shit, that I would love to know myself. It's still unclear. I spoke to the fire captain, me and a few other of my neighbors that live in the same building as me. He told us they were going to investigate and that's it. But we heard a rumor since we been here that one of our neighbors ran to the store and left a pot on the stove. I don't know." She shrugged. "This is fucked up, though. I can't believe it."

"I know. Shocked me to hell when you call."

"Yep. Lalah was so shook up from seeing those flames they gave her something to help her sleep." I looked over at Lalah. She was sleeping so peacefully. Lalah was about eight years old now. I remembered when she was a baby. Time really flies.

"So where are you going to stay? Assuming you can't stay at your apartment."

"Nah, they are condemning the place. The Chief from the fire department did give us that much information." Katrina slightly shook her head as her eyes began to fill with tears again. She tried to sniff them back. "So we are going to stay in Inglewood with my mom. She has another apartment out there."

"Apartment?" I was confused. "I thought she had that three-bedroom house over on . . ." I stalled. It had been a minute, but I couldn't remember her mom's old street.

Katrina picked up. "Oh, she ain't there no more, the landlord was a slum. She had to get up outta there. Damn roof started to cave, and he still didn't want to fix it." We both shook our heads.

"Damn, so now she in an apartment. And even still ain't it packed over there?" I remembered that was why Katrina had worked so hard to move out.

"Yeah, it's a little crowded. But we'll be ai'ght for a few weeks or so until I can get everything figured out."

"No, listen, you and Lalah can come and stay with me. I have more than enough space. And you are more than welcome."

"Ah, Precious, you ain't gotta do that. It will be cool."

"Hey, you already know I ain't taking no for an answer. So," I shrugged my shoulders with an end of conversation vibe, "did you drive your car here?"

"Actually, no. Lalah and I came in the ambulance, so I have to go back and get my car from the apartment."

"Cool, then. Soon as they release you, I will drive you over to pick it up." My cell phone lit up with Promise's name. I had tried calling her on the way here, but her phone had gone to voicemail. So I'd left her a message to call me back. "Hey, I'm going to take this, you know the reception bad in here."

Promise's name faded as the phone dropped the call. I found an exit and stepped outside and dialed her back.

"I know you ain't trying to ignore my call," Promise said, as soon as she accepted my call.

"I'm sorry, I'm at the hospital and phone ain't getting no reception."

"Hospital?" Worry instantly penetrated her tone.

"I'm good, I'm good," I assured her right away. "It's Katrina, her apartment caught on fire."

"Wait, what? Is she okay? What about Lalah?"

"They are both fine. The doctors just had to check them over. Lalah was a bit hysterical from the shock, but other than that they are cool. They should be getting released soon."

"How did the fire start?"

"Well, Katrina does not have that information right

now. It was from another tenant, though. Her entire building was evacuated and she said the building is being condemned. So, it must be pretty bad."

"Wow. Well, just thank the Lord they are okay. Shit's crazy though."

"Right. That's what I said." I sighed.

"Is it anything I can do?"

"Actually, there is. Can you open the old location dry cleaners for me in the morning? Katrina of course won't be in, the other girls can't do it, and I have a meeting."

"Sure, I can do it. I will call Dee and have her open the salon. I got you."

"Thank you. I'm going to take Katrina back to pick up her car. I offered to let them stay at the house with me."

"Good. That was my next question if she needed a place to stay."

"Yeah, they good on that tip."

"Ai'ght then, well, keep me posted."

"I will, and I should be to the dry cleaners about an hour after you open. My meeting will be short." We had a frew more then ended the call.

By the time I got back to the room, the nurse was inside giving Katrina the release paperwork for her and Lalah. We headed to her apartment to pick up her car. From there I told Katrina to follow me to Target. It was late, but I wanted to pick her and Lalah up some things they needed right away.

The building had been condemned, as the chief had said. Katrina and all the people in her building had been referred to the Red Cross for any immediate needs, but we all knew how they worked out in reality. At Target, with Katrina protesting all the way, I purchased them night-clothes, underclothes, and hygiene necessities. I even had

Katrina pick them out an outfit for tomorrow—we could go shopping the next day for more clothes. Afterward we headed to the house. After hot baths, they both fell into bed exhausted, and I did the same. The night had turned out not to be a relaxing movie night, but I was grateful all the same that Katrina and Lalah were safe and sound.

Chapter 30

"Oh my God. Thank you so much for this drink." With desperation I accepted the glass of champagne that Promise handed me. I wasted no time tasting it. "Ahh," I sighed as soon as the bubbles slid down my throat. I was at Promise's house for drinks, and she had already delivered. "I drove over here with my feet heavy on the pedal for this drink. This day has been long." I went in for another drink and held my glass out for her to refill.

"Well, that much is clear. I'm glad I could be of some assistance in your alcohol craving," she teased.

"I know. You are the bomb, dear sister."

"Well, if it's any consolation, I needed this drink too. Precious, today at the salon was a hot-ass mess."

"Wait, please don't tell me Brandy had her ass back up there?" That was the first person who popped in my mind.

"That bitch is not crazy. I think I have made myself clear to her. But anywho, no. Apparently, one my clients and Dee's clients are dating the same man. Wait . . ." She paused. "I said that wrong. One of them's married to the man that the other one is dating. To make a long story short, one found out about the other and the shit hit the fan. Before we could stop it, they were punching, scratchin', and biting each other."

"What?" I was surprised.

"Girl yes, messed up my whole damn day. I threw both they asses out."

I laughed. "Listen, it's too much action going on up there lately."

"I know, right? I'm seriously thinkin' about investing in some security. I just never wanted to set that kind of vibe up there."

"I feel you. I mean, your salon is one of the most elite here in LA."

"And I don't want nobody to mess that up. What you think I should do?"

"I don't know. Maybe you can find one of those upscale security companies that have exclusive business. The guys dress up in suits like bodyguards so they can do valet as well."

"Hmm, that's a good idea."

"Yep, I'll call up the company I use tomorrow and see what I can get set up for you."

"Thank you, Precious." Promise smiled, then sipped from her glass.

"Oh, and I want to thank you for opening up the dry cleaners for me last week at the last minute."

"Hey, it was cool. How is Katrina and Lalah? I been meaning to stop by the dry cleaners or run by your house to see them. I sent her a thousand dollars through cash app the other day to help out on anything they might need."

"She told me you did. She was really grateful. I gave her a couple stacks last week as well to go shopping. They lost everything."

"Mane, that is so messed up. I couldn't imagine losing everything in the blink of an eye."

"I know. Shit be crazy like that sometimes. They not at the house though. Lalah goes to school all the way on the south side, so I gave her the keys to Dad's house and told her that they could stay there until she gets back on her feet. You know, getting a crib and everything."

"That's what's up." Promise agreed with my decision. "Have they heard anything about what caused the fire?"

"Faulty wiring. She just found out two days ago from the fire department."

"Mmm, mmm, these damn people building shit fast and backward these days."

"That's exactly what I said. If it hadn't been for the fire department, they wouldn't know what caused the fire. Slum landlord knew that shit was crap and too cheap to call a electrician out. I told her to sue they shady asses."

"She better. Makes no sense."

"Yeah, well, the good thing is she was actually in the process of getting a house. Now she says she gone put the speed on it. I told her not to rush, but you know Katrina. She is very ambitious. And I like that about her."

"That's good. It helps me know they gone be okay. Oh, and Dee and Toya took up a collection for her. I think they'll meet up with her this weekend for lunch and give it to her."

I could only smile to see how everybody had Katrina's back. It was a good feeling. "She gone be in tears when they give it to her." Katrina was emotional like that.

"Is she back at work?"

"Now, you know how Katrina is about her job. I did fill in for her the first two days after the fire. But I have been spending a lot of time at the club dealing with these vendors and such. It's really becoming a lot. I need to bring someone up in there to manage the place, but I don't want to hire anybody yet." I was really faced with a dilemma. I knew that bringing someone in to manage was a huge deal. I had to be careful and smart.

"How about I come in a few hours a week and help out?" Promise volunteered. "I been working a lot less hours at the salon. You know, seeing less clients. I really been focusing on just managing it. Kinda frees me up a bit more."

"I'm mean it sounds like a good idea. But are you sure? Because right now it could really help me out."

"Then you got me. By the way, how is business going over at the club? Sales and whatnot? I haven't been out since our birthday."

"Booming. That club stay packed just like you predicted. I'm glad I listened to you and didn't sell it back to the bank." Because of Promise's encouragement, the club was open and raking in the cash.

"Dang, Precious, I have been missing out. I have got to spend more time up in there shaking my ass too. One thing is very clear, I ain't been partying enough. Major crisis." We both laughed. "So, what did you think about Christopher?"

The name blew a blank. My eyes shot to the ceiling to think fast, but I got nothing. So I asked, "Who is Christopher?" Then it hit me soon as the question was out my mouth. "Wait, you mean Christopher the realtor?"

"Yeah, Christopher the realtor." She gave me a duh look and filled her glass with more Champagne. "What other Christopher would I be speaking of?"

"I think you asked me this before." I thought I'd remind her. "He was fine, seems smart. He also seems like he is really focused," I added. But was curious why we were revisiting a conversation about him. "What's up?" I wanted to know.

"He has been calling me up trying to take me out."

"Hmm . . . what about Quan? Thought y'all was all tight and shit."

"He ai'ght and everything but we ain't married." She rolled her eyes.

"All true. But don't make me have to lay that nigga to rest if he gets stupid."

Promise laughed out loud. "Yeah, these niggas think they be married to you without giving you the ring or even a verbal commitment. They think commitment automatically comes because they are spending some time and money. Hmph, they are funny." At that statement we both laughed. That was true and it was probably not one female that would not agree. But like she said, she was not married, so whatever she decided to do or when she decided to do it, I had her back.

Chapter 31

Already I could feel the strain ease a bit at the club with Promise's help. She had been coming in a couple days a week as she said she would, meeting the delivery trucks, meeting with the staff, opening up so the DJ could get in on time. All type of things that really helped me out. My days were still filled with meetings with Plies, and of course the crew on certain days. I still had to make sure my product was adding up with the money, and I still flew out twice a month to Miami to meet with Pablo about my reups. Not to mention I had the two dry cleaners, where I picked up the deposits and handled all of that. Like I said, my days were busy.

Today I was at the club. I was in about three times during the week balancing books, counting inventory, and thinking of even more ways to capitalize. That was just the mind of a business owner. There was always the next step. Something always had to be next. Today I wanted to throw out a new idea with my bartenders that I had been pondering for the past few weeks. Tyrone, one of my two bartenders, was always brushing up on his craft and tightening his skills. Shareta was my other bartender. She was young, smart, and ambitious. She was in cooking school; her dream was to become a top chef. I liked them both.

"So, I was thinking we need to bring in some new drinks. You know, some new, catchy, with a kick. The name has to say it all."

"Oh, yeah, now you are speaking my language." Tyrone's smile was all teeth and jaw. "I got this one drink I been working on. Garanteed to knock you off your feet but the taste so good, it keeps you coming back."

"Okay. Sounds just like what I envisioned." I grinned.

"And I got the names," Shareta chimed in.

"Well, we can get started working on this sometime this week. Let's schedule a day where we can come in, mix drinks and throw names around."

"Cool," Shareta and Tyrone said in unison.

"Now, these new drinks should add to our business. I want to start opening up on Tuesday and Thursday from noon until six. Can each of you work at least one of these days for those shifts?"

Both Tyrone and Shareta smiled and said yes. "Okay, okay, cool. I will leave it between you two to pick which day you want to come in. Maybe y'all can rotate it. Or if you decide you want to have that same day every week, it's cool wit' me."

"I'm cool wit' either?" Tyrone shrugged his shoulders.

"Aye, me too. Now, I'm ready to name these drinks. I have so many names in mind."

We all chuckled. My phone lit up. It was Plies. "Hey, I need to get this. Maybe y'all can throw some names back and forth for a minute." I stepped away. "Aye, what's up?" I asked as soon as I was out of earshot.

"Yo, I need you to meet me at the spot."

As soon as he said those words, I ended the call. I knew something was up, and I had to get going. After telling Tyrone and Shareta I would hit them up later with the date and time for us to meet, I bounced. The spot was about a half-hour drive away from the club. Traffic was not nice, so I didn't make it in my usual time. I pulled in, made sure I was locked and loaded, and made my way inside.

Inside, Plies's mode was beast as he laid it on me. "Your boy Black and his sucka-ass niggas back on they death wish." I looked at the tall, skinny, mahogany-toned, beady-eyed boy strapped to a steel post in the middle of the warehouse with his mouth duct taped shut. The air was on, but he was all sweaty, staring at me.

"This particular bitch-ass nigga goes by Crow on the streets. He is the one out here sneaking in our block . . . selling to our people, and sold one of them a bad hit. Yeah, nigga out here living bold and shit," Plies hissed.

I eyed Crow from where I stood as I processed Plies's words. Plies sucked his teeth and started to back up. "See, his ex-girl been hanging out with Case, and apparently she been doing some pillow talking. So, my man Case paid one of his coppers and told Case when he would be on the block, then he pointed him out. And we snatched his ass up."

I continued to glare at Crow. His head dropped. The blood from his dreads was dripping onto the floor. I was sure he had probably been hit in the head with the butt of one my crews steel. "Get Black on the phone," I finally replied. "Let him know that we need to meet ASAP."

"No doubt." Plies wasted no time getting him on the line. Black agreed to the meet. Mob and Case accompanied me. I told Plies to hang back with Crow.

I sat down at the table, and across from me sat Black. Like I said in the past, he was not a pretty sight. He was the same color as the burnt soot on a stove and his personality matched. The guy was ugly inside and out. If I never saw him again it would be too soon, and I was sure he felt the same way about me. But we had business, so we were stuck.

I wasted no time throwing my eyes onto his. That was really the meaning of my meeting. I needed to know if he had anything to do with one of his crew violating me.

"We meet again." He gave me his ugly grin that was outweighed by his sarcastic smirk.

"I guess some things can't be avoided," I replied.

"Well, what is so important that you have to pull me away from my main bitch? Now she mad at me." I knew he was trying to piss me off. That was one of his strong points.

"Just handle it the same way you handle all your bitches. Those pockets," I said sarcastically. I was done with his jokes and small talk. "Now the business . . . I got one of your crew. Crow." I pronounced his name as if it stung my tongue. "Word is he been sneaking onto my blocks selling to my clients. And selling bad shit, no less." I laid out what he was being accused of. "I need to know . . . did you send him?" I asked straight out.

Black normally wore a scowl on his face that was sometimes hard to determine. The line of his jaws seemed to push forward. His forearms relaxed but his chest muscles seemed to tense. He knew shit was serious. But I also knew right then he had nothing to do with it. Because it was one thing I knew he knew for sure, I was not to be fucked with. My crew was determined, and they always made that clear. War could be started with the click of my finger. It was live or die when it came to me. That much he was sure of.

Black lowered his chin and met my eyes straight on. "That fool planning his own funeral."

"I figured as much. Some things can and should never happen. That's one of the game's first lessons." Black nodded in agreement. I sat up and made it clear to him that it would be handled. But I made it clear that if at any time I found out that he had anything to do with it, we would personally speak again.

"Crow, how long you been in the streets?"

It was clear Plies had roughed him up some more while I had been out. But he was still alert. His eyes were wide, wild, and aggressive. I motioned for Mob to remove the duct tape from his mouth.

As soon as the tape came off, he gagged, spit up a bit of blood, and took in a big gulp of air. Mob slapped him. "Answer the fucking question!" he demanded.

"Long enough," Crow answered, breathing hard.

"So, you know the rules. I mean, I'm sure you knew them before you even jumped in the game. Where you grow up?"

"Inglewood," he said proudly, still breathing hard.

"Old, Inglewood. So, you a smart boy. Ain't shit in Inglewood say dumb." I eyed him. He allowed his head to drop. "You sneaking in on my block dealing, and dealing that bad shit?" I accused.

"Nah, it ain't like that," he denied. "I ain't sold shit on yo' block and I damn sure ain't sold no bad product. Somebody lying on me . . ." He tried to catch his breath. "Like you said. I grew up in Inglewood, I ain't stupid."

I nodded. "It wouldn't be smart," I added.

"I work for Black. That nigga keep us wit' plenty work. I ain't got time for other plays."

"Crow, there comes a time in a man's life when he got to own his shit and know that he fucked up. Being greedy ain't never served no one a positive purpose. You were caught red-handed in my territory."

Crow's whole face seemed to start twitching. "Bitch, fuck you." He was upset. Mob, who was still within touching distance of him, raised his fist, but I stopped him. Crow gazed at me with his untrusting beady eyes. "You think your crew the shit. Think you run LA. Bitch, you don't own shit. I deal the streets and I SERVE WHO I CHOOSE!" he yelled at me with spit dripping from his bottom lip. "What made you ever think it was okay to take the best blocks and boot us out? Nah, Black was straight pussy for agreeing to that bullshit. I would never let a woman take shit from me."

"Hmmph." I remained calm and composed but made myself clear. "Well, Crow, you are stupid for not being pussy enough to know better. What you did was wrong. See, in this crew we stand on and swear by our product. We guarantee it. We don't fool our customers into thinking we serve them good, safe product. And we especially don't kill them with bad product." Even though I knew that selling drugs to people was wrong, I found some comfort in knowing that if they were buying from us, they were at least buying a safe product. Crow had taken that right away from someone.

"Fuck them junkies. Fuck you think I give a shit about them," he boomed. "A high is a fucking high. Either way, it takes you out your misery for a time and in some cases forever," he said with no remorse.

I had enough of him. "I was kind of hoping you would say that." I turned to Case, who stood to my left. "Hook him up," I ordered. A smile spread across my face as I turned back to Crow. "We brought this in special for you. And I guarantee it will put you out of your misery FOREVER!" I emphasized.

Case walked over to Crow with a needle in hand. The needle was filled with just enough bad heroin to do the job.

"Aww hell naw. Please. Aye, listen. No. No." He kicked and fought. Mob and Plies held him still. Case raised the needle in front of Crow and squeezed off a little drip. And with Crow screaming for dear life, Case eased the needle deep into his neck. I watched as he kicked and kicked, then his body began to jerk. Foam erupted from the corners of his lips. His arms, no longer held by Mob and Plies, fell limply to his sides. He stopped moving. It was over. The same senseless pain he had inflicted on another was now his fate.

Slowly I turned and left the building. This killing thing was never easy. And I still couldn't believe I was watching it being done.

Chapter 32

I had fought against my decision all day but finally gave in and decided to keep the plans I had made with Austin. He had invited me to his house for dinner. I had declined several times but I finally relented, only if he would let me have the food catered and allow me to pay for it. Reluctantly, he had agreed. I really wasn't comfortable going to his house but eventually said fuck it, threw caution to the wind, and pointed my whip in the direction of his house. Driving steady, I kept up with the other cars as I navigated the streets of Hyde Park where he lived. While Hyde Park had its reputation with crime and other news articles that some might deem it bad, I chalked it up to the streets of Los Angeles. There was always a story to be told.

After sitting at several red lights and stop signs in different areas, I finally turned on to West Fifty-sixth Place and listened as my GPS located the correct house address and confirmed I had reached my destination. I slowly pulled into the concrete driveway, paused on my brakes, and silenced the ignition. It was only six o'clock, so the sun was still shining, and I was able to get a good look at Austin's house. It was a cute villa, with nice landscaping.

The area seemed decent enough, and I only saw a few kids out. They were engrossed in posing for pictures on their cell phones.

I got out of the car, slowly walked up to the door and rang the doorbell. Austin answered right away. "Hey." His face lit up as soon as he opened the door.

"Hi." I smiled in return.

"I see you didn't have a problem finding the place." He stepped to the side and gestured me in.

"Not at all. I'm an LA girl, remember." I chuckled.

"Well, welcome. It's not much but I call it home." I looked around from where I stood at the door. So far, I liked it. He took me on a tour, and his house was lovely. It was a nice size. Make no mistake, a house in Hyde Park could easily run you some big dollars, and I was sure this one cost Austin a good five to seven hundred thousand.

"Your home is beautiful," I complimented as we made our way back toward the living room.

"It's an investment. I love my neighborhood. I grew up around this way, and when I graduated college and landed my first teaching job, I wanted to give back to my community, so I figured one of the best ways to do that was to live in my community. But now I'm ready to get my dream house. So, I'm putting this one up for sale next year."

"Hey, look at it this way, you will be giving someone else a chance to put down roots and build in this community." He shook his head in agreement. The doorbell rang.

"And that should be our gourmet meal. I'll be right back." He excused himself.

I pulled my phone out and answered a few texts while Austin brought in the caterers and showed them into his dining room to set up. I heard him thank them as he walked them out.

"Welp, everything is set up. If you follow me, we can eat."

I wasted no time getting to my feet. I was hungry—I

had skipped lunch to be sure I had room for what was in store. The table was laid out with fried catfish, spaghetti, greens, mac 'n' cheese, cornbread, different desserts. You name it, we had it. We both sat down and dug in.

"I'm stuffed." I sighed as we sat down to watch a movie.

"Me too. I think it's been a long time since I ate that much. I'm so busy being in class all day, then I try to get to the gym to work out. Weekends I normally have some type of speaking engagement or I'm grading papers. So, I really don't get a lot of time for home-cooked meals. Mostly, quick stuff or carryout."

"I'm guilty of the same thing," I replied.

We had agreed on watching Tyler Perry's *Why did I Get Married*, and after watching it, debating, and analyzing it, we decided that we did not understand some of Tyler Perry's merits, but the move was good all the same. Austin put on some music. I wasn't sure about that, but I had already set my sights on leaving soon, so I didn't make a deal out of it. R. Kelly's "Honey Love" blasted out of his speakers. I was surprised that he had chosen that, but I was a fan of old-school.

"Will you dance with me?" He stood in front of me with his hand out. Normally, I would have said no. But instead, I stood up.

I let my mind roam free as we danced. Austin had gotten really close, and it didn't feel bad at all. He brushed his lips up against my neck and my heart sped up. I was enticed by his cologne, and the feel of his body engrossed me. Things were definitely heating up. Then his hand branched out and I felt it moving up my shirt. The sense of DaVon touching me crept into my mind. I opened my eyes. I caught Austin's hand and stopped him. I stepped back from his embrace.

"I'm sorry," he apologized instantly.

"It's okay. But I'm not ready for that." My phone beeped and I reached down to the couch next to me and picked it up.

"And that's fine. I'm not trying to rush anything."

I read the text from Plies. "Um, listen. The food was good, I enjoyed myself, but I gotta go." I picked up my keys and purse and turned to leave. I felt Austin gently grabbed my arm.

"Do you really have to go? I really didn't mean anything by—"

I cut him off. "It has nothing to do with that. But yes, I have to go."

"You are a busy woman." I could see the disappointment on his face. One of the main reasons I did not want to date.

"Austin, remember I told you I am a busy person. I don't have a lot of free time." I looked him straight in the eyes. "This type of stuff . . . dating, being romantic, or being romanced, all that comes last in my life." I didn't mean to sound insensitive, but it was the truth. I turned to leave.

Again, he gently touched my arm. I stopped, slowly turning to face him. "Listen, this is what it is with me. It's complicated. I'm not an open book. Now, I gotta go." I hoped I was clear.

"I hear you," he said. "I'll call you."

Without replying I turned and left. Somehow I still got the gut feeling that he would not give up. But I wasn't sure why. It really wasn't that deep. LA was full of women that would grovel over a successful man. Why hound me?

Chapter 33

"So I'm sitting in the house all comfortable, minding my own business on Saturday. I had got up, cleaned up my crib, was watching some television. You know, just chilling. I really hadn't planned on the leaving the house, but I had a taste for some ice cream. Finally, I said forget it, it's nice out, I'll run and get me some. Tell me why I get outside about to climb in Dell's car, start it up because he had mine. I back it out and start driving. Suddenly, the car starts making this noise and the street was feeling extra bumpy to the point I had to stop. I get out the car and realize the front tire is flat, but not just that, it actually looks cut. Like in shreds. Then I realize the back one looks the same," Toya said.

"What the hell?" Dee's mouth flew open. She had just walked back in from bringing one of her clients to the front. Her next appointment wasn't for another half hour. She wasted no time sitting in her seat for a break.

"Oh shit. What's happened?" Promise asked. I was sitting in her chair while she styled my head. It never mattered when I came to the hair salon—there was always a good story full of drama to be told. I sat quiet and listened as it was about to unfold.

"So, something tells me to look at all the tires. All four are cut. Then finally I notice that somebody wrote in some type of black ink on his passenger side door, 'Tasha.'"

"Tasha? Who dat?" Dee's eyebrows raised to the roof. She had a Sprite Zero fountain drink on her station. She reached for it and took a squeeze.

"Say no more. This got Dell and one of his hoe's name written all over it." Promise broke the case. I shook my head in agreement.

"Girllll." Toya smacked her mouth. "So, I called his ass and told him to get over there. He gets there asking me what happened to his car. I ask him who the hell is Tasha. He don't get mad. He calmly tells me he don't know a Tasha and that the vandalism was clearly meant for someone else's car."

"That figures," Promise said.

"Hmmph, it don't surprise me to know he said some dumb shit. That nigga been slow," Dee added. "But I tell you what, since Tasha started fucking it up, you finish it by putting sugar in his tank." Dee offered up some advice.

We all laughed. "I know, right. I'm sick of his ass," Toya said.

"I mean, the fact that he was not upset is a dead give-away. You know niggas be in love with they vehicles. You mess that up, they gone trip," Dee said.

"That's a given," I threw in. I normally kept quiet but I had to say it.

"I already know. That's why I didn't even try to argue or debate with him. I put his ass out. Enough is enough. I'm done with him this time. This shit is ridiculous. It's just been too much."

"I'm glad to hear you say this. And I hope you stick to it," Promise said.

"Yeah, 'cause you know he gone be trying to crawl back with empty lies. The only way for you to get rid of him for good is to get you another nigga," Dee said, then smiled.

Promise agreed. "Yep. And you know what they say about getting under a new nigga to get over the old one." We all laughed again.

"I'm a living testament to that one." Dee raised her right hand.

Austin walked in carrying two bags filled with wings, fries, and carrots. He had been blowing me up for a few days and I wouldn't answer. I was just too busy for preliminary. But today I had answered, and when I told him where I was and that I was hungry, he offered to stop by with lunch for everyone. When I told him wings, he said no doubt and that he would be over. Everyone stopped talking as he stepped into the area. The aroma from the plates filled the room.

"Hey," he said to everyone. "I didn't mean to interrupt."

"Aww, never mind us. You are good," Promise said.

"Everybody, this gentleman with our good smelling lunch is Austin." I introduced him.

"Hey." Everybody spoke in unison.

Promise showed him where he could set the food down.

"So, Austin, where you from?" Dee asked.

"LA south side, born and raised."

"Well, I guess that's a crazy question. Probably most of us from the south side." Dee grinned.

"Right," Austin agreed.

"Me too." Toya swirled around in her chair. She was on a break until her next appointment.

"You look a little familiar, though. I might know you." Dee said.

Austin chuckled. "I get that all the time. Someone saying I look like somebody they know. Guess you can say I have one of those faces."

"Yeah, you know, Austin teaches over at the university. He is a professor." Promise smiled.

Austin walked over to me. "Thank you for bringing the food. It smells delicious," I said.

"No problem. It was worth it to get a look at you." He tried to speak softly to me. Dee, Promise, and Toya were laughing about something else. "Well, I gotta get back for my next class."

"Again, thank you." I smiled at him.

"Well, it was nice meeting all of you." Austin waved at the girls before exiting.

"Precious, girl, he is fine, fine," Dee commented as soon as Austin was out of earshot.

"And a professor. Damn, fine and successful. Do he have any kids?" Toya asked. Excitement was all over her face. One would have thought Austin came to visit her.

"Nope," I answered.

"Oh hell, yeah. He a catch." Toya smiled.

"I been trying to tell this twin of mine." Promise grinned.

"Does he have a brother or cousin?" Dee threw in.

"Right." Toya cosigned her with a high five.

"Calm down, thirsty one and two," Promise joked with Dee and Toya.

I just looked at them and smiled. "I mean he is cool and everything." I again downplayed it. "Now, let's eat some of these wings before they get cold." I stood up.

"Stubborn as an ox and ain't no changing her," Promise declared. And I knew she was probably right.

Chapter 34

I rolled my Louis Vuitton suitcase out of Miami International Airport and loaded it into my rented SUV. I was here for my quarterly meeting with Pablo and Penelope about my product. I arrived a day early so that I could meet up with a retailer named Sarah Bradshaw who sold wigs, hair weave, you name it. Promise had told me about her and I had heard through the streets that she sold to a lot of businesses out in LA. I was really considering opening up a hair store. Today I would meet up with Sarah to look at some hair and discuss prices and quality.

After reaching my hotel I checked in, went up to my room, got settled in, took a few business calls, then headed out to meet up with Sarah.

"Hi, my name is Precious Cummings. I'm here to see Sarah Bradsahaw." I told the receptionist at the front desk.

"Yes, Ms. Cummings, she is expecting you." She picked up the phone and notified Sarah, then stood up and walked me back to Sarah's office.

Soon as she opened the door, Sarah, a tall milk chocolate female who looked to be about thirty-five, stood up, introduced herself, and shook my hand.

"Finally, It is nice to meet you," Sarah said.

"Likewise." My eyes quickly darted about the room. There was a doll head on a stand with a lace front honey blond wig in a bob.

"I'm glad you could stop in while you were in the city. I take it you are interested in starting a business in hair?"

"Yeah, I'm really considering it. Right now I just need to get some background on the product that would be essential to the potential business."

"Well, my hair is top of the line, and it comes in from Korea. I go over and handle all my product myself. Right now, as you might already know, I am one of the top sellers in the game. Of course, I sell at wholesale. And I can promise you some of the best quality hair being sold, anywhere."

"I'm definitely interested in quality."

"Over here this wig was made out of Polynesian hair. Please feel the texture." She invited me to touch the blond wig. I lightly touched the hair. It moved and fell piece by piece, side by side, right back into place. It felt as natural as the hair on my own head.

"See how naturally the hair gracefully falls back into place. My hair is one hundred percent guaranteed. How about we sit down and talk numbers and distribution?"

"Why not . . . One second, though." My cell phone started to chime. It was Plies on the other end letting me know that his flight had been changed and he wouldn't get in until late that night. After I ended the call I got down to business with Sarah.

After the meeting I jumped in my vehicle and decided to head back to the hotel. Plies and I had planned to have drinks and discuss a little business but since his plans had been delayed, I had nothing else to do. Penelope was in Puerto Rico and her plane wasn't scheduled to land until ten o'clock in the morning. Oddly, I wasn't in the mood to go shopping. So the hotel and room service was what it was.

I pulled up to the valet at my hotel just as my phone started to ring. "Hello," I answered.

"Hey, Precious." I recognized the Southern drawl of his voice right away.

"Marlo." I said his name but tried to hide the surprise in my tone. I didn't have a clue why he would be calling me.

"I didn't catch you at a bad time, did I?" I guessed I didn't do a good job at hiding that surprised tone.

"No, it's fine. What's up?"

"Well, I heard you were in the city and was wondering if you would like to grab a drink or something."

Now I was being put on the spot and a bit confused. For one, how did he know I was in Miami a day early? And two, he was calling me up asking me out to drinks? "I, um . . ." I was at a loss for words but bounced back quickly. "How did you know I was in Miami?"

"Penelope. She told me you would be in today." I shook my head while smiling. I should have known it was her. What was she up to?

"Now, did she?"

"Yeah, she guilty . . . what about that drink?"

My first thought was to say no. But for some reason, maybe it was the dare in his voice, I said, "Yes. Where at?"

"Oh." This time he almost stuttered. I guessed he had expected me to turn him down or my swift answer to his dare. "Well, okay." I almost laughed at his hesitation. He was really surprised I had agreed to go. "It's this bar downtown that has the best shots in Miami," he declared. "I'll text you the address. Can you be there in twenty minutes?"

"Yep, soon as you text me that address."

"Ai'ght, stand by, it's on the way."

"Cool. I'll see you there."

A valet driver stepped up to the driver's side door. I let the window down and told him never mind. My cell phone notified me that I had a message. It was Marlo's number. I swiped the message, retrieved the address, and entered it into the GPS. I pulled out of my hotel parking lot and back into traffic. I pulled up to the bar in exactly twenty minutes. I found a parking space and got out. Just as I stepped in front of the bar, so did Marlo.

"I see you keep your promises." Marlo smiled at me.

I chuckled at his words. "Um, I don't remember making you any promises."

"You agreed that you could be here in twenty minutes."

"And that was not a promise, it was an answer to your question."

"Oh, is that how you see it?" He reached out his right arm and pulled the door to the bar open. I smiled as I stepped inside. We walked over to the bar and had a seat. A bartender approached us for our orders.

"What would you like to start with?" he asked us.

"Give me some Vanilla Jack with a splash of Coke and two olives."

"Give me a shot of Jack with some Coke."

"So, you still running the city." I laughed. I decided to break the ice. The bartender passed us both a drink.

"Oh, you do have jokes."

"A few." I smiled.

"Well, in that case. You know how I do. I'm always on my Shaft shit," he joked.

"I see, I see." I chuckled, then took a sip of my drink.

"Real talk. How have you been? Glad to be back in LA full-time?"

"Yeah, it's cool. That's my home. Keeps me busy." I hunched my shoulders nonchalantly.

"I feel you. Busy is my middle name. It isn't often I get out for a drink. And not discuss the play."

"Wait, are you trying to tell me you ain't the life of Miami." I laughed again. "I'm not even trying to believe that."

"See, you full jokes, tonight. Is that who you think I am? The party man of the three O five? I mean, I do occasionally bring the city out . . . butttt." He smiled.

"I bet you do. I don't doubt that at all."

"No doubt. So what brings you out a day early?"

"A bit nosy, huh?" I was on a roll pulling his strings.

"Now see, that hurt."

I watched him playfully stab at his heart as if I had hurt it. I smiled at his antics and took another sip of my drink. "You funny. Ha ha. Nah, really I might have another possible business venture brewing."

"Ah, no doubt. New businesses are always a plus. But really, I just wanted to make you keep your word on having that drink with me. Remember, last time you turned me down."

"Yeah, that. Well, you know that was a busy day full of surprises. I kinda had to regroup. But I'm glad I came through tonight. This drink poppin'." I raised my glass as if to salute.

"Nah, you are going soft right now. You gone have to at least take a real shot. That Henney, or Don," he dared me for the second time in one night. But I was wit' it.

"Never soft. Not the kid. And what you know about that Don?" I playfully challenged him.

"Listen, whoever made Don Julio had me in mind. You better fact check that."

"Ai'ght, we about to see." I smiled. "Bartender, two Don Julio shots . . . apiece." I winked in Marlo's direction.

"Two, at the same time . . . Okay. I see you didn't come to play. Bottoms up, then."

The bartender put the shots down and we started downing them. Those two turned out to be our first two rounds of six. Needless to say, I left the bar lit. I was tore up from the floor up, but I played it off well in front of Marlo. And if he was tore up, he played it off well too. He walked out of the bar standing up straight and not missing one step. I had to admit we had a good time. We laughed and joked about mostly nothing I could remember. But when my eyes opened up from a long night's sleep, I remembered the shots right away. My head was pounding. My stomach was twisting. And my cell phone was ringing off the hook.

"Hello." I reached for my phone slowly.

"Aye, you good?" Plies's voice came through the phone.

"Yeah, I'm cool. What's good? Your flight make it in last night?" I could see the sun shining through my window.

"Yep. I called you a couple times this morning. Thought we could grab breakfast, talk business. You ain't answer after the second time so I thought I'd give it one more try before I light up Miami."

"I know, right?" I chuckled. "Nah, I'm good, though. We can still grab that breakfast."

"Nah, it's almost time for the meeting."

I sat up and looked at the time. "Ah, snap. I done overslept. I better go I'll see you at the meeting." I jumped out of the bed as fast as my headache would allow me, jumped in the shower, and dressed. My first stop would be a convenience store for an Extra Strength Excedrin. Talk about hung over, I was riding the rails.

I sat through the first part of the meeting praying my headache would subside. And my stomach would keep its acid contents inside. Finally, by the time Pablo wrapped, both had started to ease. I played it off, though, and kept a straight face and good posture because business was business. Plies's flight was before mine, so as soon as the meeting was over, he was out of there. Penelope snatched up me as soon as he left. She walked me out to my car.

"So how was your early flight in yesterday? And how did your meeting go with Sarah Bradshaw?"

"Everything went good. Sarah had some good whole-sale deals with the hair. I think I'm going to start out with some bundles for Promise's salon. That will give me time to set up shop for the business. Just got to tie up some loose ends on that."

"Okay. Sounds good. I hate I wasn't here yesterday so we could grab a drink or two."

I knew she was going to get to that.

"Hmm, I think you took care of me in your absence. Penelope, how could you tell Marlo I was in town a day early?"

"Well, you know, I didn't want to leave you with nothing to do. I wanted you to enjoy yourself."

I just looked at her, smiled, then twisted up my lips, letting her know I knew she was up to something.

"Precious, you know Marlo likes you. I know he asked you when you would be back in town, the last time you were here. And since you been gone, he has asked me if I knew when. It actually took me a while once I knew before I would tell him, because I know how you are. But finally, I gave in and told him. Why not?"

"You and Promise with the matchmaking ideas. You two just don't stop."

"Maybe. But, how did it go? Besides him coming through drunk. Pablo had to see him before the meeting this morning. When I tell you he looked trashed, he looked trashed. I asked him what he got into and he told me Don Julio shots with you." I couldn't do nothing but smile. Now I realized he was playing it cool just as I was when we left the bar. "And let me just say you played it good in the meeting, but I can tell you're hungover too."

"Wait, really?" I grabbed my phone and turned on the camera to look at my face. And while I looked good, my eyes told the real story. "Damn. I thought I had hidden it. Penelope, I let him dare me into taking those shots. I feel like absolute shit. But other than that. I actually enjoyed his company. But that's it." I held up my hand to stop her overjoyed smile that took over her face.

"Well, I'm just glad you agreed to go."

"See never doubt me." I grinned. "But anyhow I need to get back to my hotel, get packed, and get to this airport. My flight leaves in four hours."

"Yes mam, Ms. Precious. Until next time." Her cell phone rang. I headed for my rental and she headed back inside.

Chapter 35

It was ten o'clock in the morning and shit was already crazy. My flight from Miami didn't touch down in LA until seven o'clock this morning. The LAX airport was wall to wall packed as usual, and the interstate was just as packed on the ride home. By the time I made it in, I was so tired I fell into bed fully clothed. An hour or two later, Marlo called my phone and told me Pablo needed my crew back in Miami ASAP. According to him a few of his blocks back in Tampa had been shut down, so he had to send some of his crew out there to open up some new territory.

Right away I called Plies and had him get Mob to the spot. I quickly jumped in the shower, brushed my teeth, and rushed out the door in record time. Thankfully, the interstate traffic had calmed down. I pulled up and made my way inside.

"Hey, I know I pulled you guys out of pocket this morning with our shipment just coming in. But you also know that's our way of life, the unexpected and staying ready. So, it can't be helped. Shit done jumped stupid in Miami, so I need y'all to get the guys back down South."

Right away they all eased to the edge of their seats with the look on their face that said, "Beam me up, Scotty."

"As you can see, we game." Plies spoke up. Mob nodded.

"Things pretty much will be the same. I want to send Rob, Case, and Don P. Now I know Don P and Ced both running they own territory now since they been promoted. Mob, like I said before, Ced is strong. And since he been running his own territory, he ain't missed a beat, and he has been tested. So, have him hold down Rob spot like he did last time. But have him hold Don P's down too."

"Ai'ght. He got that," Mob replied with assurance. I also knew without a doubt whatever was going on, Mob was going to make sure that shit ran tight on all ends.

"Mob and I will get them all briefed right after this," Plies said.

"Cool. And, Plies, I need you fly out for two days and meet up with Marlo. It's a bit of work you two need to put in. Marlo will give you the details once you touch down."

"No doubt." Plies nodded.

"Mob, I will need you to fly on the second day to meet up with Plies to finish off some orders. He will have all the details by the time you arrive. While you both are gone on that second day, I will have Ced hold the operation down with me backing him up, of course."

"Let's get to work." Plies was amped.

"Damn right." Mob followed up.

"What time we fly out?" Plies asked.

"Yes, I will get those scheduled in a few minutes and everyone will get a notification. I want Rob and Case to leave first thing tomorrow morning. Plies, I will get you on a red-eye, and Don P's flight will probably be tomorrow evening. Mob, I will have you a red-eye for the day after tomorrow." Mob nodded. He was always down for whatever.

With that, I dismissed them so they could have their meeting with the guys, and I could get the flights set. I hopped in my car and set out for the club. I had an order coming in and I had to open up for Shareta. We had started opening the bar two days a week for early hours, and today was Shareta's day. I hadn't given her or Tyrone keys yet, so Promise or I had to let them in so they could set up.

I pulled up to the club to find Shareta and the delivery man were already parked outside. "Hey, I tried to call you to let you know the driver was here early. He said one of his orders got canceled because of a fire, so he came straight here." Shareta met me at my car. She always got to work early.

"You called me? My phone hasn't rung."

"Yep, called you three times," Shareta clarified. I looked at my phone. No missed calls. Then I remembered that sometimes in that warehouse where we met, calls didn't come through.

"Welp, I hope he wasn't waiting long." I jumped out and unlocked the door.

Inside, while Shareta signed for the order, I sat down in my office and booked the flights for all the guys. I had accounts where I could book flights for them at any time without it being traced back to me. Once their flights were booked, they would all get a notification.

By the time I was done with that, I needed a drink. But I decided to go light, so I had Shareta hook me up a margarita.

I wanted to relax, so I headed up to one of the VIP rooms to just sit back. I took my first drink and closed my eyes. I opened them to see Promise stepping inside VIP with me. Her eyes were bulged out of the sockets and bloodshot, and her face was wet with tears.

"What's wrong?" I stood up.

"Where have you been? I have been blowing your phone up. It kept going straight to voicemail." I knew then the warehouse had blocked my phone's connection. "I came by here when I realized what time it was because I knew this is where you would be."

"Damn, I had a meeting with Plies and Mob at the warehouse. Sometimes it won't take calls. What's up? What's wrong?" I wanted to know.

Promise burst out crying and flew into my arms.

"What is wrong? You are scaring me." I hugged her tight.

"It's Dee. Precious, she was found in her apartment a few hours ago. Dead . . . She was murdered."

Stunned, I stepped back to look her in the face. "Wait. What? What you mean she was found murdered?"

Promise shook her head as if she was agreeing with something. "Just that. This morning she didn't show up to work. I was running late, so Toya opened up the shop. When I got there, she asked had I heard from Dee. I told her no. Then her appointments started to show up. We called and called. But she never answered. Finally . . ." Promise paused and took in some air. "When Toya got a break, she went over to her apartment. When she got there she called and told me that Dee's car was there, but she was not answering the door. I told her to call the police for a wellness check. The police got the office to open the door. And they found her. She had been shot and was un-responsive . . . dead." Promise threw her hands in the air.

"Damn, what the actual fuck!" I was too stunned for words. "I mean, who would do this to Dee? She got ene-mies?"

"Hell no. I mean, we all know Dee talk shit. But people love Dee. I ain't met nobody that don't like her since I been knowing her. And she done took me out in LA and intro-duced me to a lot of people since I been here."

"What the cops say?"

"So far, jack shit. By the time I got there they were questioning Toya and some neighbors. They wanted to know what brought Toya over to the house. Toya explained about her not coming to work, which was odd. They asked us did she have enemies just like you did. But other than that..." Promise shrugged like she was clueless. "And the neighbors claim they ain't heard or seen shit."

"This is some crazy shit." I sat back down and grabbed my drink.

"Please, please. Get me a drink too." Promise sat down next to me, then dialed Toya, who was out in the car, and told her to come in.

"Oh, Toya is with you?"

"Yeah, she was too fucked up to drive after all this."

"I can't blame her." I called down and had Shareta bring up two more drinks, since I was sure Toya would want one too. I also told her to bring us each a shot. I really wasn't in the mood for liquor since Miami, but at the moment it was needed.

Toya came in, eyes bloodshot, hoarse from all the crying she had been doing. She downed the shot and drank the margarita so fast I had to blink twice to be sure it was gone. I called Shareta up and just told her to bring the bottle of Jack up to us, because at the rate Toya was drinking, she would be running back and forth.

Eventually, Reese, Katrina, and Tara, who I had not seen in a while since she stopped working at the salon, all showed up all in shock. We all just pretty much sat in peace and quiet and drank. The whole ordeal was mind boggling. I could not believe my day. I had to ship my guys out at a moment's notice to Miami to help hold down Pablo's territory—which I didn't mind one bit. I was lucky to have a team that was down for whatever, whenever. I knew that was hard to come by. But the absolute worst was Dee being killed. It made no sense as far as any of us could understand. Not one of us had a clue as to what or who could have been her undoing. Dee was cool people, but somebody clearly thought different. I shook my head and took another shot. I would be hungover again, but this time it couldn't be helped.

Chapter 36

"I just wanted to let you know that my realtor finally found me a house that I fell in love with."

"Really? That's good." I was happy for Katrina. I was at the new dry cleaners early, picking up the deposit. Already I had been by the club and the old dry cleaners to pick up those deposits. I had a long day ahead of me so I decided to make dropping the deposits off at the bank my first priority.

"Yep, I mean it's not much, but for my very little first house that I will be owner of, I am proud. I think Lalah and I will be happy there for a long time."

"Hey, I'm proud of you. You have been setting goals left and right and they are all lining up. Being a home-owner no matter what is a huge accomplishment. I know your mom is proud too."

"She is, and my sisters are too. Hell, I just got to make sure neither one of them try to move in." Katrina chuckled. "But they're all getting themselves on track now. Everybody is working. So, it's all good."

"Hey, you are a good role model. I think it's safe to say you are rubbing off on them."

"Yeah, I like to think so." Katrina sighed. "I stay preaching to them. Maybe they do hear me. But listen, I want to thank you so much for allowing me and Lalah to stay at the house while I got everything together. It was a huge help."

"Aye, it was nothing. As long you two were good."

"Good is not the word I'd use. I'm gone missing staying at Mr. Larry's house. I fell in love with it." She chuckled. "But I will be closing in like two weeks, so I should be out maybe a week or so after that once I get all my stuff delivered to my house. I'll get you those keys back soon as I am done."

"That's cool, no rush. And be sure to let me know if you need any help with anything."

"I will. So, has anyone heard anything about Dee? What happened? Who might be responsible?" Katrina shrugged her shoulders with the question. Those same three questions had been bugging us all, but no one had the answers.

"Nope. I ain't heard nothing. Shit just crazy," was my dry reply. I couldn't do anything but shake my head just thinking about it. It was a sad conversation to have.

"Mane, this is just jacked up. But . . . something bound to come to light." She sighed again with frustration. The door opened and a customer walked in. Katrina and I both greeted her. I told Katrina I had to get going.

Out in my car I thought about Dee as I started up my vehicle. I couldn't believe no one was talking in the streets. Even Plies and Mob said that they hadn't heard anything. I had given a big chunk of change to pay for the funeral. I would have paid for the whole thing, but Promise had insisted on doing her part. She had closed the shop down for a full week in honor of Dee's death. She had only been dead three weeks, and the shop had been back open for a week. I had been by twice and the atmosphere was just not the same. Everyone knew that Dee was a big part of the shop. She kept things alive. She talked much shit, and it was appreciated. It was all love.

I pulled up to the bank and found a parking space. I was not prepared to get in the long lines that I knew were brewing but I didn't like using the outside bank drop box, so I had no choice but to deal with it. Reaching for the deposits, I hopped out of the car just as my cell started to ring.

"Hello."

"PRECIOUS!" Toya screamed my name. I knew her voice right away.

"Yo, what the fuck is wrong?" I knew without a doubt it was something, and my heart sank to my knees.

"TWO GUYS JUST THREW PROMISE INTO A BLACK TRUCK!" Again, she screamed while talking in huge pants.

My legs felt weak, as if they were about to give out on me. I grabbed a hold of the hood of my Mercedes. "Three guys did what?"

"They got PROMISE!"

Tears instantly soaked my face. I could not breathe. I popped the lock on my car, threw the deposits onto the seat, and sat down. I slammed the door shut and sped out of the parking lot toward the salon. "PRECIOUS, PRE-CIOUS, PRECIOUS . . . ARE YOU STILL THERE!" Toya screamed my name over and over.

"Yes." I tried to talk and breathe. I had to get ahold of myself so I could think. "I'm on my way to you."

"What do you want me to do right now? Should I call the cops now or wait until you get here?"

"No, don't call the cops. You sit still. I'll be there in a minute. Who is at the shop with you?"

"Nobody. The girls are not due in for another hour."

"Okay. Call them up and tell them Promise is closing the shop until further notice. She has family business."

"What?"

"Toya, just do it." I hung up the phone. I hit my steering wheel so hard my hand ached. I dialed Plies and told him to get to Promise's shop with Mob ASAP. I drove like a bat out of hell until I pulled up to the salon. Inside I found Toya distraught.

I headed straight for the office to look at the cameras. "Tell me what happened. What did you see?" I questioned Toya.

"Okay. We got here, Promise and I, at the same time. She unlocked the door, we came inside and started to set up. She left her purse in the car and went out to get it. I realized no sooner than she was outside that she left her keys on the counter. Now you know the doors are automatically locked until we manually unlock it on the security module, which we don't do until we open up. So, I knew she wouldn't be able to get back in. I headed up to the front to unlock the door, and just as I reached for the door, I saw two guys throw her into a truck and speed off."

"Did you see their faces? What did they look like?"

"No, they had on those hooded masks. But they were both tall. They were dressed in all black. And they were black because they had on short-sleeve shirts."

Plies texted and said they were outside. I sent Toya to let them in. I continued to view the tapes and I saw just what Toya described. The truck was a basic black Ford Explorer SUV. I couldn't see the tag number.

"Yo, what the fuck is really going on?" Mob asked. Mob knew Promise well. He used to hang out with her and Clip sometimes and double date.

"I don't know. Toya called me up and said two guys threw her in the back of an SUV. I looked at the camera. To be honest, nothing stands out."

"Play that shit back." Plies stepped over to the cameras. Mob was on his heels.

I wiped at the tears that had flooded my face and tried my best to see through the blurriness that they caused. I played it back while we all watched.

"It has to be something there. Yo, this shit ain't connected to what happened to y'all home girl Dee?" Mob asked. That same question had plagued my mind from the moment Toya said somebody snatched Promise up.

"I can't be one hundred percent sure, but it's possible. I don't know." I was unsure.

"We can't get no cops involved in this shit. It's a street situation. I don't know what happened to Dee, but that shit ain't popped open yet."

"Naw, no cops. But we don't fuck around that way anyway. We the motherfucking cops." Mob punched his fist into this hand. "These niggas wishing on that dirt."

I threw my hands to my head and sucked in air. I tossed my head back for a breath, lowered my gaze to Plies and Mob. Toya stood next to me, visibly shaken. "Listen, find my damn sister. I don't give a fuck who you have to kill. But find her. She is all I have. Put the word out on the street that I have a reward for two hundred thousand for whoever got the info that gets me to her."

"You ain't said shit but a word." Mob rubbed his waist where I knew he was holding heat.

"Don't you worry, we gone handle this." Plies assured me.

"I'ma head out to the house. Just hit me up." Plies and Mob nodded as they headed out the door. I looked at Toya. "I don't know what the fuck is going on, but I'ma keep you wit' me. This shit done got stupid."

Toya shook her head in agreement. We jumped in our whips and she followed me out to the house. I didn't want Anna to know what was going on, so I sent her home early. My nerves were so shaken I didn't know what to do. I poured myself and Toya a drink. I didn't want to drink too much because I need to be alert. Toya dozed off while

I stared at my cell phone and thought about Promise. I re-played in my head the day she had showed up at the dry cleaners claiming to be my sister. I remembered the hurt look she had on her face when I all but denied her and called her an imposter. Tears swelled up in my eyes know-ing that I had hurt her. But I smiled knowing how close we had become. Then my heart skipped a beat when I realized I couldn't live without her.

An unknown number popped on my phone. "Hello," I said anxiously into the phone.

"Yes, we have her. And if you want her back it's gone cost you two million."

"Yo, WHO THE FUCK IS THIS!!" I yelled into phone.

Toya jumped up so fast she almost fell off the couch. "Who is it?" she asked. Her eyes were bloodshot and seemed as if they would pop out of the sockets.

"You don't ask no questions." The voice was clearly male but it was muffled, so I knew they were trying to dis-guise their tone.

"Is she okay?" I asked again. This time I tried to sound calm.

"Two million. Wait on my next call."

"But—" Before I could say anything else, the call ended.

"What they say? They got her?"

"They want money. Two million dollars," I said, as I dialed Plies's number. "Get the fuck out here to my house. Now." I ended the call.

Plies and Mob walked through my doors less than twenty minutes later, so I knew they drove every bit of a hundred miles per hour to accomplish that.

"What's up?" Plies asked soon as he was in front of me.

"I got a call. Some guy. He just said they have her and they want two million to get her back."

Mob started laughing, but his laugh turned cold. "Two

million dollars. Yo, who da fuck is these pussy-ass niggas. I'ma put a bullet in that ass. Niggas must think I done went soft. No, fuck that. I'ma GUT THESE NIGGAS LIKE A FISH!" Mob boomed and hit his chest.

"My nigga Mob is dead right. We can't let you pay them niggas. Pussy-ass niggas pushing up daises before tomorrow morning. I promise you that." Plies pulled out two nine-millimeter Glocks and sucked his teeth.

I held up my right hand to stop them from talking. I had heard enough. "Enough, now what I won't do is play Russian roulette with my only sister's life. I can't do that."

"Prec—" Mob opened his mouth to say something, but I shut it down.

"Listen, I'm going to make a run and put the money together. They are going to call me back, so I want y'all to stay put. If they call before I get back, I will hit y'all up right away. Don't worry, we will get Promise back and then we will take care of the trash." I snatched up my keys. "Don't take your eyes off Toya. Keep her safe." Toya was on the couch, balled up, still crying. She wasn't cut out for this type of life.

"Did you recognize the voice over the phone?" Mob asked.

"Nope, they had it disguised."

Mob shook his head with anger.

I jumped in my Range Rover and drove over to my dad's house as fast as I could, praying I didn't get pulled over. I had built a secret vault into the house that I kept spare money in, and I had well over two million dollars securely stuffed inside. I had duffel bags already on deck at his house. It took me a couple hours, and I used a lot of muscles that I didn't know I had. But I bagged up what I needed and headed back to my house.

Plies and Mob were sitting in the den with Toya chopping it up when I returned. We all just looked at each other. They knew from the look on my face that I had not heard anything, and I knew the same from the looks of them. I sucked back the lump in my throat and blinked twice as hard to hold back the tears that were screaming to get out. I offered them a drink. We all took a shot and then sat in silence. I wasn't in the mood for talking, not even about the matter at hand. My mind was all over the place.

It was nearly midnight, but finally my phone rang. My hand was so shaky when I reached for it I almost dropped it.

"Hello," I said, trying to keep my voice straight. I didn't want to sound fragile or tough. Just neutral. I had nothing to prove over the phone, that would come in due time. The disguised voice told me where to come to make the drop and assured me I would receive instructions once I was there.

Plies and Toya loaded up in Plies's Beamer and followed me. Mob refused to let me ride alone and lay down in the back seat of the Range. As I pulled up to an open area that used to be parkland, the phone rang and I was told to get out of the car and drop the bag in the center. I could see the truck that I had watched on the camera parked a few feet away from where I was told to drop the money. I was told that Promise was over to my right in the far corner.

I wasted no time dropping the money, jumping back into my whip, and heading straight for the tree to find Promise. My heart was pounding so hard it felt as if it would pump out of my chest. The black truck pulled up alongside the money, I didn't look back to see who re-trieved it, but I heard the tires speed off. Mob and I jumped out of the truck. And there Promise was, laid up against the tree. It was clear she was unconscious. I screamed out for Mob as I noticed the bruises and blood on her clothes. I was scared to touch her, afraid I might hurt her, but we had to get her to the hospital. Mob gently picked her up per my instructions and laid her on the back seat. I sat in back with her and placed her head in my lap. She seemed to be breathing good, and her heart had a steady rate. Mob drove fast, jumping red lights and weaving in and out of vehicles that were in the way, until we reached the emergency room.

For the next three hours the doctors poked and probed at Promise and questioned me about what had happed to her. I knew in some conditions like this they would contact the police, so I had to be careful how I answered the questions because that was the last thing I wanted. I explained to them that I found her at her home unconscious after a guy she had been seeing had been threatening her. She was still unresponsive, but the doctors said that she would live. While they weren't sure how she had received the bruises, they confirmed that she had taken a beating of some sort. But they claimed they wouldn't know the extent of her injuries until she woke up. I was devastated.

I didn't know who would want to kidnap and beat Promise. It was just as odd as Dee's untimely, unexplained murder. The difference was I would move heaven and earth to find out who harmed Promise. Whoever thought they could do this to my sister and live to talk about it was mistaken. LA wasn't big enough to hide them. And I hoped they enjoyed some of that two million before it was quitting time, because their days and each breath they took was numbered. That was no threat but a fact. And it was going to be a painful one.

Chapter 37

Beep, beep, beep . . . Beep, beep, beep. My eyes fluttered open and I almost forgot where I was until I saw Promise lying in the hospital bed. The constant beeping that had forced me awake was the fluid IV drip they had her hooked up to. Toya was sitting in a chair across from me, her eyes still closed. She must have made her way back to the room when the nurses changed shift.

The sun was now shining through the window. When I had dozed off it was still pitch black outside. I looked over at Promise. She was still out but looked to be peaceful. A nurse had come in about two hours ago and said everything still appeared to be stable. Her blood pressure, heart rate, and oxygen levels all seemed good. But her body was pretty much still in shock, which probably explained why she hadn't woken up.

I stood up, walked over to her, and touched her hand. It felt warm. I watched her chest move up and down as she breathed. That brought me comfort, knowing that she was breathing on her own. She really just appeared to be sleeping.

"Good morning." I turned around to see Toya standing

up. She walked over and stood on the opposite side of the bed from me.

"Hey," I said.

"Any change?"

"Nah, all her vitals still good, though."

"Good. I can't wait until she opens her eyes."

"She will." I wanted to smile but couldn't form it on my face. My cell phone rang. I gently placed Promise's hand back onto her side. The ringing stopped but started right back up.

"Hello," I answered.

"Meet me down in the waiting area," Plies said. I ended the call without questions.

"I'm going down to talk with Plies. Stay with Promise. Do not leave her side for any reason."

"I won't. I promise," Toya assured me. I didn't trust anything.

I stepped out into the hallway. It was just as packed as when we arrived. People were moving everywhere. I had to step around a doctor and what appeared to be a family of about six hovering around him. They all looked worried.

Finally, I reached the end of the hallway. Across from a nurse's station were some double doors and four sets of elevators. And right next to that was the waiting area. The area was big—there were three big television screens to cover the area. It was empty besides Plies standing in a corner.

"How is she?" were the first words out of Plies's mouth. He looked like shit, as I did, so I knew he had not gotten any sleep.

"She's alive. But she hasn't opened her eyes yet." The words left a sickening feeling in the pit of my stomach. It stung at my heart, the hurt something I could not describe. A conversation I did not want to have. I'm sure all of that was written over my face. Plies backed off.

"Is Toya still here with her?"

"Yes." I answered. "Why?" Immediately shot out of my mouth.

"I need you to take a ride wit' me. Follow in your vehicle." The look on his face confirmed for me that this was not a question but a must.

"Let's go." I really didn't feel comfortable leaving Promise, but whatever this was it could not wait. The ride was too long, or at least longer than I needed to be with my own thoughts. Finally, we pulled up to a brick house in Inglewood, one of many we had stashed around the city. DaVon used to take me around to these houses when he was alive. Sometimes he would stop and go inside, other times he would just drive by to make sure nothing looked out of order.

I had been to this house a few times. It was huge inside. There was a soundproof basement that was guilty of silencing many cries for help. There were also big rooms that had been used for meetings or stash. You just never knew.

I followed Plies inside, and he led me straight to the basement. Right away, I knew. Don P stood behind a guy who was sitting in a chair with his head hanging, a black nylon-looking sack over his head. Mob was sitting on a couch that was close to the bar we entered. He looked up at me and pointed his gun at the unknown assailant.

I paused in my spot. Plies continued to the middle of the floor, then turned to look at me. I went to ask a question, but the lump that I had been fighting in my throat from pure sickness at the entire situation filled my airways again. I watched as the assailant, whose hands I noticed were tied behind his back, tried to move his body. I could hear muffled sounds, which told me his mouth was probably tied. I silently cleared my throat.

"Who is this?" I asked. But I wasn't even sure if I was really ready to hear the answer.

Plies gestured for Don P to remove the sack from his head. I almost stumbled backward at the familiar face that was staring back at me. I mean, he was beaten and swollen, but even through his puffy eyes and swollen lips and blood draining from the right of one of his cheekbones, he was recognizable. Quan gazed at me and moved his head, trying to speak.

"Yep, this bitch-ass nigga right here." Mob stood up and cocked his gun. I raised my hand for him to lower his weapon.

"This who we got," Plies said, his lips tight. I knew he didn't want to have to show me this. "Word came through on the streets, and we got 'em. He is responsible for what happened. All of it."

"You tellin' me Quan is responsible for Promise being kidnapped and beaten?" I asked the question that Plies and Mob had both basically just answered. But I had to ask it just to believe it.

Plies nodded yes.

"Fuckin' snake-ass nigga done violated. I wanted to shoot this motherfucker on site but I knew you wanted to see him first." Mob was amped up.

Tears attempted to escape my eyelids, but I sucked them back. It was not the time for crying. "Take the gag out of his mouth."

Quan gagged and sucked breath as soon as the gag came out of his mouth.

"Man, stop acting like a fuckin' pussy," Don P said.

"Aye, Precious, listen. Don't believe any of this shit . . ." Quan tried to suck in air and talk at the same time. His right eye was swelling by the second. "You of all people know how I feel about Promise. I love that girl. SHIT! I would never do anything to hurt her or put her in harm's way."

I listened to his words and gazed at him closely. I thought of Brandy's words as they played back in my mind. I looked at Plies, then back at Quan. "Now, I heard what you just said. And trust me when I say I understand when somebody back is against the wall. Kinda like yours is right now. But I'm gone ask you this. Is what they say true?"

"Naw, naw, hell naw . . . These niggas in these streets is lying on me. Mane, so many of them jealous of me. Jealous of my come up. Fuckin' lies."

Mob rushed over to where Quan was sitting. He picked up a chain with so much force it swung out and knocked over a pipe that was next to it. We all watched as he forcefully wrapped it tight around Quan's neck. Quan tried to scream as bubbles of spit popped out of his mouth. "Ain't nobody playin' wit' you, nigga. We ain't here on no bullshit. Cooperate or die!" Mob squeezed tighter, then loosened. Quan seemed to turn blue, he gagged so hard to catch his breath.

"Listen, the only thing for you to do at this point is reveal what you know about what happend to my sister. I do think you know who I am, and I think you knew all along."

Quan's eyes seemed to get smaller and his begging turned to anger as I watched his jaws drop and his shoulders stiffen. The corners of his mouth seemed to quiver and form into the shape of the Joker. "Tell you what I know." He tried to chuckle, but it sounded more like a gurgle. It was clear he was in undeniable pain. "Nah, fuck that. I only wanted Promise's money, which the bitch never gave me, and some pussy." Again he tried to force a laugh.

"So, is that all my sister is worth to you?"

"Yep, and to SUCK MY DICK!" He spat in my direction. I still kept my cool.

Don P took his gun and hit him in the back of the neck. Plies rushed him and hit him in the jaw. "Watch yo' mouth, nigga," Plies warned.

Mob laughed. "Now look at you wit' yo' sucka ass."

"It's okay, guys," I said, still calm. "So, what you tellin' me is, you beat my sister unconscious for pussy, money, and a blow job." I laid it out to him as a statement, not a question. "Hmmph." I grunted. "Give me a minute to let this all-sink in."

I slowly walked over to him, standing in front of him but a ways back. I reached back and pulled out my nine-millimeter. I pointed the gun at his right knee and shot. I watched as he screamed out in agony.

"No, no, please," he begged as he watched me slowly point at his left knee and pull the trigger. "AGH, AGH YOU FUCKING BITCH!" he screamed. "I knew you were crazy." This time he cried out.

I laughed out this time. His facial expression was funny, but my pain was worse. I didn't consider myself crazy, but after what he had done to my sister, it was possible. I needed revenge. "You know, it's funny that you would call me that. But you know what? You ain't seen shit yet . . . Mob, Don P. Open his legs and hold them," I instructed them. I aimed the gun at my target, his penis. "This little piece of shit will be the next to go, unless you tell me why you and whoever you conspired with tortured my sister."

"You don't scare me. I ain't tellin' you shit, bitch." He screamed but it wasn't loud. His pain was at a ten and I knew it. I thought about making good on my threat, but I wasn't done with him yet. So I walked closer to him and shot him in the foot. He whimpered, this time barely above a whisper, but the pain must have been too great for him to scream. I stepped closer to him, and this time I placed the gun between his legs. "I will count to three. After that this thing you call a penis will be hanging from a light pole in Compton." This really was his last chance. I placed my finger on the trigger. "One.Tw—"

"Keisha was my sister," he screamed before I could get the word "two" completely out. The sound of Keisha's name caused me to blink, and my trigger finger almost went limp. I closed my eyes tight. I pictured Keisha's face for a brief moment. The bitch was really becoming a constant in my life, alive or dead.

But one thing was clear, the problem was at hand. Both my eyes popped back open, and my finger once again gripped the trigger. "So, you took revenge on my sister to avenge your own."

"Damn right," came out of his mouth, just above a grunt.

"Damn right." I repeated him. "Well, I hope it was worth your balls." Without a second thought I pulled the trigger.

Quan screamed out in agony. He body started to shake in the chair, his lips started tremble, and then in a broken but steady voice, he said, "Austin said it was the only way."

"Did you say Austin? Austin the professor?" I asked, unsure if I had heard the correct name. And the correct person. His head dropped, but he managed to nod.

This time my breathing became broken. "What does he have to do with this? How do you know him?" I flung the questions at him. A million thoughts attacked my mind. I had been bent so far over in Quan's space I had to stand straight up. For a minute I was certain I saw a red flash before my eyes. My eyes fell back to Quan. Looking at him, I could see the snake he was. I realized that his ex Brandy, while crazy like him, had only been trying to warn us. Quan's breathing turned to pants, his chest going up and down slowly but aggressively. He was dying, but too slowly for my liking. With the state he was now in from the pain and bleeding, there was no way he could answer any more of my questions. He was of no more use to me. "Like a wounded horse, you need to be put out of your misery. So, tell your bitch-ass sister I said hi." I squeezed off two rounds. Both landed in the upper torso. The pressure from the shots pushed his body back. He never made another sound.

"I'm out. I need you all to take care of the rest of this." They knew exactly what that meant. I strolled off in the direction of the door. I felt as if I was carrying a load of bricks from the sure shock of all the betrayal I was being faced with. But I was not overly surprised. It just proved what we all knew was true. Your enemies were most times at your front door. I would put them at my back door— the back door, the back yard, and in the dirt. Niggas had yet to learn that even though I was a female and was brought up as a young lady, prim and proper, I was also DaVon's lady, a hustler's queen. Simply put, I was not to be fucked with. Some people just needed to be reminded. And I would rise to the occasion.

Chapter 38

Now Austin's face was in etched in my brain, even the sound of his voice. And something about him bothered me. Perhaps it was from the day I met him at the gym. Whatever it was, I had either pushed it away or ignored it. But now it was crawling up and down my skin like a spider that I would have smashed immediately. Who was he? How did he know Quan? Why was he giving Quan advice on how to get to my sister? And the thought that Keisha was Quan's sister was shocking. I had known she had a lot of sisters and brothers, but I had never known them all.

An almost uncontrollable uneasiness gripped my stomach. I had to breathe in deep several times to hold back the vomit that wanted to spill from my mouth. But I was determined to reach my destination, Austin's house. So I drove at top speed. I could see, but I felt as if my vision was blurry. I was sure my blood pressure was sky high. But not even that slowed me down. I turned the corner onto Austin's street and hit the lights on my car. I parked a house down from his because I didn't want to give him too much heads up I was coming. It was nighttime and no one was hanging out, which was surprising me. Not that anything would have stopped my mission. I had come alone because this was an issue I wanted to handle alone.

I walked up his driveway, stepped onto the porch, and tapped on the door instead of ringing the doorbell.

"Precious." He said my name in a surprised tone as he pulled open the front door. His eyes were wide, but he smiled. It was clear he wasn't expecting any company. He had on a pair of loose black Nike biker shorts and a white wifebeater.

It was hard, but somehow, I forced a fake smile. "Hey, I hope you don't mind me dropping by unannounced." I shifted my weight from the left side to the right. "But I was in the neighborhood . . . so I decided why not?" I shrugged.

"Oh, it's fine. Why don't you come in?" His words were welcoming, but I could tell he was caught off guard.

"Sure." I stepped inside. He closed the door behind me.

"I actually just got in from the gym. Was about to hop in the shower. So, don't judge me." He let out a chuckle, but it seemed forced.

"You good."

"Come on. Let's go into the living room." I followed him inside. My thoughts were all but walking in front of me. I was still trying to figure out my next move.

"Can I get you something to drink? I have Coke, champagne, water, you name it." His actions came off fake to me. The more I thought about it, this was the way he acted most of the time, but I didn't recognize it was not sincere before.

"I'll take some water. My throat a lil dry." I rubbed my throat for good measure.

"Just take a seat and I'll be right back." He rushed off toward the kitchen.

I quickly glanced around the living room and tried to spot out my move. I heard him coming and stood off to the right of the entryway that he would use to get back into the living room. Walking fast, he stepped into the room.

"I went . . ." He paused in his words and steps when he didn't see me sitting on the couch where he had obviously expected to see me lounging. He started to turn, but before he could, I put my gun to the back of his head and clicked off my safety. I wanted him to be certain of what to expect if he made any sudden moves.

I could feel the tenseness in his body. It was like he turned to stone. "How about you drop that gun," I instructed him. He was surprised I had got the drop on him first. I laughed. I couldn't help myself.

"Hey, hey, take it easy with that thang." He referred to my gun as he slowly leaned down to place his gun on the floor. I kept mine close to his head. He raised back up, still tense.

"I guess you thought I would rather have that piece of steel than the water I agreed to."

"Naw, naw. It ain't like that."

"Naw . . ." I was surprised at his language. When we had been together, he always used correct English. "So, when a college professor starts talking like that? Hmmph, you are normally too proper for your own good."

"Come on now. Please . . . let me explain." He had the nerve to try and reason with me.

"Well, that's a fresh approach." I was sarcastic.

"It's really not what it looks like." He tried to explain.

"Sure, it's not." Obviously, he thought I was dumb. "Let me think. So, you brought that gun in here to me as a gift? Or maybe you wanted to show me your new gun that you received as a gift?" Boy, please. "How about you sit yo' ass down over there on that big couch, and keep your hands up where I can see them." I eased the gun off the back of his head so he could make the move.

He walked over slowly toward the couch. "Now slowly turn around to face me and sit." He did as I told him. "I think you know why I am here."

"I—" He started to speak but I shut him down.

"Listen, just shut the fuck up for a minute." He stared at me. "Quan is dead, okay? The nigga gone. Lights out. No coming back." I wanted to be clear. His face dropped. His skin seemed to loosen around his cheekbones. "So please . . . don't waste my time with lies." His eyes left mine for a brief second.

"I want you to tell me how you know Quan."

His eyes roamed my face, and for a moment they appeared to have no emotion. His eyes then went to the floor and scanned it. Suddenly he lifted his head, looked me directly in the eyes, and said, "Quincy was my brother."

I could have stomped both my feet and screamed, but at this point I was not surprised. This shit was crazy. Sinister even. There was nothing else for me to do. I giggled. Austin looked at me as if I was a madwoman. "Oh, so you and Quan linked up." It was all making sense to me now. "Well, ain't this a bitch. Y'all really played us." I chuckled.

"Damn right. And believe me when I say I ain't done yet, BITCH!" Spit flew out of his mouth and I watched it fly across the room and land in the middle of his floor. It was disgusting. He wore this look that I could not explain. It kind of gave me a chill, but I wasn't sure why. Somehow I got the feeling he was more evil than Quincy. But he had me fucked up.

"Oh yeah, nigga. You done." I squeezed off a round and hit him directly in the left shoulder. I had placed a silencer on my gun before I exited my vehicle, but Austin screamed like a bitch and bucked off the couch as the blood from his shoulder ran down his arm and filled his hand as he tried to hold the wound.

"Nigga, sit yo' ass back down and stop that screaming

before I shoot you in the other one," I threatened with my finger still on the trigger.

"Bitch, go fuck yo' self." He voice was weak.

"No, you go fuck yo' self. Pussy ass. You and that fuckin' weak-ass nigga gone stage a coup on my sister. Why, though? What reason did you have?" I still didn't know.

"Bitch, you think we don't know?" He looked at me confused. "We know what you did to Quincy and Keisha. I knew that you were going to meet Keisha that day at the club and what her and Quincy had planned for you. He told me. I tried to talk him out of it. I told him I would end you. See, I wasn't always no professor. No, these streets could have been mine. But I decided to change. Nah, I gave that shit to my brother. See, I used to be DaVon's homie. I put in mad work for that nigga. But I walked away. My brother couldn't, he wanted to continue to work for DaVon. Thought he would get that number one spot right next to him. But DaVon wouldn't bring him in. So, Quincy wanted to make his own way. Meaning he wanted me to end DaVon, get him out the way, but I said no. DaVon was still the homie. When you stepped into that spot, I agreed. But when the time came for them to make their move and get you out of the way, they couldn't wait on me. They were impatient. I tried to tell them I would handle it. But nope, I had a speaking engagement that day, and they decided to go ahead without me. I warned them that he might be on to them. But once again they didn't listen to me. And when they disappeared, I knew it was you and fucking peon Clip. So, I clipped his punk ass."

My eyes bulged. "So, you did that. You is fuckin' crazy." I shook my head. "Damn, nigga. You more evil than that sucka-ass brother of yours."

He tried to chuckle but held on to his arm. He said, "I've been told that a time or two. And that bitch Dee,

yeah, that hoe talked too much, that is why I shot her."
My jaws dropped at that. "Yeah, see that bitch recognized
me, I knew it would only be a matter of time before she
figured out who I was."

To say I was stunned was an understatement. I remembered the day he came into the shop and Dee said he
looked familiar. He had laughed it off saying people always mistook him for someone else. "You killed Dee?" I
still asked.

"See, that big-mouth bitch used to fuck Quincy. I was
in the car with him twice when he met up with her. You
know these hoes be gold diggers. She was one of them. He
used to drop her off cash and shit." He talked about it as
if it was normal.

"Damn, so you killed Dee and convinced that dumb-ass
Quan to kidnap and beat my sister. All of this over two
bombs. Yo' bitch ass unloyal, lower to the ground than a
snake-ass brother and that slut Keisha." I shook my head
at him in disgust.

"Bingo, bitch. You figured it out. The plan was to make
yo' ass suffer, take yo' money, then put you in the dirt
where you belong." The words slithered out of his mouth
at me.

"Hmm. Okay ... Well, I hope Quincy and Keisha are
worth yo' life. See, had they been a little bit more loyal
than snakes, they might still be able to suck breath ... It's
a shame you about to die for shit."

"Nah, I'm about to die for family."

The fact that he thought Keisha and Quincy were
worth his life was comical to me. Those two people were
selfish and only ever thought of themselves, and I doubted
they would have even taken a beating on his behalf. Like I
said, his heroic stand on their behalf was comical, but it
was his choice, and I had no problem to oblige him.

"Hmmph, well, rest in family, nigga." I pulled the trigger and hit him right between the eyes. The silencer did its job, making no noise, but I could literally hear Austin's brain bust inside as the bullet marked its territory. Imagined the inside of his head looked like a split watermelon on a hot summer's day. His body slumped backward onto the couch. Blood drained out the front and back of his head and down both sides of his mouth. His eyes were wide open and stared blankly into the ceiling. I put my gun away and exited as I had entered, through the front door. I wanted to kick myself for not reminding Austin that life was a bitch and then you died.

Chapter 39

"Don't forget to bring a spoon so I can eat my ice cream. I swear, if it gets any softer it will be a milkshake."

"Dang, I keep forgetting. I got you, though. Eat those cashews you had to have." I stood up and headed toward the kitchen. I had been at Promise's house keeping a close watch on her since she had returned home from the hospital. And when I say the girl was spoiled and bossy, she had it bad. But at this point I didn't care. She could have whatever she liked. But she was also very independent. If it were up to me, I would wait on her hand and foot, but she was not having that. She had been released from the hospital with strict orders to rest. That had been two weeks prior, and I could tell she was getting restless.

"Finally . . ." She fake frustrated sighed as if she was upset with me. Then grinned. "You spoil me rotten. Thanks, Sis."

"Your pushy self." I bounced down on the other edge of the sofa and picked up the Ruffles potato chips I had been snacking on.

"Mmm, I swear this is so good." She savored a spoonful of the lemon custard ice cream. "Tomorrow I'm going to go out and make a run for some more. I can't go without it."

"You don't have to go out. I will grab some and drop it by early before I get busy." I never said it, but it was obvious I was not ready for her to start leaving the house yet. The thought of her going out really put me on edge, especially going out alone.

"Precious, come on now. I been cooped up in this house for weeks now. I gotta get the hell outta here. Go somewhere . . . to grab this ice cream is a good start." She smiled at me. I didn't return her smile.

"Well, how about I pick you up and we ride together?" Clearly, I was being overprotective.

Promise burst out laughing. "Precious, really. What sense does it really make for you to drive all the way over here to pick me up only to turn around to go back to the store? You are trippin', Sis."

"There is nothing funny about that. And really I don't mind. I ain't trying to save on gas," was my only defense.

"Look, I get that you are worried. Really, I do but you don't have to do that. Besides, I'm about to start getting out of this house anyhow. I will be returning to the salon soon, as early as next week." She snuck that one in on me. I had no idea she was considering work so soon.

"When did you decide that?"

"Today, actually."

"What's the rush? Toya's doing a good job running things. And I'm in there everyday checking in."

"Yeah, I know. And trust I appreciate all of you. But it's time for me to get back at it. I need to get busy, and first things first is me returning to work."

I really couldn't argue with that, and there was no real reason she couldn't return to work besides the fact I wasn't ready for her to return. "Hey, those hair sales are doing good too. Toya says the clients can't stop bragging about the hair."

"I told you they would. People like being able to get good quality hair from their beautician. Cut out the middleman."

"Yep, I know. So, I was thinkin' about looking for a spot to sell the hair, as well. For the people who don't get their hair done at the shop. I know the plan was not to have that extra traffic in your shop, once the word is out about the hair."

"No doubt. And I got some good ideas on some locations."

"Cool. You call up the realtor and set up some showings."

"Okay. I think sometime next week should work out. I think I'll make Monday my first day back at the shop."

"I'm sure the crew will be glad to have you back."

"Damn right. Mimosas first thing Monday at my booth."

I shook my head with a chuckle. "You will never change. But I will be by for mine." We both laughed. It felt so good to be here and laughing with her, because for a split second when she was kidnapped, I feared we might never do it again.

"Well, listen, I know you are probably missing your bed, so you can start spending more nights at home. I'm good here. And I really appreciate you taking care of me."

"Wait, I get the feeling you are trying to get rid of me."

Promise closed one eye and leaned her head to the side, then popped her closed eye open. "Hmm, well, kinda. I need some privacy."

"Privacy? For what?"

"Christopher is coming over," she revealed with a grin that seemed like it would not end.

"Christopher who?" I played dumb just to annoy her.

"Don't start that mess." She rolled her eyes at me. "You know you remember him."

"I guess." I shook my shoulders in a nonchalant manner. But I was curious. "So, when did you start talking to him?"

"Well, actually we have been talking off and on since we first met through him showing you properties. But lately we been talking on the phone a lot. Couple of nights ago when you were asleep, I invited him over."

"So you got strangers up in here while I'm asleep?" I was being petty.

"He is not a stranger. Stop whining." She sat up and checked her phone. "I needed him to take care of me while you snored," she teased.

"Haha, you should be a comedian. But real talk, are you ready for this?"

"Ready for what?"

"Seeing a guy. I mean, with the last incident still so fresh." I didn't want to say Quan's name, but there was no question who or what I was speaking of. I also hated to bring up the situation. I was sure it had triggers for her.

Promise's face turned stone, but not from fear—from anger. "Mane, FUCK QUAN!" She yelled. But then she calmly breathed in deep and sighed. "Besides, you handled that. Right?"

She knew the answer, but I confirmed with a nod then mouthed, "Yes." That was my solid confirmation.

"I know what happened to me was fucked up. Trust me, I hate that nigga for what he did to me. Both them niggas. But I won't sit around and give up on life. I won't allow it to lessen my trust. I refuse to live like that. However, my eyes will be a little bit wider and my instincts broader. But that shit will not hold me back . . . and my advice to you is to get on with your happiness."

I think we both knew that was not about to happen. My happiness was the last thing on my mind. My sister and my business were all I had brewing at the moment. I was about to say that, but the doorbell rang.

Promise's face lit up with a smile. "I think that will be Christopher."

"Yeah, I'm sure. Traitor." I accused her and stood up.

Promise wasted no time skipping to the door. I was on her heels. She opened the door and Christopher stood there grinning like a kid in a candy store at the sight of Promise. Something told me he was really fond of her.

"Hey, I hope I didn't interrupt anything." He looked past Promise at me.

"Oh no, you are good. You remember Precious?"

"I'm sure he wouldn't forget me after that huge commission." I half smiled, with my arms folded across my chest. I wasn't in the mood to be fake. I didn't have anything against him, but no dude with my sister right now would get a happy reaction out of me. Promise eyed me with a warning to knock it off.

"Yeah, that commission was nice." He chuckled.

"Aye, I'ma get going. Promise, I'll call you later." I stepped past Christopher and outside into the evening. The sun was about to set, and it felt peaceful out.

I really didn't have any pressing business, so I decided to head home. Moneybagg Yo's "Yesterday" pumped out of the speakers. I turned it up, jumped on the interstate and let the Porsche loose. Just as I was about relaxed into the song and the speed, it was all interrupted by a call. "Hello," I answered, not really in the mood to be bothered.

"What's good?" Marlo's Southern accent came through my phone. I was surprised to hear his voice. But I always played it cool, and this time would be no different.

"Burning up this interstate," was all I could come up with. I was wondering what this call was about. Was Miami in need of me and my crew again? It hadn't been that long ago that we had to slice up and get out there and help hold things down. And truth be told, if Pablo and Penelope needed us again, I was down. Without even a doubt.

"So, what happens in LA on weeknights?" That question was odd to me. I thought about his question for a minute. Then it hit me. Was he in LA? I wasn't ready to ask, so I played along.

"I don't know. I'm a businesswoman. I stay busy." I went silent again and waited for his response.

"Busy, huh . . ." He seemed to think over what I said. "Well, I'm in your city and I'm lookin' for a drink." I couldn't believe he was in LA. I had to fight to hold back the surprise that would have been in my tone if I didn't suppress it.

"You are lookin' for a drink, huh?"

"How about you join me? I hate to drink alone."

This I had not been expecting. A drink maybe, but with Marlo? "Actually, I was headed home. But how about tomorrow?" I offered instead.

"Nah, I fly back out tomorrow." The disappointment was in his tone. He had not tried to hide it.

"Tell you what, how about you come out to my house?" The words just slid out of my mouth; I was shocked to hear them myself. I guessed I felt guilty for turning him down. But I really was in no mood to go out anywhere. Home was where I really wanted to be.

"If you shoot me that address, I can come through in about an hour."

"Cool. I'll text it to you when I hang up." We ended the call and I followed through with the text. When I arrived at the house, Anna was just leaving for the day. I jumped in the shower, then changed into another pair of jeans and a crop top tee. No sooner had I hit the stairs than my doorbell was ringing.

"You didn't tell me you live in Bell-Air," Marlo teased when I opened the door. "I only ever glimpsed this on TV."

"Ha ha you have jokes, huh? Come on in." I laughed. "I'm glad you didn't get lost."

"No chance of that happening."

"I know you want a drink, so follow me." I headed toward the huge bar room. Never had I felt like this before, but I felt like Marlo's eyes were all over me. I wasn't sure if that made me uncomfortable or not.

"It's huge in here."

"Yeah, it's pretty big. But you get used to the space." I kept walking to the bar. "Now, what can I pour you?"

"You have Don Julio?" He laughed and I did too.

"No, I don't think you can handle that and drive back to your destination tonight."

"Wait, are you saying I can't hold my liquor?" He smiled.

I held up my right hand as if I was swearing on a Bible. "Hey, don't shoot me. I'm just the messenger of facts."

"Hmph, we might need witnesses. But for now, I'll take a shot of Hennessey and you can add a little Coke."

"Now, that I can get you without approval." I chuckled and pulled down two glasses. I would have the same thing.

I poured our drinks, walked over, and handed him his. "How about a movie?" I offered.

"That's cool." He tasted his drink.

I turned on Prime TV and found *Boyz n the Hood*. We agreed on that as the movie of choice. But right away we started talking. "So, what brings you LA?" I had to ask. Call me nosy, curious, either way I couldn't help myself.

"I have a sister out here," he revealed, and it shocked

me. We had talked a few times about LA, and he had never mentioned that.

"I didn't know that."

"Yeah, she is attending UCLA. Say she had to get out of Miami. LA was the pick." He didn't seem too happy to have his sister living in LA.

"UCLA is a good school . . . but you don't seem very happy about her being there."

"Aye, I agree with that. UCLA is a good school. But I would have rather her close. It's only her and me. We are all we got. You know how that goes."

It warmed my heart to see how he felt about his sister. "Welp, I never had siblings growing up."

"Aye, they can be a pain now. Always in your stuff, won't leave you alone. But having that bond is like no other. I wouldn't change it for the world." He smiled. But then his mind seemed to shift, and confusion caught his expression. "Wait, you said you didn't have siblings. What about Promise, your sister? Your twin?"

"You have a good memory, huh?" I sipped my drink. "Yeah, I do have Promise, but that kinda came about later in life . . . but that's another story for another day." I was ready to change the subject. Getting all up in my personal business was not on my schedule.

"It's cool. But how about another drink?"

"Guess I can go for round two," I said, then downed the rest of my drink. I poured the drinks, then attempted to hand Marlo his glass. Instead of reaching for the glass he gently reached for my free hand and pulled me to him.

The feel of his body caused me to swoon. He leaned into the crease of my neck and whispered, "I have been wanting to do this since I first laid eyes on you." I could not believe the words coming out of his mouth, and I would have protested, but being in his arms felt so good.

Gently, he took the glass from my hand and set it next to him. Leaning his face into mine, his lips brushed mine, and without hesitation I wrapped my hands around his head and pulled him into me. We kissed deep and hard for at least two minutes.

Marlo's hands seemed to roam my whole body. His hands gripped my butt and caressed my back and then my neck. I was on fire for him. I felt a longing between my thighs that I was sure had died along with DaVon. I tugged at Marlo's belt and the buttons on his pants until he was free of them. His member was so hard that I moaned as I reached out and stroked it. Before that I think Marlo had relieved me of my clothes.

Marlo laid me down on the floor and kissed my lips, then licked all the way down to my love, where he sucked until I screamed. I ordered him on his back as he slid on protection. On top of him, I wasted no time sitting where he stood at attention. "Damn you feel so good inside," he moaned as I slid further down. Closing my eyes, I rode him like the stallion he felt like until we both spilled over. Lying on his chest, I realized I fit him like a glove. For the rest of the night, we rode each other like it was the last time either of us would ever have a ride. Morning came before we knew it. I went to meet up with Plies. Marlo caught his flight out.

Chapter 40

"So which one of the girls you want to hire?"

"I think we should go with the April chick. She had the most availability and she did retail for seven years," Promise said. We had interviewed about twenty girls for a cashier and stocking position at the new hair store. The store was scheduled to open in a week. We were here today to stock some of the inventory.

"Yeah, I was thinking her too. And with Toya picking up a couple shifts a week and you coming in, I think we should be good for now on help."

"Yep." Promise agreed. "We can always hire someone else if we need help." Once again, I had given Promise 50 percent of the business. From now on I didn't want to do anything if it didn't involve her. Well, besides the dope game. She had no interest in that. And I seconded that. Legit was the only way I wanted her to go.

"The shipments will be coming in on Monday mornings. I think you or I should be here to sign for shipments. This way we can verify inventory right away."

"I'm good wit' that. We'll just play by ear which one of us can be here each Monday."

"We can do the same for deposits."

"Cool." Promise slit open a box with a box cutter. I hung hair onto a rack.

"Whew, this is like exercise, hanging this shit up. Some of these bundles are heavy." I stood on a step stool, hanging hair onto racks.

"Tell me about it. I'm like shit, I'm gone cut my hand with this box cutter." Promise examined her hands as if she was looking for cuts.

"You can stop looking. Trust if you had cut yourself, the pain would speak up loud and clear." I chuckled.

"Facts." She laughed. "So, have you heard anything from Mr. Magic Stick?" I turned and playfully rolled my eyes at her. I knew without a doubt she was talking about Marlo. I had told her all about the night we had spent together.

"Oh, so you got jokes?" I threw a bag of hair at her.

"Hey, don't shoot the messenger. I figured Marlo had that sweet dick. I just didn't tell you because you be trippin'."

"Well, he does have that," I decided to admit. "But shit ain't like that with us. We did what we did and that's just that. We cool."

"Hmmph. Cool, huh? Well, ain't nothin' wrong wit' that. But I think he is feelin' you more than you think. Or maybe you know and just refuse to admit it. You are stubborn as a bull."

"Nah, we both out here in these streets gettin' money the hard way. Ain't no time for feelings, I keep tellin' you that. But you refuse to hear it."

"Yeah, if you say so."

I was about to respond but my cell phone rang. Reluctantly, I climbed down off the step stool to retrieve my phone. "Hello," I answered.

"Hey." Marlo's voice was apparent as usual.

"What's up," I replied. He was silent for only a few seconds.

"I need you to book a flight and come out to Miami. Like ASAP." This was becoming a habit. But I was prepared to step up, and my crew was too.

"Yep, I can do that. Should I book for the crew right now or . . ."

"Nah, I don't need the crew. Just you." That was a surprise to me. "Listen, I don't have time to talk. But I need you to catch a flight. Hit me up when you touch down." With that he ended the call.

I glared at the phone screen. I tried to rationalize what he had just asked me to do.

"What's wrong, Precious?" Promise had been watching me. "Book, that sounds like a flight to me," she added before I could answer her initial question.

I was sure I had sort of a blank stare on my face, but that was because I didn't know what to think of Marlo's request. Promise's whole body seemed to move to the edge of her seat. I knew I had better tell her something. "That was Marlo." I turned the cell phone toward her as if his face was on the phone.

"Okay, wha'd he say?" Her facial expression read *spit it out.*

"He asked me to book a flight like ASAP and head to Miami."

Promise's cheekbones went forward into a huge grin. "Precious, he ready to see you. Hell, maybe even put a ring on it."

"A what? You are trippin'. No, that's not it." I stared back off into space.

"Then what? Is it business?"

"Hmm." I thought over her question and Marlo's request. "That I'm just not sure of. Normally, well, at least the last time he called me out, he had me bring the crew. But I asked about booking a flight for them and he told me no. I haven't heard from Pablo or Penelope." I shrugged my shoulders with uncertainty. "Maybe I shouldn't go until he gives me more details."

"Why not? You don't trust him?"

"I don't trust SHIT!" I expressed with eyes dead fixed on Promise. "I think you know that in my line of work. I can't. That was one of the first lessons DaVon taught me. And clearly that has been proven to me many times over and over."

"I guess you're right. But my heart is tellin' me he legit. I don't know what the dude wants. But to harm you I don't think is nowhere on his list."

I sighed. "I don't know what's up with him. I haven't heard from him since he left LA. And he calls me up today out of the blue requesting I jump a flight. I mean, don't get me wrong. What happened with us and the way we left it is cool wit' me. I ain't lookin' for nothin', but . . ."

"Well cool, then you can say that to his face. But what's with 'but'? Sounds like hesitation to me."

"Maybe it is. Promise, I just don't know."

"Precious, just go. Catch the flight." Her words urging me to go rang in my head. As much as I hated to admit it, there was something about Marlo. The vibe. Honestly, we seemed to vibe good together. But I would not admit that out of my mouth to anyone. DaVon had been the last and only guy I had ever vibed with. How could Marlo be the second? No one held a candle to DaVon, or least I didn't think so.

Fifteen hours later my plane's wheels pointed downward, hit the paved runway, then slowed until the plane came to a complete halt. I had safely landed in Miami. I departed the plane, still unsure as to why I was there, but I was anxious to find out. I stepped outside of the Hertz rental car agency and headed straight toward the lane that held my vehicle. Once I threw my luggage into the truck, I dialed Marlo.

"Did you make it?" were the first words out his mouth. Normally he would first say a simple "hey" or something, but not today.

"Yep, just got my rental," I informed him.

"Good, I need you to meet me like yesterday."

"Cool, text me the address."

"Done," he said, then ended the call. I didn't know what was up, but my thoughts were that Marlo had gone and got real rude. But now was not the time to hold him to it. I put the address in the map on my phone and allowed the GPS to take me my destination. I would check into my hotel later.

I drove for nearly twenty minutes before the GPS finally led me to a gate with a security guard sitting inside a booth. I pulled up and gave my name, and sure enough they were expecting me. Once inside I drove for another five minutes until I found this huge house. My guess was Marlo's place. Marlo almost lived in a mansion like Pablo and Penelope, except there was no butler outside. I parked in the huge circular driveway. Before I could ring the doorbell, Marlo opened the door.

"Hey," I said casually. Marlo looked as good as he normally did, but something about him was different. His face had a heaviness to it. Some might call it stress.

"Hey, come inside." He invited me in.

Talk about beautiful, his house was it. There was no

butler at the door, but I quickly saw two women dressed in maid outfits go two separate ways. I was sure he needed them, as big as the mansion was.

"So, I take it you live here?" I asked, more for confirmation than anything.

"Yeah, I sleep here most nights." I wasn't sure how to take that answer. Was he trying to tell me he was secretly married, or did he sleep in the trap? Who knew in the life we led. I decided it was not my business to pry.

"Oh, I just assumed we would meet somewhere less personal."

"No, this is fine. I've been to your house, remember." He felt the need to remind me. "Let's go into one of my offices." He led me down the hallway into a room. If this were only one of his offices, I could only imagine what the second one looked like. There was nothing in this office to long for. It was complete with a bar, a full den, you name it. "Can I get you something to drink?"

"Nah, I'm good. But I would like to know why I'm here. What's up?" I couldn't handle the suspense any longer. My nerves were beating at the pit of my stomach. If I had a drink, I might throw it back up from nervousness.

Marlo poured a shot of Jack Daniel's, then downed it. Something was wrong. I cleared my throat for him to spit it out. He looked at me.

"Penelope and Pablo have both gone missing . . . Possibly murdered."

My mouth didn't move, but his words swirled in my head in circles until I felt dizzy. I was sure a bead of sweat had formed on my forehead.

"Marlo, what do you mean they are missing and possibly murdered? Where does this conclusion come from?" I glared at him so hard, for a moment his form seemed blurry.

He poured another drink, then downed it.

"Would you please say something other than turning up that damn shot glass?" I was now irritated. I couldn't even picture Penelope hurt or bleeding. Pablo either, for the matter.

"The shit is crazy . . . Pablo called two days ago and said he needed me to come out to Saint-Tropez. He and Penelope were out there checking on some business with her stores. Said he needed me to come out and meet with some people about a deal that he had been working on for months. I told him cool. Got me a flight out and went to the spot they own there. This place is really secluded, they don't invite many people up there. And when they are there, unless they bring people, they are alone. No house-keepers, butlers, none of that. They like to keep it simple there. Kind of do-it-theirself-type living when they up there. Well, I get there, and everything on the outside looks normal. I ring the doorbell, knock and all that. No answer. I call both their cell phones, no answer. Finally, I try the door and to my surprise it's unlocked. Make my way inside, immediately I see the place is tossed, blood everywhere. But no Pablo, no Penelope."

"Okay." I shook my head up and down. I wanted to make sense of this. "Well, have you tried anybody they might know? Asked around about them?"

"Nah, that's not how they move. People don't know their moves like that."

"What about their bodyguards?"

"I told you, when they are in Saint-Tropez they chill on that shit. Since the island is full of rich people and shit, they lay back. Be comfortable and shit. I've been telling them forever they should always have their security on deck. Penelope say no. Pablo give in."

"So, you tellin' me you think somebody took, harmed, or killed Pablo and Penelope? Just like that?" I just had to say it out of my mouth to make it make sense.

"It's possible." His eyes were bloodshot. "I know the shit sound impossible that anybody could get to them. But . . ." He seemed to stall. I could tell he was out of words.

"Marlo, do you know what you are saying? Who the fuck would dare?"

"And that I will find out. But now something else has to be handled."

"Something else?" I nearly yelled as I repeated him. "Dude, what the fuck could be more important than finding out what is going on with Penelope and Pablo at this very moment?" I looked at him as if he were a madman with three eyes on his forehead, because in my mind the man was talking pure nonsense. I closed my eyes and breathed in deep.

"I have been summoned down to Peru to meet up with Salvador." Both my eyes popped open at the mention of Salvador's name. Salvador was the godfather of the United States, Mexico, Spain, and most of Europe. He was the truth, the light, and the death of many.

"Salvador." I could only repeat his name. "Did he say why?"

"Precious, are you kidding me?" This time Marlo looked at me as if *I* was a madwoman with three eyes on my forehead. He poured himself another drink, lifted it to his lips, and swallowed.

"Maybe it's about Penelope and Pablo? Maybe he knows something." I shrugged. "That could be good, right?" I offered no certainty in my voice. There was just no way that I could, but one thing I knew for sure was when Salvador came calling, you had no choice but to come on down. But what I still didn't understand was why I was here. Why did Marlo beckon me to Miami if he was leaving?

"That brings me to why I asked you here. Well, besides the fact that Penelope and Pablo are missing. I need you to go with me to see Salvador."

I wasted no time. "Ah, hell no." I didn't hesitate. "Why would I do a crazy-ass thing like that?" This whole situation all of a sudden seemed bizarre to me. I looked at Marlo sideways. Was he hiding something from me? Here he was calling me out the blue, then telling me Penelope and Pablo had just vanished into thin air? Or possibly lay buried somewhere? Nah, I couldn't trust shit.

"Listen—" He held up his hand to explain, but I cut him off.

"Marlo, I ain't going nowhere with you. As far as I know, you done killed Penelope and Pablo. Maybe you trying to take over," I threw at him.

His face dropped and the hurt from my words seemed to push him backwards. "Don't insult me, Precious. You worked with me for damn near a year now. Penelope and Pablo introduced you to me. Don't you trust me?"

"Nah, I don't trust shit. That's the game, and you and I both know how that goes." I reminded him of the rules. I couldn't even believe he of all people had the nerve to even bring up the word *trust*. Trust got you killed. Quick.

"He asked for you too." He dropped the words, which exploded in my ear like a bomb.

"Repeat that? He who?" I turned red inside and out.

"Salvador. I was instructed to bring you too."

I stumbled back a bit. I rubbed my forehead then looked at Marlo. "Why? Why does he want to see me?

How does he even know my name?" I knew the question was stupid, but my heart was beating so fast I had to know.

Marlo shook his head. "I don't know. I wish I did. If I had to guess I would say it's because you are running one of the most successful hot spots in the US."

His guess was probably right. "So this is probably the same reason he wants you as well."

"Perhaps. And I'm sure he knows what is going on with Penelope and Pablo. Either way, we have to go. We have no choice, Precious."

DaVon's face once again clouded my mind. The sacrifice I had made to keep his legacy going. How would he take this information? Would he buckle under the unknown? Before that question could fully leave my mind, I knew the answer. DaVon wouldn't think or question it twice. He would grab his passport, book a flight or charter a private jet, and be in Peru as soon as possible.

"Let's do it," I said, not sure where the courage to utter those words had come from.

A huge weight seemed to lift off Marlo's shoulders. "Cool. I chartered us a private jet. We leave in six hours," he announced. Once again, he moved like DaVon. I could only gaze at him.

Suddenly I realized I wanted to shower and relax a minute before the flight. "Okay, I'm going to check into my hotel, get a shower, and meet you at the jet."

"No, you don't get a hotel. Just stay here, shower, rest up, and one of my drivers will get us out to the airport."

"Nah, I don't want to intrude."

"I insist."

I really was tired from my flight and didn't feel like driving to the hotel. So I caved. "Okay. I'll take you up on your offer."

"Good. Now, can I get you that drink you turned down when you first got in here?"

"I guess under the circumstances, I will. Make it two shots of Hennessey."

"I got you." I could tell he wanted to smile, but he cuffed it.

After all the information he had just laid on me, a drink would be a life saver. The flight to Peru would take hours. I would have a few drinks on the plane in between naps and pray to God by the time I was standing in front of Salvador, I was of sound mind and not drunk. Silently I sighed.

Chapter 41

The whole ride to Peru seemed so surreal. I tried not to think about anything in particular. I wanted my mind to be as clear as was possible. Promise had been blowing me up since I got to Miami, trying to see what was up. The conversation wasn't one I could have over the phone, so I told her that Marlo and I were taking a trip to sort some things out but that I would be back in a few days and I would fill her in. Even if she had been in my face I didn't know if I could tell her where we were going and who we were going to see. While she didn't really know anything about Salvador, she was no fool, and Peru and the meeting probably would add up. Especially if I told her Penelope and Pablo were an unsure case of death or kidnapping.

Peru was scorching when we stepped off the jet. There was a black SUV with a driver and two guys who looked as if they worked for the Secret Service waiting on us. They told us Salvador was waiting to see us. And they of course were our appointed transportation.

Marlo looked at me, then opened the door for me. I climbed inside the SUV and braced myself. We drove for nearly an hour before pulling onto farmland. The driver continued on for a few miles. We passed horses running free behind secure white fences with guys who I assumed were stablemen attending to them. Finally, the SUV came to a halt in front of a modest-size ranch style house.

The car with the two Secret Service type guys had stopped before us. They both got out, and one opened the door on my side for me to exit. I hopped out and stood to the side and waited for Marlo to exit. We both fell into step behind the guys. We were led into the house, to what one of the guys referred to as the parlor.

"Parlor? Where are we, in Mayberry?" Marlo whispered and I wanted to laugh.

Inside we were told to wait. Two other guys stood in the back of the room silently. Marlo looked at me and I at him. We said nothing.

"Welcome to my home." A tall, middle-aged, Hispanic-looking guy with thick curls greeted us. "I'm Salvador." It was clear that English was not his first language, though he spoke it well. But his Spanish accent would not be denied. He said his name as if he was signifying that he was king. It was clear he was proud of who he was.

"We came as we were summoned." Marlo spoke up first.

"And not a minute later," I added. I felt stupid for saying that, but I was truly at a loss for words. It wasn't every day I was summoned to meet one of the most notorious men in the world.

"You two will be taking over Pablo and Penelope's spot, meaning you will be sitting next to me, reporting to me." To say he didn't waste any time or beat around the bush would have been an understatement.

I wondered if he himself was sure of the words he had just let slip from his mouth. Did he have any idea what he was asking? And why would we be taking over Pablo and Penelope's spot? What about them?

"With all due respect," Marlo's voice interrupted the room. Salvador reached into the pocket of his shirt, pulled out a cigar, and put it between his lips. Marlo went on. "I think right now the focus should be finding Pablo and Penelope. We can't just give up and—"

Salvador cut him off. "Listen, no worries. There is no need." Salvador kind of smirked. I looked over at Marlo. "Pablo, Penelope." He shrugged. "They have been put to bed. It's night night for them." He shrugged his shoulders again.

My heart sank to my feet. I understood. Marlo asked the question. "Put to bed. Like, what does that mean?"

Salvador looked around at some of the men in the room and laughed a hearty laugh. Again, I looked at Marlo. "He questions Salvador." He stopped laughing and looked at Marlo. "That bitch. You know she tried to cross me. Beautiful always to me. Always. I say to her, Penelope, I'm Salvador. Beauty as you are, but even your body will never cloud my vision. She laughs. Okay." He shrugged his shoulders, then placed the still unlit cigar between his lips. "She goes to Saint-Tropez and gets rid of my child." He rubbed his stomach.

I couldn't believe my ears. Penelope had been pregnant with Salvador's baby. "Pablo, he always weak for her. He help her. He knew it was against my wishes. The money and power that I give to him go to his head. He thinks he can be rid of Salvador. Thinks he can test Salvador. Can you believe he tried to send henchmen after me? After all I do for him. The bitch, she in his head. But no longer." He waved the conversation off. He was done with it.

"Are you saying you murdered them?" The color seemed to drain from Marlo's face.

The color almost drained from mine as I watched Plies step into the room. "Yes," he said, and I knew he was answering Marlo's question.

"What are you doing here, Plies?" I was trying to suck in air from all the shock I was receiving.

Plies looked me in the eyes. "I'm here tying up loose ends."

I looked at Salvador, then back to Plies. "What loose ends?" I wasn't sure I was ready to hear his answer.

Salvador produced a remote and turned on the TV that was on the wall facing us all. A clear, bloody picture of Penelope and Pablo appeared. Marlo stumbled slightly but caught his balance.

I gazed back at Plies. His eyes seemed blank. "You did that?" I asked. "Are you working for him?" I referred to Salvador.

Instead of Plies speaking, Salvador jumped in. "Do you really think that when I found out a woman," he said it as if he was almost disgusted, but his face remained calm, "was taking over one of my biggest drug supply areas, that I would just let it be? No. I needed eyes. Close eyes," he stressed. "You see, Pablo was always weak for the ladies. So I had to do it. All I had to do was find the lowest snake in the pile." He looked at Plies.

Plies wore an offended expression.

"Yeah, that Clip. He had real loyalty. And there was no way he was going to spy on DaVon's woman." His name sounded kind of choppy coming out of Salvador's mouth. "And I can respect him for that, but I needed help."

"So?" I mouthed and waited for answer.

"Yeah, I was on my way to make that nigga an ace in the hole. But somebody bodied him before I could heat his ass up," Plies spoke up.

"But . . . that was—" I stopped short of saying what was on the tip of my tongue. Plies was supposed to be Clip's boy. "Hmmph. The fucking game." It was clear to me.

"Damn right. And the price was right. I was gone blow that nigga brains out without a second thought. Just like I did with that bitch Penelope and her pussy huband Pablo." He said it as if it was a badge of honor.

Salvador shook his head. "Something else to learn. Snakes don't live long."

Pop!

One of the guys standing in the room with us stepped up behind Plies. We watched as his head exploded and his body dropped behind it. I had to step back to keep blood from getting on me.

Pop! Pop! The same guy stood over Plies and pumped two more bullets into the back of his head.

Salvador turned the TV off, then looked from Marlo to me as if everything was running on schedule. "See, you two, I have watched you for a long time now. And I am positive you have what it takes to be what Pablo and Penelope couldn't. And now you will get your turn."

"Turn." Marlo spat at him without releasing actual spit. I saw the rage that edged over his entire face, the same that had turned mine blood red. The hate I had building up in me for Salvador was immense. I saw myself pumping two bullets right between his eyes. The feeling was so strong I felt nauseated. Marlo's lips got tight. I watched him closely while never taking my eyes from Salvador. "Do you really think I would work for you now? Huh? Do you know who I am?" Marlo beat his chest. He hit it so hard I thought I heard a rib crack.

Salvador chuckled again. A chill went down my spine, but it was no match for the rage I had for him. I was not afraid. "I didn't want to believe it at first," he said. He didn't look at Marlo, he seemed to stare off into space. "But I know you are Pablo's son."

This time I stumbled. The room seemed to spin. I looked over at Marlo. I thought of Pablo's face, and it was right in front of me. Marlo was black, that much was true, but he was the spitting black image of Pablo. How had I missed that? Why was it hidden from me?

"So you a snake and a liar too?" I asked him.

"Precious, no, it's not like that," he tried to explain to me. I snatched my face away from him. I didn't want to look at him. I thought of Penelope too. I thought she was my patron. But that too had been a lie.

"Listen, this is business. You two can finish this lover's quarrel another time. I need you to get back to the States and await my word. Get me a lighter," Salvador commanded. "And put them back on the jet!" he yelled at his workers, suddenly seeming angry.

The room seemed to swim. I started to move my feet. *Pop, pop, pop, pop, pop, pop, pop, pop, pop, pop, pop, pop, pop!*

"*Agh, agh, agh, agh, agh!*"

Connect with U s

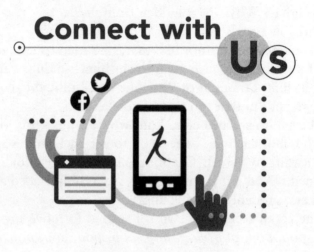

Visit us online at
KensingtonBooks.com
to read more from your favorite authors, see books
by series, view reading group guides, and more.